Mangoes On The Maple Tree

Acknowledgements: A section of this novel in different form previously appeared in *What Was Always Hers* (Broken Jaw Press, 1999).

Excerpt from *Days and Nights in Calcutta*, copyright 1977, 1986, 1995 Clark Blaise and Bharati Mukherjee. Reprinted by permission of Ruminator Books.

Cover art by Greg Charlton
Copyedit by Richard Cumyn
Design and in-house editing by the publisher, Joe Blades
Printed and bound in Canada by Sentinel Printing, Yarmouth NS

Simultaneously published as BJP eBook 40, ISBN 1-896647-80-4 (PDF), with distribution via http://PublishingOnline.com.

The publisher acknowledges the support of the Canada Council for the Arts and the New Brunswick Culture and Sport Secretariat-Arts Development Branch.

Broken Jaw Press
Box 596 Stn A
Fredericton NB E3B 5A6
Canada
www.brokenjaw.com
jblades@nbnet.nb.ca
tel / fax 506 454-5127

National Library of Canada Cataloguing in Publication Data
Uma Parameswaran
Mangoes on the maple tree / Uma Parameswaran.

Also available in a PDF format.
ISBN 1-896647-79-0

I. Title.

PS8581.A688M36 2002 C813'.54 C2002-904378-6
PR9199.3.U53M36 2002

Mangoes On The Maple Tree

Uma Parameswaran

Uma Parameswaran

BROKEN JAW Press

Fredericton • Canada

"Family, family, family. In India, all is finally family."
— Clark Blaise, *Days and Nights in Calcutta*

Chapter 1

Jyoti Bhave sat on the couch in the family room, her polisci book in her lap. It was probably nearing three o'clock, she thought, looking at the beam of light that fell across the Ping-Pong table that stood half folded in a playback position at the centre of the room. Another beam, from the other pane of the same large window, fell on a framed picture of one of her childhood crafts that her mother had proudly placed by the side of a framed *peepul* leaf painting. The peepul leaf had been painstakingly dried and painted upon by a pavement artist on the streets of Mumbai. Her own handicraft consisted of her attempts, in Grade Five, to dry a red maple leaf and paint a white polar bear on it. Her mother, Savitri, had framed each of the two leaves in similar gold-painted wood frames, assuring eleven-year-old Jyoti that the white blob on the maple leaf was as clearly a polar bear as the fruit on the peepul leaf were bananas.

The April sun pouring in through the basement windows to the southwest turned, and soon it was not bright enough to read. But it was bright enough to resist the chore of getting up to turn on the lights. Jyoti stretched her legs on the ottoman and looked at a ceiling panel that Krish had covered with multi-coloured stars taken from a sticker-sheet three Christmases ago. She loved the brightness of their bi-level home, with large windows on all four sides. Winter had made its unmistakable presence felt here as everywhere else in the city. The windows on the opposite wall were half covered with snow, even though Jayant and Dad had spent all of Monday morning shovelling the driveway at the back of the house and clearing the sidewalks, helped sporadically by Krish and herself. Radio and television stations were still gushing about it being the blizzard of the century, surpassing the 35 centimetres of November 7, 1986, and 35.6 centimetres of March 4, 1966. Not since Environment Canada had started keeping records in 1876 had Winnipeg experienced a bigger blizzard. There seemed to be a touch of pride in some of the newscasters' voices for their home and native city now valiantly picking itself up after the 43.2 centimetre snowfall of the past weekend, of which a record 37 had fallen in a 24-hour period.

The wind had a way of piling the snow at an angle so that the windows looked as though they had a diagonal slash across them. If their sidewalk around the house had been on that side, the wind blasting its way along the bay would have blown it away, and Jayant would have saved himself two hours of shovelling each time all these years. No one ever used any of the sidewalks except for the one from the back lane. The postman and newspaper boy cut right across the front lawn from one mailbox to the next, and everyone else came in by the back lane and back door. But Dad was a stickler for clearing the paths, and the boys grumblingly had to join him every time he went out in his ski-pants and heavy parka.

No more shovelling for Jayant. On the other side of the staircase that divided the basement into a small family room and a large rec room lay Jayant's stuff. His clothes were strewn around an open suitcase; the light blue Adidas bag she had given him for his seventeenth birthday was half full. She should be happy he had selected that bag over any other from his half-dozen sports duffel bags, but all she had felt the last few weeks was an engulfing sadness. She looked at the clothes hanging over the back of a chair with a jogging suit topmost; at his squash and tennis rackets, Ping-Pong bats, flute case and running shoes on the floor. Three sweaters she had given him over the last two years were piled on the folded Ping-Pong table. She felt a spasm of searing ache, sadly happy that her gifts meant as much to him as to her.

For three months his conversations had so revolved around this projected year-long junket that each member of the family had developed their own particular way of teasing him. Krish had an elaborate gesture of showing "it" coming out of his ears; Priti, their nine-year-old cousin, had a knack of rolling her eyes into a squint, and Jyoti said a martyred, "Oh no!" whenever he started saying anything to do with the trip. They would never admit aloud that they were proud Jayant was taking to the road with Brendan, Jim and Bob, and that they loved the young men's animated and zany arguments that went on every weekend. They bragged to their friends about Jayant's ambitious trip, but at dinner every evening, they razzed him about how his junket was going fizzle or blow up.

All their best times, as far as they could remember, had been at the dining table. Sharad had long ago established a family custom that no matter where they were the rest of the day, they should be home for dinner, unless they had a valid reason — and he was sole judge of its validity — for their absence. They bitched about it, but came just the same, knowing as they grew older and complained more that the custom had kept them close as a family.

Now that Jayant was actually packing, the periodic bursts of emptiness that had sent Jyoti's stomach into a cramp were becoming permanent, as was the dull pain in the back of her head. *Too close*, Jyoti thought, *we're too damn close, and that's why I am bleeding inside as though it is the end of the world.*

When Jayant came out of his bedroom at the farther end of the basement, the rec room leapt into brightness; Jayant always turned on all the lights wherever he went. He stacked more record albums on the table and went back to his room.

Jayant is leaving home. A cuckoo clock inside her popped

that statement, flaring the dull pain into another spasm of searing ache. She could understand the emptiness. It was natural. Only fifteen months separated them in age, and any authority she claimed as elder sister was in exaggerated fun. They could just as well have been identical twins.

Her feelings of apprehension and resentment were more complex but still understandable. She was afraid for his safety; the car they planned to drive to California, and then east or south or wherever fancy took them, was a 1976 Pontiac, a relic from the age of monsters. They had repaired it over the last twenty weekends, in Bob's father's three-car garage, changing just about everything but the chassis, scraping and painting the outside, fitting it with a stereo deck and a horrendous muffler, or lack of one, that made it sound like a Concorde. They drove it as rashly as they drove their motorbikes. And so she was afraid. Jayant was immature, had always been rash. Though at nineteen he was six inches taller than her, not too long ago he had been a thin little boy with soft girlish features and large eyes, a spindle-legged waif who was always falling and hurting himself. But at twelve he had gone to the other extreme, tough-bodied and hyperactive, always getting into trouble for bullying others, climbing forbidden trees in the Bania's orchard where jackfruit and mangoes were grown commercially, hanging out with the kind of company "that misshapes one's moral spine" as Dad repeatedly yelled at him whenever he was caught. Jyoti had invariably covered for him or even abetted him in his escapades.

And then they came to Canada. End of Chapter One.

Now he was leaving home. End of Chapter Two. End of the age of innocence. The immemorial rites of initiation had changed in form and age but were essentially the same as those that had sickened her in the recent rerun of Alex Haley's *Roots* — that particular episode of the boy's initiation in distant

Africa: separation, blindfolded walk into the forest, three days on his own, and then the return, only to feel the clean guillotine-swift fall of the axe that initiated him into manhood.

She did not want to think about it, but Jayant had stolen her hour. At Christmas she and Pierre had decided they would have a July wedding and move to Edmonton. But before she could talk about it, Jayant had announced his plans and the whole family had revolved around him since then. She had not told her parents about herself and Pierre. What should have been open celebration was now a furtive affair.

Jayant was leaving first, making her feel guilty for the hurt Dad would suffer, losing them so close upon each other. Dad and Mom wouldn't adapt easily to the empty nest, especially since she was marrying Pierre and not someone of "our own kind," as Dad said even after all this time in this country. They wouldn't be able to take it. Or maybe they would. They were parents. Perhaps acceptance would come as naturally to them as resentment did to her.

But closer than this emptiness, beyond these fears, deeper than the resentment, all of which flared from time to time into anguish, was something that was frightening because it was so pervasive. Despair. A dull despair as at some inevitability. A primal feeling. A deer nimbly running towards the lake but braking of a sudden, sensing a tiger near, then moving forward again, driven not by its parching thirst but by a sense of inevitability. Kalidasa must have described it somewhere, for they had a way, the Old Masters, of combining breathtaking tenderness with nightmarish violence. Infinitely more moving than those who showed the violence of life through violent images. Separation, blindfolded walk into the forest, the circumcision blade; Shakuntala's deer, blue water, tiger.

She was exaggerating. For pittoosake, he was just going away for a year, and she too had to leave at some point anyway. But she could feel a pall enveloping the family, not just the five of them but the whole family: Priti and Vithal and Aunt Veejal and Uncle Anant; Pierre; and others, shadows now, but hers, their family. It was all around her, the smell and sound of it running in undulating waves and spastic vibrations; if she stretched her hand she could touch it. It was dry, hard, cold and stiff, like a dead hand.

What did the buffalo that roamed the prairies feel when they smelt gunpowder from the muzzles of a guns stalking their band? What did the Incas feel when they heard Spanish horses galloping through their land?

Jyoti remembered every new moon day the purohit would come with *darbha* grass, and her grandfather in his red-bordered white dhoti and shoulder cloth, sacred ash striped across his forehead and torso, his sacred thread dipped in turmeric, would sit on a wooden plank facing east. Sprinkling water with darbha grass, he would repeat the mantras that called upon their ancestors to assure healthy continuity of the family.

Where was the *kusa* grass that would help them through this pall of inescapable happenings, where the Gangajal that would cleanse them, sustain them, resurrect them? Was there a way out of Abhimanyu's labyrinth, some way they could bring to surface the cumulated power of their ancestors that reposed within them?

"Oh jeesus, where's my backgammon set?" Jayant was rummaging through the games shelves at the far end of the rec room. Scrabble, Trivial Pursuit, Clue, Blurt, Othello, Perquackey, Chess, Checkers, Yahtzee, Ludo, all the board games neatly stacked on the mahogany bookshelf were being thrown every which way. He ran his fingers through his hair.

Jyoti rose and went into the alcove at the far left, which was Krish's corner. She found the backgammon set on top of Krish's electric train set. The box was bound in leather, soft to her fingertips, its red and black suede insides seemingly fragile. Who could blame him for being upset?

"That kid needs a belting." Jayant took the box and set it alongside his rackets. "Talk of the devil," he added, as Krish came running down the stairs shouting, "Howdee folks!" Krish, at ten, still had some baby fat on his face and thighs, but looked very like Jayant because he went to great lengths to do so; he wore his hair, wavy black like Jayant's, just below his ears and he flicked it up with a movement of the neck the same way his brother did.

"How come you're home so early?" Jyoti asked.

"Second Wednesday, you know? Teachers have to have their monthly pow-wow. Suits me fine."

"Jeesus, I don't remember having so many in-service breaks in my day."

Krish walked up to the table tennis table and flipped through the record albums, pausing to admire his present favourites before going to the next. "You taking the whole collection?"

"Hell, no. You're welcome to all of them. I'm just sorting the ones I want copied for use in our car."

"You're really leaving, eh?"

"By next week I'll have you out of my hair, kid. Great, eh?"

"How long d'you think you'll be gone?"

"I've told you a hundred times, kid. A lot depends on what kind of jobs we get along the way."

"Maybe your money will run out before you reach the coast."

"Nah, we'll pick up some dough some place."

Krish shifted from one foot to the other. "I'm going to miss you, Bhau." He stopped himself short, realizing he had used a forbidden word. Back in Pune, he and all their cousins his age had called all older brothers and cousins Bhau as was the custom, but Jayant had shed his Indianisms fast and he had dinned it out of the others with his derisive taunts. "Oh shit, do you have to call every one Auntie or Brother or Uncle? And if you must go for all these crappy familiarities, say Auntie Vee, not Vee Auntie, for chrissake."

To make up for his lapse, Krish spoke loudly and brashly, "Jeesus, I'm gonna miss you, Jai, especially on Wednesdays' flyers route. They're so damn heavy. Can you give me a hand today?"

"Out out, bozo, you and your paper route!"

Krish wasn't quite sure if Jayant was being good-humoured or angry. But when Jayant kicked his Adidas bag clear across the room because it didn't have what he was looking for, Krish took the cue and left, whistling to cover his disappointment.

Jyoti moved to the table and drew a dart out of the quill that lay on it. She ran her fingers over the smooth red plastic, and pressed its gold tip on her finger. She looked at Jayant's black eyes, his nictating lower lids. He looked like a Kathakali Ravana. She threw the dart at the dart board on the far wall above the games shelf. It hit the second circle of metal, bounced off a boxed board game on the shelf and fell to the floor.

Jayant sat on the floor sorting through his books and filling a carton to be taken for the Children's Hospital Book Market. It made her think of a day, soon after Jayant had started school, when they had missed the school bus home. Or rather, he had. Seeing he wasn't there, she jumped off the bus, which left without her. Two minutes later Jayant came running towards her and she stared murder at him, shaking her fist, waiting to shake his insides out. Their school was nowhere near the regular bus route, and they would have to walk home. Her uplifted fist dropped when she saw tears rolling down his long lashes and down his cheeks as he watched the bus disappear around the corner.

"What we gonna do, Sis?" he gasped through his sobs. She put her arms around his shoulder and they sat on the culvert at the school gate until he'd had his cry. Then, hand in hand, they walked the two miles home.

Softly Jyoti said, "Krish and Dad, especially Dad, will miss you."

"Let him. Time he knew he's never going to live his dreams through me. Jeesus, just because he was almost, but never quite, Number One in anything he did. The way he's been after me all my life, to drive that crummy ball ping ping back and forth."

Jyoti looked at the cabinet that separated Krish's alcove from the rec room. The top and bottom shelves were cluttered with trophies, but the shelf at eye level had just half a dozen small silver cups on black bases — Jayant's first prizes won back in Pune, kept polished and in place by their father. Sharad himself had won several cartons of bigger silver cups that had once been on these shelves, but he had removed them about four years earlier when Jayant first entered the Manitoba Open. "My son is going to fill those shelves, just you wait," he would tell his friends. And Jayant had, with table tennis, and later with squash, trophies.

"No one can be so good at anything unless he enjoys doing it; besides I've seen your face when you are playing in a tournament; so don't try to pull that one on me."

"Big deal. Provincial champ in a crappy basement game." He threw a dart at the board.

"I'm glad you're pitching out," Jyoti said coldly, "and I sure hope it gets into that thick skull of yours that we're different, and no matter what we do, we are never going to fit in here. Take to the road, get high, sleep around, but still and all …"

"Fuck off, Sis, you'll see."

"All the swearing, all the in-jargon, you can swear all you want, but you're never going to be one of the boys. Not that I see why anyone would want to be."

"Don't you come at me with all that crap about morals and Hindu values and the whole hogwash. I've had an earful from Dad all these seven fucking years. Him and his pipe dreams about India. Why the hell didn't he stay there? A nuclear scientist, he was there right from the beginning, Trombay, Tumba, the whole bit. He'd have been a director of an Indian Institute of Technology or some national lab by now. Instead, he quits the place and rots here, selling houses, jeesus, a crappy real estate broker, just one step better than an encyclopedia salesman."

"He's not a con man, for pittoosake, people need houses, and," she added more assertively because she did not quite believe it, "encyclopedias too."

"Sure, sure, as much as they need a hole in the head. You remember where I got my *Britannica*? In the miscellaneous classifieds. I saw this phone number, watched the price go down from $360 to $120 over three weeks. I went there — a shitty little bed-sitter, this young couple. God, nothing in that room cost more than twenty bucks, and here was a thousand-dollar *Britannica* dumped on them by some smooth-talking salesman who'd sold him on how the encyclopaedia could educate him in applied electronics. Jeesus." He picked up a Ping-Pong ball and squeezed it in the palm of his left hand. As he raised his hand to run it through his hair, a faint smell of camphor from the ball wafted up, arousing nebulous memories of another place, another time.

Jyoti's face flushed with anger and she was about to say something, but stopped herself knowing her voice would tremble like the last leaf of autumn. She picked up a lime-green-glo-ball from the sofa and whammed it down on the floor. It bounced from floor to ceiling, ceiling to floor, up down up down.

Jyoti said, "It couldn't have been easy for him to pack up everything and move here at age forty, and it's no bed of roses here, mowing the lawn and painting the house and doing a hundred menial chores which used to be done for him by servants in the luxury of his ancestral home."

"Some house that, a sprawling shambles handed down untouched from the time of the Peshwas, where you have to walk half a mile to get to the shithouse. Jeesus, we haven't lost anything on that count; even he couldn't think so, else he wouldn't have signed it away without a second thought. And he wouldn't be so sentimental about that ancestral shack if he were back in Bombay.

"And you wouldn't be mouthing vulgarities. Have you ever heard such language from Dad? Ever?"

"He speaks like out of a book, and a mighty bore of a Victorian tome, too. Sententious half the time and sentimental the other."

"Stop that, Jay, just stop. You know why he came here, for us 'to live without tension and yet with dignity'," quoting him, " 'to give our children a healthy environment where, because one doesn't have to kowtow to politicians and the body doesn't have to scrounge for food, the spirit can aspire to higher experiences than this sorry world allows.' "

Jayant laughed sarcastically. "That's a load of crap meant to rationalize his failure. And the irony is that he isn't even sure he's found all that in the promised land. Higher experiences, hah! A real estate salesman. You know what your trouble is, kid? You're on the moon with that Pierre of yours, holding hands and singing moonshine into his brown black hair. If you'd get laid a couple of times you'd stop hearing all those preachy echoes of Dad's slogans."

He looked at her, and there was something in her eyes that drew him sharply against the wall of recognition. In a whisper he said, "You haven't, Sis, have you?" Even as he said it, he realized she had.

"Good luck, little brother," she said. "When you come back, Dad will fix you up with an upper middle-class, fair-skinned, homely Brahmin bride, as the matrimonial ads say when they mean home-loving. Virgin of course."

Jayant grabbed the darts from the Ping-Pong table and zinged them at the board in lightning sequence. All three lodged in the inner circle, one dead centre. He picked up his jogging suit and blindly rushed up and out, slamming the outside door.

Jyoti walked upstairs to her room and unbuttoned her cardigan with fingers that trembled in response to his pain. She flung herself on her bed.

She was about eight or nine, Priti's age. Jayant, whose school, only for boys, though run by the same Roman Catholic Mission as hers, had a longer December vacation and he was already in Delhi, visiting cousins. In the inter-class recitation competition, Jyoti had been chosen to represent her house, as class sections were called. She had a talent for memorizing poems overnight and this was not the first time she had competed in the 24-hour-speakathon, as it was called. That evening, as she memorized the selected poem, the import of the lines hit her:

> Oh call my brother back to me!
> I cannot play alone:
> The summer comes with flowers and bee,
> Where is my brother gone?

She burst into tears. The scenes were so clear — Jayant run over by a lorry; Jayant in the Yamuna, his usually curly hair straightened out and streaming behind him as he floated feet first; Jayant tripping along the railway tracks and being scooped up and flung away by the engine's cowcatcher. She cried herself to sleep, sure Jayant was dead in some corner of Delhi. She went to school next day, her stomach knotted with cramps. But she couldn't withdraw, for that would be letting down her team. And so she sing-songed her way — ti dum ti dum ti dum ti da — so that the meaning didn't matter.

When Jayant returned a few days later, they quarrelled and argued as always; and two years later, when someone two grades lower than hers recited the same poem, Jyoti snickered with her friends at its sentimentalism and they teased the poor girl to tears.

"Pierre Pierre Pierre." She chanted the name the way she might a mantra that would resolve all her problems. But Pierre was also a problem. No, she wouldn't think about it. God, how she missed him; if he were here, she wouldn't be thinking of problems; they would be too busy doing things. Oh, she could sleep forever, she was so tired. She lay on her bed, her fists clenched. They had hardly relaxed when she woke a short while later. There was work to be done.

Never mind Pierre, never mind Jayant, her polisci paper was due Friday, and exams started next week. Jyoti got into her winter clothes, thinking, *God, will the winter never end*, and set out for the library.

Chapter 2

Savitri entered a quiet house. She came in by the back door and stood on the stairwell, unbuttoning her coat. She stepped into the kitchen and placed a pile of scribblers and her handbag on the dining table. Then taking off her gloves, she leaned against the wall and pulled off her winter boots. Placing them in the boot rack by the stairwell, she called, "Jyoti? Krish?" No one answered.

Savitri was entering her forty-second year with a skin that had not aged since she was thirty. The first layers of middle age fat lay becomingly on her for she had always been softly curved, her elbows and shoulders rounded on her petite figure, her unobtrusive features setting off her marble smooth skin. She had a small forehead framed by thick wavy hair that curled lightly by the end of the day despite her tight chignon. She was wearing a well-fitting suit—black skirt, a gray coat with black in the collar, and a silver-gray blouse. Her hands deftly picked hairpins off her coiffure as she carried her coat to the front closet.

Krish entered the kitchen from the hallway to the bedrooms as Savitri returned. "Hi Mom!" He was dressed for hockey, helmet in hand. She tousled his hair as she walked past him and he said, "Aw, Mom!" and patted it back.

"Rushing off already, beta? Is Jyoti home? Have you had anything to eat or drink? Don't run off on an empty stomach."

"Aw, Mom. Not a chance I'll neglect my poor stomach any

time, and you know that. I got rid of all the overripe bananas for you."

"So I see, beta. And a pint of ice cream, too, I suppose," she laughed, putting his A&W mug into the sink. She took the glass jar from the blender base and rinsed it out before half filling it with water so the banana pulp could soak and loosen off the walls of the jar.

"I was going to do that, Mom, honest, just as soon as I had ..." He trailed off, watching her wiping spills off the countertop. He smiled sheepishly. "I'll put the kettle on for you," he said turning the knob for the burner on which the kettle was already sitting.

She tousled his hair again. "You are my little golden chore-boy, Krishna, what would I do without you?" She picked up the kettle, emptied it into the sink and half filled it with fresh water.

Krish opened his mouth to an O. "I forgot about the fresh water. But I know what comes next." He took the teapot from the cupboard and washed it under hot water.

Savitri took down the tea canister. "Go see if Jyoti is home."

"She was when I went out on my flyer route, but if she's still around she's quiet as a mouse."

Savitri took her books to the study she shared with her husband, and returned. "Her room door is open," she said. "Don't be late for dinner," she added, watching Krish button up his jacket.

"No way. We have hockey practice at seven."

"If it's at seven, what are you doing in all this gear now?"

Krish placed his helmet on his head and dribbled an imaginary ball across the tiled floor. "Pick up some game on the bay. Don't worry, I'll be home in time. Say, Mom, can I have a toonie for sharpening my skates?"

She opened her bag and took out her pocketbook. "Anything else?"

"Hot chocolate?"

"Finished your flyers already?"

"Yah. We got off at 2:30 today. Second Wednesday, remember?"

He sat on the steps and zipped up his boots, helmet by his side. Savitri disappeared into her room and came back a minute later wiping her face with a hand towel.

"Mom, me and Mike want to go to Saints Roller-Skating this Saturday."

"And you need a chauffeur?"

"Only to pick us up. Mike's dad will take us there. And I need a new math scribbler. I got ten out of ten in spelling AND in dictee. I almost blew it on "pirouette" but took out the second "r" just as our scribblers were being collected. Hey, Mom, have you seen my comb anywhere? The dark blue one? Can you buy me another? I think I lost it. Please?" He put on his cap and gloves as he spoke, gave his scarf a final tug and picked up his helmet. "Bye, Mom."

"Just check to see if Jyoti is downstairs, beta."

She put two spoons of tea leaves and boiling water into the teapot and went to her bedroom. Krish clomped down the stairs, through the basement and up again. "Nope, Mom, she ain't here, nobody home but us chickens," he sang, as he banged the door behind him.

"Bye, my sweetheart," Savitri said, coming into the kitchen as she pleated her sari. Tucking the pleats in at her waist, she stood watching him slog his way through the snow instead of taking the sidewalk.

Savitri looked different now, very brown, softly beautiful, and somewhat tired. With her hair cascading down her back, all traces of makeup washed away, she looked even younger than in her teaching outfit. The whites of her eyes were clear, pale blue as in infants, but her tiredness showed where her brows were knit in worry. She poured herself a cup of tea and sat at the farther end of the table, her back to the window. She propped her feet on another chair and closed her eyes. She imagined the sun shining warmly on her back.

The window was an oversize one, nine feet by five, the frame undivided by wooden strips the way it was in most other houses. The kitchen too was oversize, compared to the houses around theirs. The dining area was large enough to comfortably hold a table for eight. The table was of solid oak, a handcrafted piece from the 1940s that they had bought within a week of coming to Winnipeg. Not sure they how long they would stay, they combed the newspapers for used furniture, and picked up some beautiful items for next to nothing. The dining table set was one of the priceless treasures, bought from an old couple who were moving to an apartment. Sharad had phoned the number in the ad, and asked for directions; the old man had been quite specific. They were to take the second left turn off St. Mary's, and the house was the third one to the right just down the hill. Sharad's brother in law, Anant, who had been in Winnipeg a little longer than they had, drove them over. Frustrated, they went into a gas station on St. Mary's, phoned again, and told the old man the name of the gas station. "Oh, you are almost here," the old man said, "Head back two blocks, turn right, just go over the hill, and the house is the third one at the foot of the hill."

The "hill" turned out to be a ten-degree slope, so slight, it was no wonder they had missed it. Anant laughed and cursed Winnipeggers' idea of a hill as he parked the car. The house was full of wall shelves and display cases crammed with crafts, with a colourful quilt hanging behind the dining table. Everything smelled freshly cleaned, with the smell of furniture oil overpowering all others. John and Muriel Jones, the couple, welcomed them warmly. There were photographs everywhere, over the fireplace, between wall hangings, on bookshelves. Muriel, delighted to see so many charming visitors in her home, went over the family photographs on the mantel, saying where they were now and the names of the grandchildren. On one side of the mantel were two black and white photographs, yellowed with age, framed in dark mahogany with exquisite curlicues carved on them. One was of a young man in uniform, his hair clearly blond, proudly standing with military cap in hand; the other was of the same man, and John, and two others, all in uniform. Between the frames lay a square box, which Muriel's hand cradled, as she said his name — Christopher — her brother, whose medal was all she had now. The smell of apple pie wafted from the oven in the kitchen. A Westminster clock chimed five.

That scene was etched in Savitri's memory, her first impression of Winnipeg, a friendly place of warm, hardworking people and large, closely-knit families.

In the rented two-bedroom apartment where they lived at the time, there was no room for the extra leaves of the dining table or for all eight chairs, but once they bought their own house, the table had not only the extra leaves and all eight chairs around it but several stacking chairs as well that stood in a corner by the window. It was always open house at the Bhaves, their friends often said.

It was the largeness of the kitchen and of all the windows of the house that had attracted Sharad when they were house hunting, and they had bought it even though the bedrooms were smaller than was convenient. "But let us face it, we live at the dining table," Sharad had said, "and one can always fix up minor details." Sharad was good with his hands and tools; he loved carpentry, and he had fixed up the basement so the boys had their own rooms in addition to the family and recreation rooms. The low wide china cabinet with glass doors on both sides that divided the dining area from the cooking area had been made by him to match the table. "I guess I can always become a cabinetmaker," he had joked in those days when he had hoped to find a job at university or industry commensurate with his training in nuclear physics.

Savitri shifted her neck over the contours of the old-fashioned chair to find the proper curve to cradle her. Without opening her eyes she brought the cup to her mouth and sipped. Mentally she checked off the list of chores she usually did on Wednesday evenings, but suddenly realized she could not do anything today because she had to go back to school. Pete Kozolski had gone a little too far with his practical jokes. He had given chocolate-covered laxatives to three Grade One children during recess, and one of them had taken violently sick. Pete was in Savitri's homeroom, extremely intelligent, extremely lazy and totally irresponsible. The recommended dose of the laxative was half a square for a six-year-old, and the poor girl had swallowed four. Savitri smiled. The prank was Pete to a T. But it was not a laughing matter. Since she was the homeroom teacher, she was also under fire for Pete's misdemeanours.

Pete — broken home, of course. It was not politically correct to say "broken home" nowadays. But there were more and more of them everywhere in every class each year. Savitri wanted to transfer to another school division, away from their own area, for she felt she was prying into her neighbours' bedrooms.

But why was she breaking her heart over Pete Kozolski when her own home was on fire? While taking grocery bags out of Sharad's Volvo last evening, which she had taken out for emergency shopping, Savitri had come across an packaged condom, and remembered that Jyoti had borrowed the car last week. Jyoti had asked for Savitri's, "To go to the library", she had said, and Sharad had insisted she take the Volvo because of the bad weather. The condom was on the floor under the back seat. Thank god it was she and not Sharad who had seen it. Savitri opened her eyes and looked at the 8x10 photographs on the china cabinet.

All were school pictures, and so all but Krishna's were dated. Jyoti was particularly lovely in this Grade XI photograph, which was why she allowed it to stand there. She wore her long hair loose, parted on one side, as had been the vogue then. That, and her wide set eyes made her resemble the face that had flashed from covers of popular and news magazines and been emulated by models during the Kennedy years, and which had made a comeback. An elegance and a kind of seeming candour, although Jyoti's face was oval-shaped, unlike the square lines of those others. In this picture she had a faraway look in her eyes, so irreconcilable with the sullen twist of her lower lips that characterized her now.

Jayant and Jyoti, where were they? Did they know why they were doing what they were so hell-bent on doing? Jyoti, Jyotishma, my darling child, this still core of sadness that veils your eyes, this silence that pales your cheeks, when did you get it, my child?, and why? Conceived in the floodtide of my love, reared in the springtime of my wealth, when did you get it, my child, and why? In your eyes I hoped to see the flash that betimes brightens mine even now; in your voice I hoped to hear the song of the sky that comes even now to me though never so loud nor often. But you, in the floodtide of first love....

Savitri sighed, and sat a while longer with her eyes closed. The sun was on her back, framing her head and casting stray curls on the white lace centrepiece. Then she rose and energetically started getting dinner ready.

She was stirring *dal* onto the sauteed onions when Sharad came in. "Anybody home?" That was his usual greeting. "Everyone who counts, I see," he added, when he didn't get the usual Hi's from any of his children, and saw Savitri at the stove.

"You're a bit early today," Savitri said, "Would you like a cup of tea so you can have the *rassa* a little later?" She put on a fresh kettle of water. Sharad brought the day's newspaper to the table.

"Was that Jyoti?" Savitri asked.

"No, I just opened the door to see if there were any flyers. What is with Jyoti?"

"Oh nothing, I haven't seen her since yesterday, that's all."

"You worry too much, Savit. She's all right. Our lovely daughter. Don't you feel proud walking through a store with her? She looks so much like you, even the sad expression she has sometimes — it makes me so feel so protective and weak with pride. Reminds me of how protective I used to be of you. But then I remember how little you needed any protection. Always knew your own mind, didn't you. Come to think of it, I've been henpecked all my life, eh? You've always made up my mind and yours."

"Enough of your sales talk, come sit down."

"I rest my case. I sit down, I have tea instead of hot *masala rassa*."

Sharad smiled. All his handsomeness was concentred in his smile. When he smiled his face lit up, as did the room.

Savitri brought him his cup of tea. "Biscuits or crackers? I think biscuits would be better because the new brand of triticale crackers I bought last time is awfully insipid. Tastes like the mush we fed the cows back home."

She stood by his side and put her hand around his shoulder. He placed his hand on hers and leaned against her. "How about a date tonight? First I want to go over these designs I've got from McDiarmid to show you the deck I'd like to build this summer. And then ... " he smacked his lips, "don't tell me you'll be marking scribblers till 2 o'clock."

"Not unless you get hooked on a late night movie." She preferred having patio chairs on the grass in the yard rather than a deck, and she did have to go back to school, but she hesitated to tell him so.

"What a life! When one has to ask one's own wife for a date." Sharad bent his mouth to the soft roll of skin between blouse and waist. "Ummm." There was an air of being-in-love between them that had nothing to do with what they said.

Sharad was a dark complexioned man of forty-seven, with a head of black and graying straight hair. He had a lean face and a long neck that he tended to stick out and this made him look even thinner and taller than he was. He moved her hand to the nape of his neck and Savitri, familiar with his needs, started massaging. "Ah," he voiced his gratification at having his weak spot tended. "If only he didn't stick his neck out, he wouldn't have such problems," Jayant or Jyoti often said, whenever he complained about stress of work. "Or if he'd keep his head on his shoulders," they'd say. All of them loved playing on words and there were some jokes of which they never tired.

Savitri, as was her custom when they were alone at teatime, wanted to talk about matters that could not be shared with the family at dinner; but she could not bring herself to say what had been on her mind all day. She told him of Pete instead.

"The way you say it, you sound as though you admire his crooked genius," Sharad said. "Everything is flying off centre in this culture because far too much is excused on some pretext or the other — broken home, peer pressure, Dr. Seuss generation.... And teachers don't bother to tell kids clearly that right is right and wrong is wrong." He went on, elaborating.

"I was thinking," Savitri interrupted, "of those messages on radio and television and buttons, 'Have you hugged your child today?' What must a child feel on hearing it who doesn't have a parent?"

"Oh, those plugs," Sharad shrugged them off. "You are just too soft-hearted, Savit, worrying yourself sick over imagined heartaches. Everything is overdone here. Like that other plug they shoot at you after midnight, 'Do you know where your child is at this moment?' It gets to you the first time you hear it, but when you think on it, every parent who cares knows where his children are, and to parents who don't care, no sermon is ever going to have any effect anyway. Listen to this." He read from the newspaper, 'One hundred and ninety-eight high-risk kids cost system $7.9 million,' They suggest that earlier intervention would cut costs, blah blah.

"Manitoba spends 1.4 million dollars a day on these kids, can you believe that? I think they've made an error, but maybe not. On 4,500 high-risk kids. I sure would like to know what they spend on high-achievement kids; better still, why don't they provide something for everybody, like basic literacy for one thing; did you see the *Newsweek* report about illiteracy in high schools? And read this! 'Prisoners want more recreational facilities, and the new Headingley jail boss thinks he is going to set everything right.' Read this one. 'Councillors decided yesterday to hold off plans for a bylaw making parents liable for vandalism damages caused by their children.' What else do you expect? Of course they'll never pass such a bylaw in this society because, one, there is a two-in-five chance that their own children will be involved in vandalism, and two, parents and teachers are forever passing the buck to each other. No one wants to be responsible for anything, and certainly not for any person other than themselves."

Sharad went on about trust and responsibility and good moral backgrounds. Savitri trembled at the irony. When she could control her voice, she interrupted him to say, "I wish Jyoti would come back earlier some nights." She had to tell him sometime.

Sharad laughed easily.

"Don't be a worrier, Savit, she's a good girl, and Pierre is a decent boy. He is so polite, so respectful; and he looks like us too, with his black hair and eyes. Besides, you shouldn't continue to live in the prudish world of our youth. The youngsters are doing well. They have their own code of conduct and are often far more idealistic than we give them credit for. Everything depends on one's family background. Even though the situation may be similar, how one reacts to it is what is important." Sharad poured himself another cup of tea.

"I wish Jyoti would ..."

"She's out dancing, right? Don't worry, these crazes are perfectly harmless." He went on in a tone of explanation as though he knew all about it and she, nothing. "A hundred youngsters swaying and jumping together under strobe lights can't come to any harm; group activities are safety valves that each generation discovers for itself. As long as they are in a group, working off steam, they are all right. And thank god for our Winnipeg winters; nobody can wander in the bush, least of all our children."

Savitri smiled sadly, turning away to hide her face from the most vulnerable of all her charges, more vulnerable than those in her care at school.

Sharad continued to sit at the table, reading aloud from time to time items from the newspaper and adding his commentary. " 'Two Jewish students shot a Palestinian in Hebron yesterday sparking riots', okay, we got all that on TV yesterday. 'Egyptian Prime Minister called upon Arabs to be united' ... cutthroats all of them, but they will stand together against the rest of the world, more than can be said of us Hindus, that's the pity.... 'Colorado low pressure is heading north', oh no, another storm on its way.... Did I tell you I heard on the radio that Sturgeon Creek is bound to flood again ... and homeowners always raise hell whenever the City talks of building more dikes ... here it is, about Sturgeon Creek, why don't they just re-do the road higher? The bridge gets washed under, or threatens to, just about every year. These people have no sense about longterm planning."

Jayant came in. He unzipped his parka, threw his shoes down the stairs and came into the kitchen. "Whew," he said, fanning himself by flapping his parka. "I must have worked off a pound in sweat running four miles round that crummy track at Max Bell. Their lousy ventilation system is going to kill us."

He placed his hands squarely on his father's shoulders and helped himself to biscuits as he read the newspaper over his father's head. His face was pleasant and relaxed. His smile just like his father's, a little crooked and utterly captivating.

"How was your day, Dad? Did Mrs. Adrian L. Mackie make up her mind — the one who brings marbles to check the level of the floor in each room?"

"That's Mrs. Pringle. Mrs Mackie is the sweet old lady who wants a new three-bedroom apartment within half a block of her church, and there aren't any blocks with three bedrooms in that area. One of these days I'll manage to persuade her that even if all three of her children turn up with their children at the same time, they could make do for a night or two on the living room carpet. Poor lady, she really should move into an apartment before her house needs any more repairs and gets unsellable. So, how's the car coming along?"

"Guess the old girl — she's been rechristened *Ida Busby* — is ready for the road, but us guys ain't quite.... Everyone's having second thoughts. Brendan's realized he's more involved with his girl than he'd thought; Jim thinks he hasn't saved enough money to have the kind of ball he'd hoped to have and he's worried about slaving at some job en route. Bob's the only one who is firm. I'll give them a week to get over their latest hangups. And then there's the flood; won't bother us if we head straight west, but we'll see. Say, Dad, I noticed your car's been in the garage all day. Got a chauffeur driven limo or something?"

"I forgot to plug in the block heater last night. It didn't seem all that cold this morning, but it wouldn't start. Maybe I should get the battery checked."

"It isn't even two years old, Dad. Did you plug in the trickler? I'll check it out for you. Why didn't you give me a shout? We could have got a boost from Matt next door. Why didn't you call for the company car? You shouldn't have to take a bus."

Sharad shook his head. "I should take the bus more often and get used to it, son. I just can't take crowds, and that's bad."

"Come, Dad, it couldn't be all that bad for someone who's taken the bus in Bombay, hanging onto a strap without space for half a foot or even just toes. " He playfully pummelled his father's shoulder.

"All those alien faces staring at or through you. It makes me wonder, makes me ask myself, 'What am I doing here? Who are these faceless people among whom my life is oozing away?' Each of them is so self-contained, looking at me as though I shouldn't be there. All those discreetly questioning eyes that make me ask myself endless questions."

Savitri said, "I know what you mean. One feels so vulnerable. That is why I am glad I have my own car now."

"But how long can we live this way, in a shell. Isn't it frightening?"

Jayant said, good humouredly, "To each his own hangup, Dad. When I take a bus downtown, I love the ride. The Pembina strip might be an eyesore, an 'aesthetic black hole' you've said, but there's something that grabs your guts, even in winter. Or maybe it's that Stanfield billboard at the Jubilee corner, but I sure feel my spirit raring to go up the ski slopes, even if it is only with designer name underwear to hold me up and Cougar boots to centrally heat my soul. Every time I go over the midtown bridge in a bus, I get a mighty kick thinking of the Indians' canoes and Hudson's Bay Company boats. Yeah, I'd have liked to have been here seventy, eighty years ago, on the Red and Assiniboine rivers."

Sharad, who had laughed at Jayant's descriptions, now said seriously, "You've said it, son, the fascination that rivers and mountains hold.... That's why our people raised temples on every hillock and riverbank. Our people ..."

Jayant, still good humoured but with an edge of impatience, cut in, "Our people, our old country — Dad there's no our people, no old country for anyone in the world anymore, least of all for us. *This* is our land and here we shall stay."

"Roots, son, roots. I often think of our plantain trees back home. Each plantain tree leaves a young sapling before it dries up. That is why we have a pair of plantain trees strapped on the posts of the wedding shamiana or the doors of houses on all festive occasions — it is a symbol of continuity and usefulness; you know how every part of the plantain tree — flowers, leaves, trunk — is put to good use. Roots are so important. Can we really grow roots here?"

"Sure, just look outside as you ride the bus. Or out your bedroom window at the new apartment block across the varsity fields. They call it Summerland because it's summer all year long in their balconies. They have twenty-foot trees around the patio, and five-foot tropical trees inside the quadrangle, all set up overnight and all flourishing like crazy. If anything, the pollution in the air seems to have acted like pep pills."

Sharad shook his head. "That would be a most reassuring analogy, Jai, if ours hadn't died." He looked out of the window at the two tall poplars that stood between two evergreens near the fence between their yard and their neighbour's. "The centre branch didn't bloom last summer, if you remember, and you know what Matt said? He said they are Ontario poplars not native to Manitoba, and so it is to be expected that they would dry up one winter just like that," he snapped his fingers. "Looking at them now. Who'd think one of them is dead, that the core is dried up, that the sap's not likely to run up those beautiful branches so perfectly shaped one would think they've been trimmed that way? If it doesn't leaf this spring we should cut it down, he said, else it will snap in a storm. And if an Ontario poplar can't survive in Manitoba soil, what chance do we have?"

"But, Dad ..."

"Oh, it is news time." Sharad rose hastily and went off to watch television.

Jayant took his father's seat at the table, and opened the newspaper. Savitri said, "Read me the real news, beta."

"Yeah, unlike Dad, right?" Jayant laughed. "And he seems to think I'm like him."

Savitri said, "You are, beta, in so many ways. Read to me about that poor boy at Oakbank, isn't that terrible? I caught the news halfway through this morning, and heard that a five-foot-eight, one-sixty-pound guy had fallen into a snow fort he'd made, then the news reporter went on to say he was thirteen years old, just thirteen years old. My stomach knotted up, poor child."

"A lot worse is coming, Mom, they say it might go down in history as the flood of the century. I've phoned in to be on the volunteer list for diking."

Jayant read about the diking at Fargo, where the Red was expected to crest by the end of the week. "Much depends on what the ice jam fourteen kilometres south on the Bois de Sioux River does," he read. "And listen to this, Gerald Flood says in his column that blizzards like what we've just had are likely to set Manitobans leaving the province in droves. He has statistics. So, maybe I won't come back after my trip after all, eh Mom, how does that sound to you?"

"And leave behind the Pembina strip, with its Stanfield underwear and Cougar boots? You wouldn't have the heart to do that, would you?" she laughed.

"Listen to this," he said. " 'Home owners bristle at the prospect of diking.' Great, do they want to go under or what? Check this out, Mom, {many people are not heeding the possibility of flooding'." He continued to read, flipping the pages, relaying information about historical tidbits. "Did you know that in 1916, there were 3,400 people of Chinese descent, and that all 163 laundry shops at the time were run by Chinese? and that today there are seventy Chinese restaurants in town? Incredible isn't it? And there are hardly four places with East Indian cuisine. How about that? Why doesn't someone start a really classy Indian restaurant? All those women who cook humungous dinners for their humungous parties, why don't they get together and start a really classy restaurant with some ambience? That'll be the day."

Savitri continued with the cooking, and when she started on the *chappaties*, the last thing she cooked every day, Jayant rose and started setting the table. Each of them had their own distinctive plate and mug, though the cutlery and glasses were of the same set. "Say, Mom, I'm going to miss my plate and mug. I've had this ever since we came to this house. 'Member the awful set we had when we were in the apartment, with big hoopla flowers all over? Ugh. We bought this at Eaton's the day before we moved here. Six years using the same plate and mug! If this breaks when I'm away, my heart will break." He held his plate to his heart dramatically.

"It's like your desk in class," he went on. "Just try sitting at somebody else's usual place and they'll stare daggers at you. We get so possessive, don't we?" The doorbell rang and he went to answer it. "Oh, hi Aunt Vee. Hi Pixie Trix. Come on in."

"I don't have the time, I have to rush off for a meeting. Is it okay to leave Priti here for a couple of hours?"

"Well," Jayant drawled, "we don't usually take in little monsters ... "

"Yeow, you mean old grizzly."

"Hello, Savit!" Veejala shouted from she was. "Don't have the time to unpeel myself of coat and boots, but I'll stop for a chat on my way back, if that's okay."

"I shan't be in, but come in just the same," Savitri shouted back, busy at the stove.

"Bye, Jai. Bye, Sharad."

Jayant closed the door behind her. "Well well well. Pixum Trixum, how many teeth do you have today?" Jayant was at this usual teasing. "I've already set the table, and there ain't no more room for nobody, not one."

"Is so, too." She playfully jabbed him and he pretended to knock her down before swooping her to the kitchen.

Soon Krish came back. When he was ready, they sat down to dinner. "Jyoti is not here yet," Sharad said. "I suppose she has her reasons." But they all knew he really meant she had better have some very good reason. For a few seconds everyone was quiet and then Krish and Priti spoke at the same time. "Jinx," they said, also at the same time, and the air cleared with their laughter.

"We used to have a long exchange instead of Jinx," Jayant said. "You kids don't have that any more? Tennyson."

"Longfellow," Savitri said.

"What goes up the chimney?"

"Smoke."

"What does that mean?" Priti asked.

"Nothing, as far as I know," Savitri said, "but it sounds good."

"We're not through yet, it goes on, Mom," Jayant said.

"Aw," Krish pretended to yawn, "how dumb."

Savitri attended to the children's needs while the others helped themselves. She gave a large serving of everything to both children because another of the family rules was that no one should leave anything on their plate, and so a large first helping of vegetables and *dal* ensured their dinner was a balanced meal no matter what they had eaten or not eaten at lunch.

"Eggplant, yuck." Krish pushed it to the edge of his plate.

"Oh, gross!" "Yummy." "Don't take a ratch." "Oh, flip." Savitri smiled indulgently at their jargon, her mind far away, her eyes periodically looking for Jyoti. Jyoti, Veejala, Pete Kozolski. Hands reaching out to her from all directions. The same hands at times needing hers and at other times steadying hers. But now she did not know whose had the need, whose gave the reassurance. Need: her world had always revolved around needs, but now the indistinctness between the hands pressed her to the wall. Pete, her helper at the last parent-teacher evening, his bright beady eyes blinking back heartache as he ushered each set of parents at designated intervals, making sure no one stayed beyond fifteen minutes; and she furtively letting her hand linger on his shoulder or head anytime she could, silently reassuring him he mattered whether he had parents or not, whether they ever came to this interview or not. But there had been other times in the course of a normal working day when in spirit she had turned to him, seeking reassurance about the worthwhileness of her job among so diverse a room of children with such diverse levels of background, performance, emotional needs. And Veejala, why was her mind turning to Veejala in sudden leaps? And Jayant, what demon had he tried to exorcise, running four miles in the track house? Hands that reached out, hands that comforted. Whose was which, which need whose?

And in the midst of all this panic was the sanity of dinner, the soothing jargon of "Oh, she took a hairy!" and "No kidding?" as Priti and Krish monopolised the conversation. Krish sometimes wanted to show that he had outgrown baby language, but with Priti around he usually fell back to her jargon. Though Priti was only a year and a half younger, she looked and behaved like a child. Suddenly Savitri's mind registered through automatic reflexes that Priti had gone too far.

"No, Priti, your shouldn't call your teacher a grizzly, it just isn't done."

"Sorry, Auntie. But it is all right to call some others a grizzly, right?" She winked at Jayant.

"Grr, I'll break every bone in your body. Crunch, crunch," Jayant said.

"Jai, you treat her like a four-year-old. She's in Grade Three," Sharad joined in.

Krish took it up right away. "Well, three," he drawled on the word the way his brother had, "that's pretty close to her mental age. What's for dessert, Mom, I have to rush."

"Fruit and vanilla ice cream."

"Can I have just the ice cream?"

"Sorry, no."

"Aw, Mom!"

Savitri brought out the dessert bowls and spoons. She scooped ice cream in each and topped it with blue grapes. Jayant's face registered distaste. Priti noticed it and winked. "I hate them, too, the seeds bug me." Krish added, "And they don't really go with ice cream, but what can you do with Mom?"

"I love them," Savitri said, "they remind me of *jamun*. Remember the marvellous purple fruit that used to drive parents up the wall because of the way they stained shirts and faces?"

"I have a Panchali spoon." Sharad held out his spoon, which had not been washed properly. Everyone laughed.

"Tell us the story, please, pretty please," Priti said.

"Aw, not again!"

"I haven't heard it for months, come on Unca Shar."

Sharad went over the story with due drama while the children interjected their own sounds and comments, most of which were now part of the telling as with all of their dinner table stories.

"When Panchali and the Pandavas ..." He paused, and Priti excitedly and Krish duly alternating said, "Yudhishtra, Bheema, Arjun, Sahadeva and Nakul ..."

"... were exiled to the forest, Panchali was given a magic pot that...?"

"... would provide as much of any and everything they needed to eat until it was washed."

"But it could not be used more than once a day …"

"… the magic would work only once a day …"

"One day, soon after they had finished their meal …"

"… every last lickety split …"

"… they had their meal at midday, not at dinner time but midday …"

"Sage Duravasa arrived at their ashram with his retinue. Panchali was in panic. How was she to feed so many guests?"

"... The cupboard was bare..."

"Aw, makes no diff. She didn't know how to cook anyway."

"She did so too."

"Nah, no way."

"Quiet. Sage Duravasa and his entourage went to the riverside for a dip. And Panchali was desperate. How was she to feed their guests? and if she didn't, how could they survive the sage's wrath, which was proverbial? He was as explosively quick tempered as …"

"A nuclear bomb"

"As Vithal bhau"

"'Krishna, brother Krishna,' help me, she prayed. And Lord Krishna appeared there, pretending that he just happened to be passing that way. 'I am hungry,' Lord Krishna said, 'please get me something to eat.' 'Wait till I tell you why I called on you,' said Panchali. But Krishna said, 'First feed me and then you can tell me'..."

"Anything everything."

"Any time all times."

"'But I've just washed the vessel clean,' Panchali wailed"

"Hnnn hnnn hn."

"Really o truly o clean?"

"'I have so too,' Panchali said."

"'Lemme see for myself,' Krishna said."

"So Panchali brought out the pot she had already scrubbed and put away. Sure enough, she was a sloppy dishwasher."

"She was a princess."

"Aw, all girls are sloppy."

"And there was a smear, a smidgen of ..."

"Spinach!"

"Dried grain of cooked rice!"

"Aw, Krish, we changed it to spinach, don't you 'member?"

"Krishna scraped it off and put the ..."

"Spinach."

"Rice."

"In his mouth and said, 'Ah, that was a good meal. Thank you. That was delicious. I am not hungry any more.'"

"And he burped."

"No, he didn't. That's bad manners."

"Did so too. Burping is a way of saying one is satisfied. You don't know nothing about India."

"Do so too. I've been there more often than you."

"What's the use? You always fall ill the day you land in Bombay."

"You're mean."

"Quiet, quiet. And just then, even before Panchali could run to pluck some fruits from nearby trees for their guests ..."

"The rest of the story is no fun."

"... the sage returned, and he said to Panchali he hoped she hadn't cooked anything, because his stomach felt full to bursting and he couldn't eat even a thimble of rice."

"And he burped, to prove it."

"And everyone who was with him said the same, they were ..."

"... full, up to here."

"And they all burped and lived happily ever after."

"No fair, you can't make changes."

"So, in satisfying Krishna's hunger, Panchali had fed all his devotees. Priti, what is Panchali's other name?"

"It's on the tip of my tongue."

"Aw, dumb. Homiensis sapiensis ignoramensis."

"Igno whatever yourself."

“I have to rush. May I be excused?” said Krish.

“Yes, be sure you rinse your mouth.”

“Aw, Mom! You don’t have to tell me that every day. I’m not a baby.”

Priti, with an alacrity she seldom showed, piped in, “His mental age, mental age.”

Jayant laughed, “Wrong cue, buddy. Congrats, Pixum.”

Krish left, but the others stayed on, waiting for Priti to finish. Jayant had not eaten his grapes. He never did. Savitri started clearing the table, hesitating over Jyoti’s plate, still hoping she would arrive before dinner was put away. As she stacked plates in the sink she thought of Vithal. Hands reaching out for help. Why was his hand there? Savitri stood at the sink, her fingers in warm suds that climbed up her wrist and popped, leaving a momentary chill on each nerve end. Why Vithal?

“I told her, ‘Donna Cloutier you’re the meanest meanie …’” Priti was saying. Donna, that’s why Vithal was there in her mind. Donna McCallum loved Vithal.

Savitri was relieved at having figured out the connection. Sudden unconnected presentiments scared her. Long ago, as a preteen, she and her siblings had spent a summer in Delhi with an uncle and aunt. It was their family custom to get together as many cousins as they could at one or other place every summer so they could grow up together. Probably the real reason was to give the parents, all but one pair, some time on their own without children running riot all summer; it was only as much work to manage ten or twelve children as two or three; moreover, the older children usually managed the younger ones better as long as they were cousins and not siblings.

Naren, who had just completed his first year of college in Delhi, had experimented with all of them on something he had learnt in psychology. Holding a deck of cards face down, each had to guess aloud what the card was and then flip it face up;

he took notes to see how many times each one got the number right and/or the suit. She'd got an incredible high score. Thereafter, when alone, she tried it out, slowly running her fingers over the back of the card before making her guess; this seemed to sharpen her ESP. It became a party game for her; while other cousins and siblings showed off their card or word games, she would show off her ESP. Then she started having occasional experiences of telepathy. Like the time towards the end of that summer when Daljit, who lived next door, fell off the terrace while flying a kite. A few days earlier, she had seen a boy in her dream, so swathed in plaster-of-Paris all over that she couldn't make out who he was. He was bragging about how it had hurt, but hadn't cried. When the accident really happened, she sobbed uncontrollably for hours and refused to talk to anyone. They gave up and let her be. Then Naren came in and soothed her; she told him she was to blame, she should have told him, told the adults what she had seen in her dream so that Daljit wouldn't have fallen. Now he'd never be able to play football for the country, as was his goal. Naren patiently explained that the boys had walked on the wall parapet every single day and were good at it; that she had always felt scared of the terrace because the parapet was just a few inches high and she was always afraid she would tip over if she leaned against it, even when her feet were on the terrace floor. She hated it when the boys walked on the parapet. That is why she had that dream. Daljit had tripped because he had walked backwards and caught a foot in the rain drain gap; if his foot had hit against the edge as it had so many times earlier he would have stopped as he and others had so many times earlier; it was just a freak accident. However, Daljit had fallen on to a charpai below and the rope-strings had saved him, except for his right arm that had crashed through the *charpai*; since he was left handed anyway, this wouldn't get in the way even of his writing, tough luck he'd have no excuse at school; and the dream was all wrong about Daljit's stoic forbearance because he had howled his head off and had been snivelling ever since.

Savitri was comforted, but later saw events and people elsewhere in space and time, sensed others' auras and feelings. They were momentary flashes always too indistinct to mean anything, and each time she was disconcerted for days. She was glad when she outgrew that stage, though embarrassed the day she found out she had lost it. It was at a party the following summer. With great éclat she took a deck of cards from someone else who had just finished a trick, and ping, got not even one right. She regretted not having practised periodically all those months, but never did try to develop those powers again. She did not want to know the future even though her heart ached now more than ever, wondering what the future held for her children.

Donna Cloutier, Priti's classmate; Donna McCallum who loved Vithal and was losing him through filigree impediments of ideals and goals. Savitri remembered the silversmiths of Pune, stretching silver strands over flame, curving, shaping them into intricate designs. One could always make out the presence or absence of that final finesse that differentiates art from non-art, that final skill which gives the touch of completeness. Filigree patterns of mind and heart bound those two, but they did not align. That was it — alignment — the missing element in some of that silverware made in Jeweller's Lane in Pune but which was always there in the jewellery sold at the air-conditioned boutiques of the main street. If only they would align.

The water was getting cool in the sink. There were hardly any bubbles left. Mr. Grierson would be on his way to school, as she too should be.

Hands in warm water, hands in suds, nerve ends feeling that subtle breath of cold as each bubble burst.

Savitri rushed through her washing. Jayant would do the rest. She went to get dressed while Priti, Jayant and Sharad continued to chat at the table. Their voices came comfortingly through the hallway as she changed into her pantsuit. Jayant was so good for Priti; the poor child needed an older brother and Vithal hardly filled the role. But Priti was good for Jayant too, she realized. She brought out his gentleness, good humour and patience, qualities he was missing all too often of late. Hands that reached out were often the same as the hands that reassured. The realization came to her soothingly now instead of panicking her.

Jayant was now relating a story about the outhouse in the far corner of the yard in Grandad's home; it had no roof and there was a *parijata* tree that shed loads of *parijata* flowers in the blooming season. He was mimicking the sweeper-woman's angry outburst at how the flowers were a nuisance, smelling up and making untidy her domain!

Savitri was about to contribute her own memories to their conversation, memories from a time when the outhouse did not have plumbing and commode, and was open not only to the sky but to the rear yard too for stray piglets. But there was no time.

"Remember the pigs, Mom?" Jayant said, as she pulled on her boots. He knew it only as a story, but spoke as though he had been there.

"One man's waste is another's food, etc., etc.," she laughed.

"What pigs? Did you have sweet pink little piglets?"

To Krish and Priti piglets meant Wilbur in *Charlotte's Web* and the three little pigs whose houses had been huffed and puffed and brought down. To her the word brought out other images, "yukky," as Priti would say if she knew. But Jayant was carefully steering the talk away to something else, knowing Priti could never enjoy their pig jokes. Oh, he was so good for Priti and she for him. Why did he have to leave? The pebbles of worry that had been rapping at random against her consciousness now coalesced into a lump of granite on the floor of her womb. *Jayant, my son, my baby.*

She had breast fed Jayant into his eighth month. He was a difficult baby. He would not have his milk at bedtime, but would fret himself to sleep and wake up close to midnight. She had got into the habit of bringing him from his crib to their bed so she could sleep. She would wake up to the feel of his little fingers moving around her breast, his open O-shaped mouth sucking at air till fingers and then lips found what they sought. Later he would bite in exasperation, asking her to give him her other breast.

Savitri opened the back door. It had just started to snow.

"G'night, Auntie."

"Night, night."

"Sleep well, Jayant," she said, wishing she could draw him to her side again and never let him go. The night was cool and still, the snowflakes quietly falling to the ground.. She stood by the garage door for a minute before getting into her car.

Chapter 3

Veejala arrived a little after half-past eight. Jayant let her in and fussed over her, helping her out of her coat, and giving her a hug.

"I got away early. I can even sit down for a minute and have a cup of coffee, if anyone cares to make me a cup."

"Polly put the kettle on!" Krish sang.

"I think some *rassa* was left over today," said Sharad. "I could check."

"I'll get you a hot cup of it." Jayant hurried to the kitchen. Veejala entered and sat on the arm of the sofa nearest the door to take off her high-heeled boots. She was a strikingly good-looking woman, elegantly dressed in an expensive skirt-suit. Everything about her was aristocratic. She had that air of confidence that successful career women acquire, and a couture that was associated with opening nights at the ballet. Her makeup was just right, discreetly accentuating her bold large eyes, curved lips and high cheekbones, while toning down her prominent jaw line and straight nose. Her hair was perfectly groomed, falling half way down her back. She wore no jewellery except a blue ground kimberlite diamond ring that flashed brilliant red and blue, and a watch with a band of exquisitely woven gold. Over and above the sum of these parts was that expression of one born and reared in the kind of wealth where money is never mentioned, where people tacitly and sometimes obsequiously accepted her superiority, where one was expected to be a benevolent despot of unbounded generosity and compassion, the kind of personality moulded over many generations, and even so surfacing in only some siblings. Sharad's features resembled hers, but he did not have any of the unselfconscious hauteur that characterized Veejala.

"Look at what we've made!" Priti, sitting on the floor, pushed an elaborate Meccano structure towards her mother, a crane carrying a hump-roofed truck with a working pulley.

"We, huh, Jayant you mean," Krish scoffed, miffed at having missed the fun because of his hockey practice. He was still in his hockey clothes.

Jayant brought in a steaming mug of *rassa* and placed it on a side table next to the recliner where Veejala was sitting. He sat on the carpet and tinkered with the crane. "You should put the whole thing on wheels," he suggested.

"What good are three wheels? You think Krish can keep any of his sets complete?" Priti said.

"Oh, flip."

Veejala reached out and ran her fingers through Jayant's hair. "I could give you a haircut before you leave."

Jayant pulled himself closer to her recliner and leaned his back against her. "An oil massage is what I need."

Veejala massaged his head, singing a masseur's song from an old movie in which the masseur guaranteed relief from all aches of head and heart — "O sar tera chakraye, ya dil dooba jaaye, aaja pyare, paas hamare ..." She scratched his hair upwards and put a clump into a hair band taken from Priti's head, much to Priti's glee. "You haven't changed since your baby days, Jay, you always wanted your head scratched. That was the only way to get you to sleep. Jyoti liked to have her ankles pressed; she still has weak ankles, doesn't she? Vithal ..."

"What about me? What did I like?" Priti wanted to know.

"Oh, my babekins, you were so undemanding I don't remember."

"You were so busy you," Sharad started, but Jayant cut in,

"You loved to have your ears cleaned, Pixie. The number of Q-tips boxes I've cleaned out babysitting you!"

"Mum, Jayant was telling me about Grandad's house. Is it really true you used to play badminton in the dining room?"

"Why, yes, it is almost, not quite, the size of a regular court, forty feet by twenty feet and almost twenty feet high, much lower than regulation height. We made the lines smaller all around to leave a bit of room outside the lines, but it didn't matter when we were under ten. At that time there used to be a partition right at the centre, a five-and-a-half foot wooden wall that used to be our net, and it was hilarious because you couldn't see the other side except through the door at either end. We spent half the time accusing each other about cheating on the service lines, which we drew with rangoli paste on the black floor. But when I was about twelve, the partition was taken down especially because of the doors. The main hall was renovated about the time my Auntie Reena got married into a family of really tall people, ookpiks as you would say. Grandfather figured he didn't want her in-laws cursing his daughter for bumps on their heads. People in earlier generations were rather small, I guess, because the doors were all so low inside the house. Have you noticed how each generation is so much taller than the preceding one nowadays?"

"Thomas Jefferson was considered tall, and he was five-foot-six," Jayant said.

"Better food, more care," Sharad said.

"Oh, phooey," Veejala said barely audibly.

"What did you do with the furniture?" Priti asked.

"There wasn't any. It was a dining hall."

"Aw, don't you remember how people in India eat at weddings?" Krish interrupted, "From those big leaves stitched together into a round plate, and sitting on the floor?"

"Every other day was like a little wedding when we were growing up. There were always shoals of people wandering in and out every day, and at least ten Brahmins at lunch most days because of some pooja or the other, a naming ceremony or death anniversary or engagement lunch; if nothing else, there was the monthly Amavasya or Satyanarayan pooja, for the dead, the unborn, the reborn, everything and everyone included in the everyday routine. Both kitchens were running full steam from dawn to dusk"

"Two kitchens?"

"But of course, two kitchens with two sets of everything; one for the cup-saucer-spoon people and one for the others."

"Aw, no kidding!"

"There was far too much kidding," Jayant said. "The place was always swarming with kids; now the kids are all from the servants' quarters alone, as I noticed last I was there, but I can imagine how it must have been thirty years ago within the family as well. Just as it is on the streets of Calcutta now."

Veejala gave Jayant's hair an impatient tug. "Irretrievably brainwashed by our newspapers, aren't you," she muttered.

"Must have been such fun," Priti said.

"Oh, I wish I'd been there. Was it fun?"

"I suppose so, I don't remember now, sweetie."

"How come you never tell me about Grandad's house?" Priti whined. "Unca Shar is the only one who tells me anything, and Jayant."

"I'll remember it all in my old age, sweetie, and tell lovely bedtime stories to your babies, okay?"

"How come you don't tell *me*?"

"Calm down, sweetie. You have only bad memories of Pune. Every time you've been there you've fallen ill with one thing or another, and so talking about your visits won't do us any good; you have this elephant-like memory of all the bad experiences that surface when we think of Pune. Besides, this is home to you, and one can have only one home at any given time. So let's not get confused as to what's what. Now, help Krish put away all this, it's time to go home."

Sharad, in a voice that took on deeper timbre because he

was so serious, said, "I think children should know about their heritage. It goves them something to fall back upon.

Veejala cut in, "If there's a crutch handy, you, and by that I mean all of us, can bet your last dollar you'll use it whether you need it or not. That's human nature. Whereas if it isn't there, you'll jolly well learn how to move around on your own two feet. And all that baggage from the old country is just a crutch. All that weight on our backs. We have to strike roots here, I know that, you know that, but we sure have a devil of a time doing it. But let's not mess up anything for the kids, okay? "

"The past is important. One must have a sense of identity, of pride."

"Sure sure, but we overdo it, Sharad; only those who can't cope with the present tend to live in the past; romanticizing the past is an escape route at best, and it can be toxic."

"About this identity and pride bit, Dad," Jayant put in, "I hear a guy out west compiled a report after interviewing apartment block caretakers and cleaning maids. He writes that most of them said East Indians were prompt with their rents and so they liked them, but they were also aloof and superior, and didn't get along with others. Too proud, in other words."

"Reports," Sharad said with contempt. "Don't believe any reports or statistics. They invariably contradict one another. In this country people make a profession of living off other people: educators write volumes on teaching methods instead of actually teaching; writers become critics instead of writing; poets have to be actors to get heard."

"Heh, Dad, sounds like you have a new client! A radical university prof., right? You've got new examples for your old theories!" Jayant didn't mean to be sarcastic, but that's the way it came out. To compensate, he said, "That's true about statistics and surveys. Someone here in Winnipeg took a survey in School Division One some years ago, and found out that East Indians were bottom of the list on dating choices, meaning no one wants to date Indians."

Veejala caught the wave of tension shooting between father and son and pocketed it. "About that report, Jay, ask the fellow to interview the same persons' employers and you'll get another story, that East Indians are very docile and easy to control and boss around. And both," she turned to Sharad, "will be true. Statistics without a perspective of cultural background is hogwash. For example, only now, after decades, it has gotten through to many that the black children of Georgia shouldn't be judged by Boston-formulated IQ tests."

Priti was not perturbed by the currents of friction in the room, but she was bored. "I love Uncle's stories," she said emphatically. "I'm going to be a storyteller at the Library when I grow up. So, Unca Shar, you have to tell me more about Pune and Panchali and everything about back home."

"Before I count to ten, you'd better put away the mess, get your things, and put on your boots and coat. Else I won't take you to Pune this Christmas."

"You mean you're going? Can I come too?" said Krish, suddenly excited out of his usual scoffing.

"We can miss school, yippee!" Priti danced.

"Ask your dad," Veejala replied.

"Sure, take him. Auntie Vee is always on wheels, and she just might forget you at Timbuctoo airport, but we'll put a label tag around your neck because we know that lost baggage always finds its way back home, eh?"

"Up up up, Priti, time to go. I have an honours seminar first thing in the morning. Oh, I hate Thursdays." Veejala took her coat out of the closet before Jayant could get to it.

"And I hate Mondays and Tuesdays and Wednesdays and Fridays as well," Priti sang as she put on her boots.

Chapter 4

Jyoti was walking along the tunnel towards the Arts Lounge when she heard her name being called. It was Rick McGregor. She waited till he caught up.

"Hi Rick!" She was genuinely glad to see him. They had been friends since collegiate days. "Where've you been? I haven't seen you in class lately."

"I dropped our anthro course. How are things going with you?"

"Okay, nothing to write home about. No wonder I haven't seen you. Why did you drop it? I thought you loved anthro."

"I did, but the guy gave me a D on my research paper last term. I thought I'd make up this term, but it wasn't worth the hassle. At least the grade won't be on my transcript, since I managed to withdraw from the course just before the deadline."

"Gave you a *D*? Gave *you* a D? No kidding. Did you talk to him about it?"

"No way. He's a tough nut to crack. The D, especially with that penalty for late submission last term, would have plopped my grade point average more than I can afford, even if I aced the exam. Forget it, though, let's talk about better things. The Kiss concert on the 29th for instance. I was planning to phone the gang this evening, once I get my English term paper out of my hair."

"Isn't the 29th a Tuesday? Sure they're here on a Tuesday?"

"And Wednesday."

"Isn't Gene Simmons kinda over the hill? Like fifty-something?"

"Are you kidding? They had the top-grossing concert tour last year."

"I read that there are always more guys at their concerts than girls. Why do you think, Rick? I mean, the guys' are lit-up like the star-spangled banner. One would think it'd be the other way around, that girls would fall for that."

"They're cool. Forget their showbiz and stunt effects — I hear they have hydraulic cranes to swing them out over the audience, but that's not the point — it's their music. They're cool. So, with all your questions, are you in or not?"

"Sure am. Wouldn't miss the gang. And the 29th suits me fine. All exams over. Super."

"Great. Martin says we can have the post-concert bash at his place. Tell Chris, could you? He's still in anthro, right?"

"Yeah, will do."

"Talk more later. Have to rush. McEachern will bite my head off if I don't hand in my paper today. And he bases his grades on the length of your bibliography. I used two books. Have to rush to the library and get another twenty titles."

"Rick, he's not going to buy that."

"You never can tell. *Ciao*."

Rick went on towards the library while Jyoti climbed up the stairs to Fletcher-Argue.

The moment she was alone, it hit her. How could she have committed herself so unthinkingly to anything without checking with Pierre? The sight of Rick had taken her back to her collegiate days, when she was part of the concert gang. The last eight months when she and Pierre had got serious had simply been wiped away during the conversation. Jyoti felt guilty, nervous. And resentful. To have to check with someone instead of being spontaneous. But as swiftly as it had built up, her resentment ebbed. It was only fair; that's what commitment meant.

"It ain't none of his business," Debra said quite categorically to Jyoti's troubled narration of her problem. "Quit gender role playing, Jyoti. Does he ever tell you where he is or will be? You say he's in Regina, but did he say what he does on these business trips?"

Jyoti wanted to be told just that, but coming from Debra, it had the opposite effect, making her want to defend Pierre. No, Debra wasn't the right person for the occasion. She shouldn't have confided in Debra. But when one has been best friends through school for six years, it becomes a habit to confide even though their paths had diverged. Everything Debra said had a trumpet peal of conviction. She would certainly get into any law school she wanted. She was so articulate; Jyoti marvelled at the way she strung out long sentences in a well-modulated voice, complete with commas and semicolons and all the unchanging vocabulary of advanced social science courses.

"You've got to stand up for your rights. You've got to develop a positive self image. Jyoti, don't you read anything? Unless we conceptualize the parameters of the problem ... I don't mean we should ignore the variables ... apperception tests conducted in Harvard show ... individuation requires that ..."

Jyoti escaped from her and went into the lounge. She threw herself on the carpet, resting her back against a vacant sofa.

She loved Pierre. She lived for their times together. When she was with him, nothing else seemed important. Their love blotted out the clouds and made a canopy, an arboretum, an indoor atrium where it was summer all year long. She trusted him; she wanted to share everything with him. She loved him and he loved her. And they were getting married. It was as simple as that. That was marriage.

Why then was she flinching at the thought of marriage,

why this resentment? The finality of it bothered her. They were so happy as they were. Why did they need this piece of paper? But Pierre was insistent. He was insistent about many things. That was one of the traits she loved in him, his insistence, his single-minded pursuit of goals, whether it was winning her to go to bed with him or his overriding business ambitions.

Kiss. What was she going to do about Kiss? After running into Rick, she noticed the posters plastered all over the University Centre near the box office: "Famed '70s fire-and-blood rockers still make a spectacle of themselves — and they're proud of it!" If a New York cop could become a hot-selling rock star, there was no reason why Pierre couldn't become a business tycoon. DVD/video stores were tomorrow's boom and Pierre was two steps ahead of everyone else. *Pierre. Pierre*, her mind chanted, oh, how she missed him. She wouldn't go to the concert. She'd tell Rick she couldn't. Pierre wouldn't come, and he wouldn't like her going without him. But she should, she should. No, there was no point going against a partner's wish, because one wouldn't enjoy it anyway once there was an argument. And of course there would be an argument. It stood to reason she shouldn't go just as he wouldn't if she didn't like something. That was marriage, trusting without question that there was a sound basis to the other's preference.

Boloney. It wasn't logical. She was simply thinking in circles, and all because of Debra's militancy. For pittoosake, she had outgrown rock concerts long ago. It was a good year and a half since her last rock concert. She wouldn't mind a jot missing that and every other rock concert in the world. But that was not the point; the point was that she felt torn and she shouldn't. Love should not be full of tensions.

She felt constricted, robbed of her independence. Nonsense. But what was sense? If only Pierre were here she wouldn't have to think. Pierre, Pierre. Sitting on the carpeted floor of the lounge, surrounded by a floating population and smog of cigarette smoke, she meditated — on her love, on Pierre, on their times together. His hands, his face, his passion, his insistence, the smell of his cologne, his skin.

She got up from the floor and sat by the window. All she could see was the parking lot. She listlessly opened her binder. Oh, how she hated studying. That would be one of the bonuses of going away, of getting married; she could just take up a job, a people-oriented job where one could coast on others' lives without being so obsessed with one's own. How had one spontaneous response to a harmless invitation rocked her so out of balance? Because it was a rock concert, ha ha. She looked out the window. The hill built by the snowplows that cleared the parking lot was white with new snow.

"Hi, Brad!" The voice was familiar. Jyoti looked up. Yes, it was Moma. Manorama Khanna was a striking figure who stood out no matter what the crowd; she carried herself like a Nefretiti on the Nile. No, like one of those sultry women who model winter furs on a horse ranch against a cumulonimbus sky; a tall, brown girl with a kind of brazen beauty and lifestyle that shocked the East Indian community. Her latest spotlight in the campus and local newspapers had been at a fund-raiser organized by the engineering undergrads — who else would think up such a thing — that was little more than a striptease auction for raising money for The Barn, as they called their special building. Engineering students bid for a dinner date with the performers. Moma was one of the stars. The articles had said she loved what she did; she did not drink, did not do drugs, did not sleep around, and please note that a dinner date meant just that and no sex, and she did have brains, as anyone who cared to see her transcript would know, so what was the problem? Some people paraded their brains week after week in television competitions, which, if anyone cared to know, she too had done in high school, and some people paraded their body for a good cause.

"Hi, Moma! You're *trés chic* today," responded the young

man she had greeted. Moma was looking extraordinarily *chic* and also extraordinarily out of place in a student lounge. She wore a plaid pleated skirt and high-lace-collared blouse under a black velvet jacket. She always dressed extravagantly, with more than average makeup, more than average heels, more than average jewellery. Her coat pin today had an expensive-looking, oversize stone; and her voice was always carefully controlled to a timbre of sexy casualness. "Enough to strike a guy impotent", Rajen had said at one of Jayant's basement parties. "I wouldn't mind trying," another guy had said.

"How are you, Brad? You never did return my CD. Is it still at Kim's?"

"Honestly, Moma," Brad said in a theatrical whisper that was louder than her voice, "do you have to foghorn my secret life to the world at large? Her hubby's got awfully suspicious, honestly, the guy is so jealous...."

Moma punched him playfully on his chest, and turned to an older woman who was with her. "Hi guys. Meet my aunt, Mrs. Khanna, from Delhi." She introduced her friends to Mrs. Khanna, a sari-clad woman in her forties, rather round all over and with a pleasant smile. Moma said, "I told her she hasn't seen anything of the U. until she's seen our Den of Iniquity."

"Wildlife in their natural habitat," said Brad.

"Hi, John!" Moma called out to someone who was walking down the other side of the room. "Come meet my Auntie from India. Auntie, John plays basketball for the Bisons."

"I wish I had brought my stilts," Mrs. Khanna said, stretching her hand to John's. "I feel a Lilliputian in Brobdingnag."

"Auntie!" (*Who else but Moma could get away with so many "Aunties"*, Jyoti thought.) "Don't throw such big words at us. This is our level of intelligence, see." She held up a styrofoam cup on which someone had punched a pattern of holes with a ballpoint pen. Everyone laughed.

"Hi, Moma !" Two other guys greeted her. Moma knew

everyone by name, unlike Jyoti who knew only faces most of the time, and greeted them with a generic "Hi" or a wave of the hand. "Alan," she said, as she gave a hug to one of the expanding circle around her, "meet my aunt, Mrs. Khanna. She teaches in a school for the mentally handicapped in India, and I thought it would be nice for her to meet some of you guys."

"Gee, thanks," Alan said.

Moma said, "More seriously, Auntie, Alan's girlfriend works at St. Amant's and you must take time out to visit there. It is quite something, the care and love between the kids and volunteers. I worked there one summer. Alan, can you help?"

He said to Mrs. Khanna, "I knew there was a reason for that hug; Moma's so good at getting others to work for her. But, this time, it's a pleasure. I'll give you my phone number ..."

"I know it, Alan." Moma claimed she had everyone's phone number in her memory. Jyoti waited for her to get him to write it down anyway, because she thought this claim about keeping all the numbers in her head was a popularity ploy, but Moma didn't.

"Hi, Jyoti!" Moma came to her, and her voice was even more artificial than usual; it always was when she spoke to people of her own skin colour. Jyoti got along well enough with Moma, but she felt that was because she had a white boyfriend.

Moma introduced her to her aunt, and added, "Jyoti has a brother Amar's age, Auntie, Maybe she'd know about the stuff Amar wants you to get for him." She addressed the group at large, "My aunt has three sons and a daughter and each has given her a shopping list yea long."

Jyoti smiled at Mrs. Khanna, who said, "I carry the list with me all the time. Yes, I would appreciate some help."

"Here, please do sit down. Can I get you both some coffee?"

Mrs. Khanna said, "No thanks, I seem to be drinking

coffee all day. Besides, it is lunchtime, I hope. One does get such an appetite when travelling, no?"

Moma dragged them both off to the cafeteria. On the way, Jyoti found out that the two were not really related; their families had been neighbours in Delhi at one time. They had hardly sat with their trays when Moma said, "Oh just a sec. I have to speak to Lynn, she looks so washed out, poor thing, I'd better check." She hurried off, chasing a girl who was disappearing out the door. Mrs. Khanna said with a touch of pride, "Moma is quite a stunner, isn't she? And she is such a warm sweet person too, so like her to go cheer up a person who is down. You too should talk to her."

Jyoti tried to laugh it off but felt very upset. "Do I look down, washed out?"

"You are a lovely girl, Jyoti, but you do look stressed out a bit."

"Exams are on." Jyoti sought an excuse. She wished she had not got into this situation; it was just as Sridhar said: one felt obliged to be courteous and helpful the moment one saw anyone who looked like they may be from India. Silly, really, because one should be that way with everyone. Just her luck that Moma should have gone off. If she hadn't, Jyoti would have excused herself on some pretext or other from this person. But, she had to face it, this person somehow made her feel she might have some answers. Like, if she had sons Krish's age, what was she doing here? Did she feel no guilt leaving them while she travelled the world?

She asked Mrs. Khanna as much in a tactful way. Mrs. Khanna shrugged her shoulders and smiled. Her mother-in-law lived with them, the children were old enough, and she'd got a rather good travel bargain. One had to see the world, didn't one?

But didn't her husband mind her coming away on a long vacation? The question sounded so blunt that Jyoti tried to cancel it. "I'm so sorry," she blurted, "it is none of my business."

Mrs. Khanna laughed. "Not to worry," she said. "Is that your problem? A possessive husband?"

"Oh no, I am not married ..." Jyoti hastened to deflect the conversation, which was getting too close for comfort. "Tell me about the situation in India."

"Not as bad as it appears from here. Things always appear much worse from the outside than they do when you are actually there."

"I didn't mean it that way," Jyoti said, thinking she had offended the visitor in some way."

"My fault, forget it. I am so peeved at the way your newspapers report anything that happens in India, always seeing the government as a radical Hindu theocracy. Don't they know that there is no way any government can be in power in India unless it is secular in practice? If anything, minorities are the ones who have the power. It is just that I am rather tired of going to parties and carrying on superficial conversations. Like how is it in India? People's questions often reveal a lot about themselves," she said. "This view from the outside happens to everyone. Me too. I was walking through Jackson Heights and Queen's in New York, and it was the most depressing sight I've seen. All those poor women from India living in all those awful, stinky, cockroach-ridden little flats. It was pathetic, but then I went to a Sunday gathering of sorts in the same area, and everyone I spoke to seemed really happy and didn't feel there was anything deplorable. The view from the inside is always different than the view from the outside. All I can say is that I am glad I live in India."

Jyoti's surprise must have shown on her face, for Mrs. Khanna quickly added, "I'm sorry. I didn't mean to put down anyone or anything, but this trip has given me a new perspective on many aspects. I've really enjoyed meeting people these last three months. The women, especially, have been so helpful."

Jyoti felt challenged by this woman. Maybe she could talk about her problems. It would be great to get another perspective.

And yet, when Mrs. Khanna created an opening with, "Let us talk about you. I would love to know more about the way people here live and think," Jyoti shied away.

"I would like to tell you, Mrs. Khanna, but you'll have to take a raincheck on that. I keep trying to see things from the outside and, as you say, they appear worse."

"Outside of what?"

She knew what she meant; if Pierre were here, she'd be inside and not so analytic. Yes, that was a help, but she really did not know what to say to Mrs. Khanna. But why not? She said, "I don't know, frankly. You're right, I am stressed out. It's because I'm seeing this guy and feel kind of guilty that I like some things he doesn't." She had said it; it wasn't all that difficult.

"But why should you feel guilty? If you decide you can get along only with someone who is exactly like you, don't you think that's rather impractical? Is that part of what's expected here? I don't mean to intrude, but I really am curious about so many things. Yesterday I met this very interesting lady, Maru, and she is taking me to the ballet tonight. She is so funny and cheerful. Do you know her?

"Oh, yes, I do. She's a good friend of the family. She is a scream, isn't she? What were you talking about?"

"She introduced me to this charming lady whose husband was a lieutenant colonel in the army back home, and who now works as a parking lot attendant. It is mind-bogglingly wonderful seen one way but just so sad seen another way. I don't know what to make of some of the stories I hear."

Just as the conversation was getting interesting, Moma came back. "Sorry I took so long, Auntie. Thank you, Jyoti, for taking care of my Auntie. So, how are you? I ran into Rick a minute ago, and he said all of you were going to the concert on the 29th. I have backstage passes, and I plan to take my Auntie to it, right Auntie?"

"Lucky you," Jyoti said to the aunt, "You're going to be seeing people and places no one who lives here ever does. St. Amant's, Kiss, and of course you will see the usual places too, I guess."

Moma picked at her aunt's plate of french fries which she had left untouched. "And how is your gorgeous boyfriend? I ran into him the other day at Earl's. Is he one handsome guy or what?"

Jyoti smiled as though gratified. But again, this was getting too close for comfort. She also regretted having confided in Mrs. Khanna, who knew Maru, who knew a great many people, which meant word would get around that Jyoti was dating someone other than "one of our own."

As she walked homeward, she chanted her new mantra. *Things always appear much worse from outside than when you are actually there.* And soon she would be there, inside the cocoon. Pierre and she loved each other. She wanted everything he wanted. They were one soul in two bodies. They would make love six times a day from now until eternity and everything will work out perfectly. That was marriage. Marriage was not bondage; it seemed so only from the outside.

Jyoti had been running almost unawares. Now she was all out of breath. She stopped in the middle of the boulevard where University Crescent curved out towards the houses. She took several deep breaths, then set out again.

Savitri was relieved to hear music coming from the basement as she returned from school. Jyoti was home and no one else was. At last, they could talk. She went down to the basement, calling out, "Jyoti!" over the blaring stereo. Jyoti was on the couch, her feet on the ottoman, books all around her. On seeing her mother, she leaned over and turned down the volume.

"Hi, Mom," she said, her voice noncommittal.

Savitri glanced at her sullen mouth and did not look again. By habit, she started putting things back in place as she spoke, magazines off the top of the television and into the magazine rack, books off the floor, socks that should go into the laundry basket.

"I don't want you to use your father's car in the evening, now on. Any time you need a car, take mine, and if I have to go out again later I shall take Dad's car. Is that clear?"

"What's the big deal?" Jyoti chewed on a piece of gum. "There isn't a scratch on the Volvo, not from me. So what's the to-do?"

"Because."

"Don't you think I outgrew that reason ten years ago, Mother?"

Savitri burst out with sudden vehemence. "We are supposed to treat you as rational adults even when you behave like beasts." She took out a packaged condom from her cardigan pocket and flung it against the back of the couch. "I don't know whether you want to prove something to me or whether you meant to flaunt this at your father or what, but I don't want this to happen in Dad's car, ever."

"Big deal, Mother, it was just an accident that it dropped out. Why would we put it there on purpose?"

"In Dad's car, how could you?"

"It was just an accident. What's the big deal?

"Not in Dad's car, never. Is that clear?"

"As for Dad, what makes you think he'll flip his lid any more than you? You help him wear his blinkers night and day. You trot him in and out of his ivory tower all the time, but surely no one could have lived here seven years without ..."

"How long has this been going on?"

"I don't think you'd really want to know. You should be happy, for pittoosake, that we are being so careful and all."

Savitri was taken aback, but she gathered herself together

with an effort. In a quiet voice she said, "I'll take you to Dr. Rogers and put you on the pill." Then she shrugged, "Maybe I am out of date there too, maybe a mother is not needed any more for that." More firmly she added, "But you will go to him, Jyoti," and after a pause, "if you haven't already, of course."

Jyoti picked up the condom and stuck it in her backpack. She remembered how much she had resisted and how insistent he had been. However, it had not happened in the car but beside it on a thick blanket that had been prickly and hateful and cold. Why had she succumbed, why did she always yield? "Ramses! Damn romantic name for a goddam rubber."

Savitri was startled at the bitterness in the girl's voice. She moved forward, instinctively seeking to protect her, but Jyoti turned away. The girl's rejection set off an explosive reaction in the woman. She said, "If that's how blasé you are about it, I pity you, Jyoti, I pity you."

Jyoti picked up several books at random and said with studied casualness, "I'd better run before you get behind your lectern."

Savitri, her hands on the back of the couch, stood still till the door banged shut upstairs. Then tears rose in her eyes. "Ramses." *When you said that, my darling, I wanted to hold you to myself, lick away your tears, smooth away your fears, take you back into myself and wrap you and keep you safe. Instead, I spoke to you as to a woman, a woman I wanted to claw and hurt.*

Chapter 5

At eleven o'clock the next morning, Jyoti was in the kitchen, having her breakfast. She was wearing her usual stonewashed denims and a loose, open-collared shirt. Her hair hung loose, uncombed. It was good to be having a lazy, quiet Saturday morning with the house to herself. Dad did the father thing Saturday mornings, sitting on the bench watching Krish at hockey practice. *Bet he's glad the season's ending*, she thought. Saturday was Mom's supermarket day, and weekends were Jayant's garage days, tinkering with their tub.*Ida Busby*, where did they get the name?

After the altercation with her mother, she had whipped back to the university. Coming in at ten-thirty had been dicey, for she had yet again missed dinner, but fortunately Sharad had been watching television, and Savitri was in her den, so Jyoti had slipped into her room and shut the door. If they weren't able to waylay her as soon as she came in, it was an unwritten rule that there would be no arguments after ten o'clock.

She had slept well, thanks to Pierre. He was super, as always. Hc had called around eleven from Regina and they had chatted for forty-five minutes. His call was always like his lovemaking. First he had asked all about her. "When did she wake up? What had she worn? Was her hair in a ponytail? What colour were her earrings and ring?" He wanted to visualize her exactly, photographically. "What had the weather been like? Had she walked or did she get a ride to the U.?" She had answered all his questions in detail, interjecting a litany of,

"I missed you, Pierre, I miss you." It was so good to hear his voice, his laughter. Nothing else mattered. The thought of Rick's concert and her mad walk home never for a moment entered her mind just as Pierre never for a moment entered her consciousness when she talked to Rick about the Kiss concert. After due foreplay, Pierre told her about himself. Everything was rolling along super (that was his favourite word and it had also become hers). He had almost finalized his deal. Ben Michalski, the present owner of the store, was a steady guy with a steady business. They couldn't go wrong with him. He was retiring, close to sixty-five and ready to drop out of the rat race, and he and his old lady had plans to do some travelling before the Reaper got to them. The store was ideally situated, lots of warehouse room, lots of parking space, just ten minutes from downtown. The place was only a village as of now, but it would be sitting up in no time. Five or six years and the city would be moving into the area. They couldn't go wrong. Oh sure, they'd get the loan. No problem at all. One had to put in money to get it back. One had to think big; one couldn't go wrong with video, it was the thing, just keep two steps ahead of the others, that's all. An electrical and hardware store in a sleepy place that was soon going to be a mega shopping plaza (he had an inside tip on that from one of the councillors). No, they couldn't go wrong. This was much better than the pizza franchise. "Believe it, this is super."

He had gone on with other details of his plans, all grandiose, all fail-proof. And she hadn't heard the best part yet, he said. He had found their dream house and had put a deposit on it. "Oh, baby, you're going to love it." Sure he worked fast, that's the only way anything gets done. But to be truthful, this was his third visit to Regina, remember? He'd been looking at this store and this house since his first visit. No, not a big deposit, but it was a private sale so the woman was being careful, as she should be, as we all should be.

"Oh, babe, don't worry," he knew just what she liked, and

she would love it, "believe you me." Four level split, sunken living room, "you gotta think big, baby, or you won't get anywhere." First thing Monday morning he'd drive down for the day, but he had to be back first thing Tuesday. "Don't worry, honey, he wouldn't get into another accident, promise," and he wouldn't exceed the speed limit, no way any cop's going to pull him off the road, no way anyone's going to know he's on suspension.

He'd gone on to talk about other details, the timeline for the video licensing, the renovations ... and then, oh, how he loved her yes yes yes he adored her, he could feel her in his arms, the aureole of her nipples between his lips, yes just relax, yesyesyes, oh it was so good, yes it would always be good because they were made for each other, yes.

Pierre knew how to rouse her, how to relax her; oh, he was a super lover. And she missed him, god how she missed him. But he had work to do, and the video franchise was a super idea; he'd better clinch the deal. "One had to grab Old Ma Fortune while she was around," as Dad said in his quaint way. See you soon, never soon enough.

Dad liked Pierre, thank god. Good old Dad. Poor Mom, she had been mean to Mom yesterday. Pierre, his hair, his hands, the smell of his cologne, his skin. Wonderful world, wonderful life.

Jyoti scooped the last little cereal grains off the bowl, and swept the toast crumbs off the table. Something was nagging her and she couldn't figure out what it was. Jayant, of course it had to be Jayant. He was leaving home. Jyoti sat on, cradling her coffee mug, unable or unwilling to put her finger on that nagging incertitude.

The doorbell rang. Jyoti came to herself, quickly took a comb out of her hip pocket and combed her hair. She went to the front door. Who was it? How exasperating the opaque glass panel was. They should have a peephole put in as were in most new doors. If it turned out to be a pair of Jehovah's Witnesses, she'd scream.

Jyoti opened the door. It was Sridhar. "Come in, Shri, oh it's good to see you, how are you, old pal? You never come in the front door. Oh, you have your car today!" Sridhar came in, taking off his parka and shoes. He was in his usual garb, a pair of baggy trousers in an outdated style and a full-sleeved shirt that hung on him loosely.

"Yeah, a weekend driver. They gave me outside parking, in the U-lot, so of course I didn't take it this year. Who wants to walk so far in the cold when the bus takes you to the basement in two seconds flat?"

"You've lost weight, Shri," Jyoti said with genuine concern, "you should take better care of yourself."

"Why the welcome mat? Something wrong? Did Krish beat you at Othello? Pierre not turn up? Mom refuse you the car? Prof. make mincemeat of your term paper? I love the welcome, but why?"

"A little of everything. But mainly because it was a relief seeing you when I expected a pair of Jehovah's Witnesses, is all. Have you noticed how they always come in pairs? Usually an older one, and a young one who always looks rather sweet, you know, kind of clean-cut and innocent-faced."

"So I have competition from there too, hnh?

"Not really, I prefer the rugged look, as you know."

"Yeah, that's why I didn't shave today."

"I was having a quiet cup of coffee. Come on, I'll make you a cup. If you swish some instant Nescafe and just a little bit of water in the mixie, and then serve with hot milk, it tastes just like back home, as you would say. I got this secret recipe just yesterday, from one Mrs. Khanna who is visiting from India. I'll try it on you. Come on."

They walked to the kitchen.

"Saturday morning and no one is home? Where's everybody?"

“Dad’s gone to Krish’s hockey game; a special game to end the season, I think.”

“That kid’s growing up fast.”

“Mom’s enjoying herself at Safeway as usual.”

“You never thought of helping her out, eh?”

“No thanks. The way she loads up the cart like there’s no tomorrow makes me gag.”

She got him his cup of coffee. He had taken the chair on the narrower side of the table. “That’s my chair, pal, don’t take my sunshine away,” she sang. “*Archie Bunker* rerun, eh?” he said, moving to the other side. Jyoti leaned her elbows on the table and looked at him seriously. “Tell me, Shri, do I look washed out?”

Sridhar peered at her through an imaginary monocle after wiping it carefully with a tissue.

“Contrariwise:

> Helen, thy beauty is to me
> Like those Nicean barks of yore
> That treacherously o’er the perfumed sea
> Dashed me to bits on yonder rocky shore.”

“Shri, be serious. I really want to know if I show everything on my face.”

“Wear your heart on your sleeve and all that?”

“I mean, like yesterday, I was feeling a little low and this woman, Mrs. Khanna, an absolute stranger from out of the blue, takes one look at me and says I needed to talk to someone. I mean that’s scary, you know.”

“Did she have a cleft upper-lip, a double voice?” He ululated.

“Shri, please.”

He stopped his antics and said in a sincere tone, but with a characteristic touch of humour, “Maybe you let your guard down precisely because she was a total stranger. You are a stiff-upper-lip person who'd rather die than shout for help. Only someone like me who's been sitting on your doorstep for three years would know something's eating you." Sridhar patted his left shoulder with his right hand. "Here's a shoulder to cry on, my beautiful, no Atlas or Hercules but it is yours."

Jyoti looked at him affectionately and put her hand on his. The blood rushed up to his face and the vein on his neck throbbed. He inhaled deeply, but his voice still had a short-winded catch when he said, "Where's Jayant? He's the only one you missed in your cataloguing."

Something had shot through Jyoti's hand and into her throat. Was this the first time she had touched him? Surely there must have been many other times in the three years they had known each other. Maybe it was the first time, because though the house was always full with Jayant's friends, and though she spent a lot of time discussing candidly all kinds of topics with his graduate friends from India, they usually followed old customs with each other. No "touching" familiarities, as they punned about it. But since she got serious with Pierre, she had become less inhibited, she figured. But that was an electric touch, was it ever. Nah, just part of her general "touchiness"over the last few days.

Hormones, Debra would say, just hormones. But how his vein had throbbed! She withdrew her hand consciously and slowly across his shoulder, but the moment had passed. Just hormones, mechanically surging up.

"Where else? Under their car, as usual. At Jim's, I suppose."

"Some host! Invites me for lunch and then disappears!"

"For lunch? Are you sure it's for lunch? I mean, you're welcome, of course."

"Sure I am sure. Not just me, the whole usual gang from Engineering, since this might be his last weekend, he said."

"Lunch! Oh, my god!" Jyoti got up and started clearing the table. "I thought it was for dinner; I'm pretty sure Mom thinks so too. I heard her cooking in the morning, but if it were lunch she'd have been back long ago." She opened the oven door.

"Yes, *palak-paneer* is all cooked, but nothing else. I'd better start something." She took out the rice boiler, measured water and rice and plugged it in as they talked.

"Have they decided when they're leaving? The roads are still bad, and the floods are quite certainly on the way. Emerson might go under on the 21st. Even if it doesn't, both the Red and the Seine are expected to peak on the 26th, and St. Mary's Road dike needs to be built up another three feet. I don't see them leaving in a hurry. Or maybe that is just the push they need to get moving before the city goes under."

"No, that won't happen with our Winnipeg," said Jyoti. "There's a charmed circle around our city. Haven't you noticed how blizzards and storms never hit us, despite all the media hoopla predicting rainstorms and snowstorms." She opened the freezer door of the refrigerator and took out a bag of peas and beans. She took a cauliflower from the vegetable shelf and picked up a cutting board and knife.

"Let me help, I could do that," Sridhar offered.

"Where you could help is with the car. Have you taken a look at it? Is it really safe? It didn't look anything like a car when they brought it home."

"Like new babies, who don't look very human either."

"Oh, please stop joking. I'm seriously worried. I wish you would check it out."

"They know what they are doing. Jim has fixed up a neat ramp at his own place, or his family's anyway. Jim and Brendan are pros; that's been their job every summer."

"But you're in Mechanical Engineering, and you've been up to your eyeballs into car building for the last year. Please do help them."

"No one's asked me and I'm not a guy that butts in."

"Why so formal all of a sudden?"

“Mine’s only book knowledge. Jim and Brendan have worked in garages since they could lift a ratchet.”

Jyoti turned her eyes from the florets that she was separating from the leaves. “Is that what they say or how you feel?”

Sridhar smiled sheepishly. “A little of both, I guess. Just one of those hangups that we intellectuals have when we come up against real life mechanics. We tend to get snooty as a way of responding to their them-against-us feeling.”

“I’d feel better if you would check the car. All their tools are throwaways.”

“Don’t worry, those throwaways from autobody shops are much better than what we usually buy. But,” he raised his hand in a salute, “I will take a look at it, ma’am, many looks at it, anything you say, ma’am.”

They laughed.

“You’re a sport, old pal. I feel comfy talking to you about my concerns.” Jyoti put a newspaper under the board and started cutting the cauliflower after throwing out the waste.

“I should feel flattered. Something else is bothering you. Out with it.”

“I’ll take a raincheck on that because things aren’t all that bad yet. Everyone is a bit nervy now that Jayant is all set to go, that’s all.”

It came again, that sudden tremor of response to something he was doing or feeling or thinking. Jyoti could feel his eyes on her, almost as tangibly as the touch of his fingers a few minutes ago. She had never taken his flirting seriously. There was too much affection, too much companionship between them for love. Surely it had to be the same way with him. Surely he wasn’t really in love with her! If he were, they wouldn’t be so much at ease with each other, would they? She was always just a little high-strung with Pierre, especially when they were with others. That was being in love.

Jyoti pushed towards Sridhar the opened bag of frozen

peas and beans from which she had taken as much as she needed. "Put this back in please. Thanks."

Sridhar replaced the bag in the freezer and helped himself to apple juice from the refrigerator.

"It is nice to have you, here, Shri, someone to talk to, to growl at, to laugh with, someone who knows all about the family." Sridhar waited and when she did not continue, raised his eyebrows quizzically.

"Everything is dandy, really, it is great to be alive and in love."

"With Pierre? And me rooted to your doorstep these three years! Is that fair?" He threw up his hands in mock despair.

"Oh, be serious."

Sridhar literally wiped a grin off his face with his hand. "Yes ma'am. At your service, Mem Sahib. What did you say is your problem?"

"There is no problem. Except that everything is so extreme, so high, so low, so ecstatic, so depressing. And so mixed up, like everything leaking into everything else so you don't know just what's really bugging you. And me never letting on. Pierre used to think I was cold-blooded until ..." she stopped. How could she be talking about such things, and to Sridhar? But even as she thought it, she knew her words were intentional, something in her prompting her that, yes, he was serious, had always been serious, and she had known it, always known it. And that she wanted to hurt him.

She did not miss the momentary stiffness and hurt on his face. He shrugged exaggeratedly. "Never let on about clammy hands and short-windedness, tingle and all, right? And you can't talk to anyone about it, right? The mental projector keeps on shooting a million angles of the same face, right? And if you don't have someone to spill it to, you just burn up inside, right? So out with it, old pal, let's sort it out. Let's start with Jayant's car."

Jyoti's colour rose. God, he was serious! About both,

though; yes, he wanted to help, but he was hurting too. He had diverted the focus from her and Pierre and himself to Jayant and cars. She was relieved he had done so.

"That was a good write-up you got in the *Manitoban* about your electric car. So, when will you be going to Detroit? When is the science exhibit or whatever it is called?"

He ignored her questions. "There's something eating into you. Something you don't know or want to know. Maybe you aren't as sure as you'd like to be about the sixty thousand dollar question, is that it?"

"What's the question?" she challenged him.

He backed out. "Will Jayant's car hold?"

The tension in the air was thick as smog. Then he decided he wouldn't back out; he pulled himself together, and said, "The jackpot question is, Does Pierre feel the same way about you as you about him?"

She flared up. This was none of his business. "Of course he does. Every fibre in your being can't quiver unless the vibes are mutual!" she shouted.

"Can't it? Can't it?" He was shouting too. Then he quickly recovered his flamboyance and his usual bantering tone. "Every nerve, every hair standing on end, and not just hair, I can tell you."

Jyoti felt a flush of heat in her nether lips. It startled her, that sudden quiver. She was swept into frenzied fantasy and hated herself for being so swept away. With biting coolness, she said, "That sounds like a wisecrack you've been rehearsing to tell the boys in the locker room. But what would you know about locker rooms and sports?"

Sridhar had been up on his feet with her first words. Now he lifted a chair and for a second she thought he would lift it over his head and bring it down on hers. He lowered it with a thud, his hands still clenched around its back frame. His sleeve button had popped and she could see the taut muscles of his forearm; he played no sports but it was clear he lifted weights, and again she felt a shooting shiver deep inside her.

"Damn you, I must be mad to come here. God, how I wish I could hate you and have done with you. Time was all of Winnipeg was brighter because of you, every day a gateway to Eden and I would go to sleep touching the tips of your fingers. But now I can't get to sleep until I've exhausted myself tearing you up, until I rip you apart night after night. Damn you, damn you."

He walked out of the room and out of the house, slamming shut the front door. Jyoti sat frozen while something within her rushed out chasing him across blinding snow down dark tunnels across dark fields deep into dark oceans of water closing over her. If she could fling herself out the door, she could follow it and be with it wherever it was so she could be whole again.

Within minutes, Jayant came in with his friends. Jyoti stirred the vegetables one last time, re-lidded the skillet and turned off the stove. She shouted a general "Hi" and carried on with her work, taking out carrots, peeler and grater.

"Hi Mom! Mom? Oh, hi, Jyoti, something smells good," said Jayant as he came into the kitchen. "Gee, thanks, Jyo, for starting on lunch. I meant to phone Mom and tell her it was lunch and not dinner but before I knew it, wham, it was noon. Wasn't that Shri whipping out of the bay at a hundred miles an hour? He told you it was lunch, I guess. Have you sent him to buy something?"

He went back to the living room. "Come on in, you guys, make yourselves at home, as usual. I'm gonna make a round of mango sundaes for everyone."

The others came in — Arun, Danesh, Vithal, Rajen and Prakash — all young men under twenty-five. They greeted Jyoti, all except Danesh, who stood awkwardly, waiting to be told what to do. Jayant pulled out a chair for him. "Sit down,

Danesh. Whoa, I forgot to do the due honours. Jyoti, this is Danesh Joshi newly come from IIT Delhi, a grad student in Electrical. This is my sister. Okay, sit down, guys."

Jayant took out several pop bottles and placed them on the table. "Help yourselves, fellas, that is if you can't wait for Chef's special sundae coming up in five minutes." He gave a running commentary on his recipe as he worked. He took out the blender and smelt the jar. "First you have to make sure the jar doesn't smell of masala." He fished two cans of mango pulp from one of the cupboards and emptied them into the jar, "Mango pulp, make sure the cans aren't dented because that means a risk of lead poisoning. Vanilla ice cream, don't ever use any other flavour, especially not cherry, and don't ever use maple syrup because both are too overpowering. Mangoes and maples don't mix. And whisk."

"Is that why we never get to see your pals Brendan and Bob and Jim?" Arun asked.

"What?" Prakash said.

"Our host's red-and-white maple leaf homies."

Jayant did not respond. He turned on the blender, and foam frothed up over the rim. He went on, as though there had been no digression, "Empty half the jar into a jug and whisk to ten. Empty some more, add milk, lots of it if Rajen is around, whisk. Pour into jug, or jugs if Rajen is around, and serve."

Meanwhile Vithal opened the oven door and the pots and skillet and sniffed at everything. "So what else is cooking, Jyoti? Let me help."

Jyoti was pleased to see her cousin. "It's anybody's guess what's going to be on the table," she said. "Mom's made enough *palak paneer* to feed an army, and *pilav* will be ready in a few minutes. There will be potato-*chhole*, of course, the gravy is ready, and the potatoes can be added as soon as Mom comes back with a bag of taters. Can't have a meal without *chhole*, of course. Here are carrots to be grated for salad. Any suggestions?"

"How about *puris*? I haven't had a good Indian meal in eons. D'you mind if I make *puris*?"

"Oh, Vith, you don't have to ask, for pittoosake, this kitchen is all yours any time you want it."

"KO, Jyu. But if you and I are joint chefing, we should ask each other, eh? No fair if I take unilateral decisions over such key issues, right? You know how messy *puri*-making can be."

Time froze. Jyoti opened a cupboard at random so she could hide her face. Why, why was she so weak, so vulnerable as to allow her whole life to be rocked out of balance by chance remarks made casually in some casual context that had nothing, absolutely nothing to do with her? Vithal was continuing his chatter as though he had not sent her reeling into a black hole.

"Mind you, there are ways and ways of doing what one wants. The easiest, though, is to get the other to decide to do what one wants to do oneself."

"Through flattery, cunning, connivance?" Jyoti asked, clinging to a straw.

"No, first play straight, play team. Only if you'd said you hate all that oil smoke or some such thing would I have to go to Plan 2 or 3."

"Which are?"

"Trade secrets. You'll have to figure it out yourself some other time when we don't agree." He laughed.

It was no use trying to find excuses for Pierre, who had made so many decisions for them with such rapidity: Regina instead of Edmonton, a house she had not set eyes on, a business venture of which she knew next to nothing. Or maybe he had not decided in haste, maybe he had been thinking of it a long time. He said he had gone to Edmonton in February and stopped in Regina briefly. When had he gone the second time, since he'd said this was his third visit? What had they talked about? Suddenly she realized she drew a blank on the last three months except for the sweet nothings of the bed. No, she was not being fair to him or to herself. Of course they had planned their life together down to the last detail. She would finish university while he set up the business; he would take his degree while she managed the business; they would have their first child three years from now, and another and maybe another.

Vithal was snapping his fingers at her ear. "Psst psst, earth calling planet J." She laughed though she dared not turn yet. "Do we have onions?"

She took a bag out of the lower shelf of a cupboard. "Sorry, only two left. But if you could wait a little, Mom will have some, I'm sure."

Vithal took a knife, cutting board and onions to the table. "Arun, it is time you washed your eyes. Cutting an onion a day keeps corneal fluid flowing clean and fresh. Here, for *raita*; so slice them very thin about two and a half to three centimeters long, while I knead the dough. Whoa, speak of the angel and there she is."

Savitri came in, carrying two grocery bags.

They all rose to their feet. Vithal took charge. "Don't everyone get up and mess up the place. Auntie, you come right in, the boys will unload whatever there is to unload. Rajen and Prakash, go to the car. One two three hup."

Savitri greeted each by name and was introduced to Danesh, who greeted her with joined palms, "Namaste, Mrs. Bhave, it is so nice of you to have me over." Vithal gave her a hug keeping his doughy hands off her. "I thought Jayant said dinner," she whispered to him. "But you seem to be doing well."

Vithal hugged her again. "You go straight to the recliner, Auntie S. and put your feet up, sing a song, have a nap, whatever you want. Lunch will be ready in half an hour if you remembered to buy onions. If not, an hour because I don't know how to cook without onions and I'll have to make a trip to the cornerstore."

Savitri laughed, "Onions and potatoes, don't come home

without them. I do have a phone call to make. But I'll join you in a minute."

"Please don't come back. There's no room in the kitchen."

Vithal took a large mixing bowl and half filled it with flour. Sridhar walked in, followed by the others who brought in more grocery bags. "Onions, here is a bag of onions." Jayant greeted Sridhar, "Hi, Shri, the way you vroomed away I thought you were out to kill."

Jyoti was turning over with a spatula the cauliflower pieces, to which she had just added curry paste and salt. The room, the voices, the people, all disappeared and she was wrapped in silence and peace. Sridhar was back.

Later she would try to figure out everything, the way his vein pulsed on his forehead, the way blood coursed along the fine capillaries of his eyes, the quiver in her own vitals, the peace that had now come unsought, all this she would relive and analyze, but now it was enough that he was here, that whatever it was that had ripped itself out of her in anguished frenzy had not raced behind him in vain.

"Me, kill?" Sridhar was his usual clownish self and no one noticed the tightness in his voice except Jyoti. "Me, kill? Gentle as a baa lamb. If anything I'm just a wet doormat for people to walk over. Nah, I had to rush to the plant science lab to take some timed readings for Kevin. He's away for the weekend." He took a chair near the window and opened the newspaper he had brought. "Here's the flood news, guys. The only ones who are going to be happy are school kids. 'A forecast of snowbound roads and storms have made administrators at Swan River announce that schools might remain closed next week.'" He went on with other details. Vithal said over the sound of Sridhar's voice, "Arun, what were you groaning about? What's on this evening?"

Arun turned the onion over in his hand. "Yeah, I was saying I can't make it to your place. I have to be at the ISL at eight."

"International Students' Lounge," Jayant explained to Danesh.

"I've been stuck with it. Thank god, the year's almost over."

"Any nice girls, yaar?" Rajen asked.

Jayant guffawed. "You kidding? Don't you know the type that comes to ISL parties? A mix of do-gooders and husband-hunters."

"Come on, be fair," Arun interjected..

"Okay I'll be fair. Most of them have hearts of gold, and intelligence in inverse proportion."

Rajen sighed. "Is there any place you can meet the other kind?"

"All intelligence and no heart?"

"You know what I mean, girls who aren't bird brains. They seem to have discontinued the line, except for one or two like Jyoti."

"Angling for brownie points not allowed."

"They must be somewhere," Rajen ruminated aloud. "When I first came ..."

Prakash interjected for the benefit of Danesh, "Rajen is our veteran fighter, his eighth year."

Rajen bowed as though he had received a compliment, "When I first came, everyone knew everyone else, I mean the Indian crowd; we used to get invited to homes. Now there are droves of us brown people everywhere and no one knows anyone. As for girls, we can't seem to find any smart girls, present company excepted, of course."

"Thanks."

"Tell me, Jyoti, what's the matter with girls, Indian girls I mean? One tries to say a friendly hello to them and they freeze up like we're making a pass."

"What's worse, they're cute and coy, or brazen and upfront, or whatever it is that fills the bill for white guys."

"Three of our girls got married to white guys this school

year. And I know some who are going steady. So what's with them? Don't we count?"

"There are three hundred who don't date white guys," Jyoti said impatiently.

"Oh, them," Arun dismissed them, "they're so conservative they'd be in purdah if their dads told them to."

Danesh, shy about entering the conversation, said in an aside to Sridhar, "The other day I was at the Patels'."

"No kidding?" Jayant said, "I thought you were all alone and lost, and you say you've been to the Patels' already?"

"Well, they are related to my sister-in-law."

"You, a gujju? Whoa, wouldn't have guessed it from your name. Thought you were from Pune, like us. "

"No wonder they've taken you into the fold."

Vithal, who had been hammering his fist into the dough said, with a wink at Jyoti, "Yeah, tell us Jyoti, man to man, let us have it, why this rash of our girls dating whites when there are so many bright chaps from India?"

Rajen added, "And keep off the double standard bit as well. We guys go out with white girls only because our own are such touch-me-nots."

"It just happens," Jyoti replied, annoyed at the turn of the conversation but not wishing to be a spoilsport. "There might be a dozen really nice guys, but a girl can fall for only one, and he might just happen to be white."

Sridhar looked up from his Saturday crossword. "Vibes, man, vibes." He gesticulated with his fingers, "Supersensitive antennae that vibrate like a jack-in-the-box the moment Prince Charming appears."

"Or Princess Charming, let's not be sexist," Prakash added.

Arun shouted, "You're all off the track? Who's talking about love and marriage? I'd like someone who'd sit with me over a pizza, or at a movie, I mean, just plain friendly friends, you know?"

"Oh, that," said Rajen, "no squeezing hands and maybe ... hmm," he swallowed meaningfully.

Jayant said in a cool voice that masked undertones of vehemence, "That's the problem, you guys are so naive the most you can think of is holding hands. Maybe if you offered to screw them you'd have them at your feet."

"Easy, easy," said Arun in a placating voice, "there's a limit to jokes in mixed company."

"Jyoti's okay," Rajen said, "she's one of us guys."

Jayant slammed the refrigerator door with needless violence. Jyoti held her breath. Was he about to explode her to the sky? So let him. Who were these guys anyway? She controlled herself.

"Look," she said, "you are like the six blind men around the elephant, each talking about a different thing altogether. And liking the sound of your own voice so much that the discussion can only go round in circles. I wonder if maybe you don't really want to date girls but only want to talk about them. There are as many kinds of dating as you can think of, but if you don't let the girls know, don't blame them. Ask Danesh about the three hundred girls you rejected out of hand just now. You have to understand that Indian girls born here are a little different and maybe they do feel more comfortable with guys born here, but there are any number of us who would love to have a chat over coffee. As for dating local style, we have to change some time or another, you know, and come into step with the world around us."

"Say, that's profound, Sis," Jayant said mockingly, "we have to change. Sounds so good when you say it, and yet you know what? Just the other day someone said just the opposite and it sounded even better. 'Take to the road, get stoned, sleep around, but you'll never become one of them. Why anyone would want to become one of them beats me.' Those were the words."

Prakash shook his head dramatically as though to clear it

of all the volleying going on around him. Danesh, feeling the inhibitions of a newcomer to a closed group and yet eager to speak, hesitantly said, "But you should make every effort to merge, since you are here to stay, Jayant. I mean this is your country. You have to try to assimilate, don't you think? The Canadians would appreciate that."

"Assimilate, my ass," Vithal growled, giving the dough one last thump before putting a lid on the bowl. "They — white Canadians — don't want us to assimilate. They want us out. We'll be squashed like bugs soon." This was Vithal's special territory and he got worked up easily. "We'll be squashed, I tell you. All these years they led us to believe the isolation was coming from us, that we were communal, parochial, closed within our cultural exclusiveness, etc., etc., but now that we are trying to merge, their real feelings are coming out. They've never wanted us and now we've become a real threat. Serves us right for wanting to be one of them. We have to stay separate from them and stay together, and we've got to show them we have as much right to be here as all those pissed-off whites who've bullied their way into this country these last three hundred years. We've got to stay apart, stay together. That's the only way."

Danesh was impressed by Vithal's conviction but still puzzled. "But that would be like living in ghettoes."

Rajen said, "Good word, yaar. But that's called multiculturalism here. Each group stays within a closed charmed circle never bothering about the others. And then, once a year, there's a three-ring circus, a zoo called Folklorama where everyone visits everyone else's cage. Hula, Calypso, bagpipes and all. Just wait for the *mela*. It comes around in August."

Prakash said, "Hey, have you thought about it? It struck me when you said "bagpipes" that Folklorama is the only time the Brits and Scots and French, the so called founding nations, actually bring themselves down to the same level as the rest of us hyphenated Canadians by having pavilions like everyone else?"

Sridhar cleared his throat and raised his hand importantly. "The Oracle speaks, silence everyone. Think about this. This whole multiculturalism hooplah that the government initiated back in the seventies is the power group's ploy, the old British formula — divide and rule. They want to promote ethnic divisions so they can perpetuate their power; first, by starting ghettoes that separate one hyphen from another as you say, but more insidiously by dividing each ethnic group within itself by baiting them with funds; the moment money comes into anything, people will squabble over it. Throw a bone and watch the fun as the dogs tear each other to pieces. That's what the heritage and culture ministries do. The minister or their hireling appears on the scene and everyone rushes to fawn, to take photographs shaking hands or hugging."

Vithal said, "That's what I mean, we've got to stay together, not squabble. Ghettoes are necessary. Look at the Jews. They were ghettoed for centuries and that was the best thing that could've happened to them. Only in ghettoes can unity thrive. They toughened themselves, did everything three times better than the others and now they don't get pushed around any more. They are on top of the world."

Rajen interrupted, "Granted; I'd even go farther and say they chose to ghetto themselves during the last little while with all their religious customs and what not; yes, they are tops, but will be so only for a little while longer. Now that they are accepted and all that, do you see the writing on the wall? They are disintegrating, just melting into the sea of mediocrity. What an anticlimax! Tsk tsk, no more Einsteins, or Schweitzers, or even Saul Bellows and Philip Roths. They're finished; gone *schlemiel*, *schlimmazel*, *kvetch*, *schlep*, all gone; *knish*, *blintz*, *borscht*, all gone, *oi vey*!"

Everyone laughed, except Vithal. "Don't fool around, man, we've got to stand tall. And, by god, we shall. We shall build our temple at the confluence of the Red and Assiniboine, and then we shall say, Okay, we are ready to assimilate. But not here, not now. To assimilate now would be tantamount to boot-licking, worse apple-polishing than your picture of what you say ethnic organizations do with ministers and henchmen, Sridhar. We've got to stand tall, man, and kick these racist bums to kingdom come."

Arun remonstrated, "Come on, Vith man, I thought you'd have grown out of the Naxalite phase by now."

Vithal was too worked up not to pounce on him. "Go ahead, be patronizing, but if you get stones and eggs smashed on your house window, you'll get action faster from them than from any goddam cop. That's the writing on the wall, comrade, that we can't expect anything from these pissed-off bastards. Living like goddam ostriches, that's what we are."

"I didn't know you feel that strongly about it, old chap," Arun said, "I'm sorry. I didn't mean to scoff at your Desh Hall friends. I haven't seen them on campus lately. How are they doing?"

"Dunno. I haven't been there. Jyo, is the oil ready for the *puris*? Yes, all set for the best item of a scrumptious meal, coming up after this break. Stay with us. I need more milkshake before I get to work on the *puris*."

Jayant passed him the jug. "You sound good, man, but your arguments don't hold water. How can we stand together with guys who'd be way out of our orbit in India? One makes friends for their qualities, not for their skin colour. Face it, man, we don't have anything in common with the other half of the local Indian crowd. They're uncouth, ribald hooligans. Do we have to rub shoulders with them simply because we happen to come from the same political entity? That's all India is, a political entity that came together as a nation after a zillion years because the British made it so."

"British, my ass." Vithal was at the stove, frying the *puris* as Jyoti rolled them out.

"Jeesus, cool it, man. I know my history as well as you do. Asoka, Akbar, Aurangzeb — all ruled all of India, but they didn't have a nation, not by a long shot."

Rajen edged in, "How about Sivaji, Jai Bhavani, Har Har Mahadev."

Jayant lightly gave Rajen an upper cut on his jaw. "No one makes fun of Sivaji under this roof. But no one."

Rajen gamely said, "How about Ram Rajya? Can one refer lightly to that?"

Danesh got suddenly excited at that. He leaned forward and cried, "You can't use that flippant tone for Ram Rajya. It has held us together. Rama Krishna Govinda — that's the truth, the only truth, and because of that we've been a nation for five thousand years; who cares about political entities based on geographical borders? Nationhood is different from who happens to be ruling. Five thousand years of culture, that's nationhood.

Jayant was as impatient. "Let's talk about us here, okay, here and now is all I care about. Give me one solid reason, one solid reason in hell why we should paw around with illiterates who troop into airports carrying kerosene tins and bedding rolls? I've seen them, jeesus, mucking up all of Heathrow with their stinking masalas and turbans. And," he turned to Vithal, "I have news for you and your favourite story about the *Komagata Maru*."

Rajen explained to Danesh, "The *Komagata Maru* was a ship chartered by a Sardarji back in 1914 to circumvent the immigration regulation that said colonials immigrating to Canada had to come straight nonstop from a British colony. It was Canada's sneaky way. If anyone praises Wilfrid Laurier and McKenzie King, you've got to sling this right back at them, so listen: the Direct Passage legislation was white Canada's sneaky way of preventing brown immigrants, since there was no direct steamer service between Canada and South Asia. The sardar got one over the Immigration guys by chartering a ship nonstop from Hong Kong to Vancouver and loading some three hundred Indians on board after shipping them to Hong Kong. But the ship was quarantined and the passengers starved off the coast of Vancouver for a month and then they were shunted back to India. A shameful, ignominious episode in Canadian history. I would like you to know and use these facts and words, call it what it is: a shameful chapter of our history."

Arun said, "Why don't you guys start a compensation thing the way Japanese-Canadians are fighting about the World War II disgrace?"

Jayant cleared the table of glasses and jug as he spoke and started setting the table. "Because Indians are so goddam divided among themselves. That's what I am trying to tell you. That sardarji — Gurdit Singh — was a cheapskate two-bit crook who led these 376 suckers by the nose even though he knew perfectly well they wouldn't be allowed to land. He was out to make money, same as the agencies and immigration lawyers of today that trade papers for cash."

"But ..." Danesh started.

"And those four hundred deserved what they got too. Many of them bribed the guy to get on board because they thought they'd get rich quick. Skid row bums led by a scoundrel."

"Easy, easy, Jayant," Arun said, "you have to forget your lord-of-the-manor past; this is a classless society."

"Shows how little you know about this society," Vithal shot back at him. "But never mind that. Jayant is himself a prime example of what he is trying to say, that our worst enemies are our own people; just listen to him giving an Orientalist version of the story. God, Macaulay would laugh in his grave. That's what British education has done to Indians, generated a whole lot of bloody brown sahibs who find fault with their own people and do the white man's stabbings for him. We've got to stand together, man, we've got to build our temple on the Assiniboine."

"Count me out," Jayant said stubbornly holding his ground. "They've brought nothing but a bad name on us. Getting convicted for rape and murder; alcoholism and wife-battering. That rat who killed a whole family last year out in B.C...."

"Easy, easy, when there are a hundred thousand people, there's bound to be a coupla crooks and maniacs among them."

"Exactly. And don't forget to read between the lines, the editorial slant of how quick the reporters are to identify the colour and hyphen of the few of us who get into trouble. They want to exploit and milk every story dry."

Jayant poured ice into a jug, filled it with water and placed it on the table. He piled the cutlery in one corner and tore the cellophane off a new package of table napkins. "Exploitation? I'll tell you about the exploitation that goes in B.C. That show last Saturday just about killed me with embarrassment."

"What are you talking about?"

"It was a documentary on farm helpers in B.C. We were at Larry's watching the game. I had the remote control. During the commercials I switched channels, and there it was. Poor illiterate Punjabis bundled off into unheated shacks eight and ten to a cabin. And who was their employer? A son of a gun sardar, that's who. I was so paralyzed with shame I couldn't press the damned button to change channels. Jim was decent enough to pass it off with a 'C'mon, you guys, get back to the game.'"

Vithal said, "You have a decent lot of friends. I'll hand that to you and to them. Real decent guys you can be proud of, and I'd be proud of you if your head wasn't screwed on the wrong way."

Rajen said, "Hey, Mr. Oracle, man, why so mum? Let's have your words of wisdom."

Sridhar had been doodling intricate designs on the edge of

the newspaper. "Let's see. My oracle says," he started reading from Joyce Gilpin's Horoscope column, "listen to this, 'Cutting yourself off from pipe dreams may be painful but necessary. Look ahead — set yourself new goals, destination.' I'm sunk, shattered, devastated, no more pipe dreams."

Rajen added, pretending to read the paper upside down from where he was, "Don't forget the last sentence. As always it's, 'Romance can be bright spot of your day.' Which brings us back to where we started, where, oh where, have all the smart girls gone?"

Sridhar said, "Maybe we talk too much and do too little, that's what Vithal is trying to say. Jay gets so het up because he emotionally identifies himself with every brown face he sees. Vithal, on the other hand, is far more detached despite his seeming fanaticism. He's calling for a political coalition. Never mind your class and cultural differences, he says, stand together."

"Hear, hear."

"I agree with Vithal, but I know I react just the way Jayant does. Okay, I know this might sound pretentious, but why does it have to be "them" and "us" all the time? White-brown, south Indian-sardar, etc., etc. Why not just you and me, one on one, individualistic like. And let time take its course. A generation or two and everything will be more even all around, like Rajen said, but the other way around. Seen one way, cultures will get diluted, but the upside of it is that we'd have a newer and richer mix within each community and within society generally, and once we have a fair degree of white-brown mix kids, we'd all be better off. Just a matter of time."

"As Mrs. Rabbit said to Mr. Rabbit, 'If we can hold out a little longer we'd outnumber the hunters.'" Arun said with a tone of finality trying to bring the debate to an end. "My stomach's held out long enough. Vithal, how are the *puris* coming?"

Savitri entered as though on cue and said, "Get started,

everyone, Vithal. go sit, *beta*. I'll take over."

"What about Krish and his dad?"

"Just as well they aren't here, because there's no room at the table."

"Mmm, everything smells so good, there may not be anything left by the time they turn up."

"Auntie S's kitchen is one big *akshaya-patram*, Danesh, just dig in," Sridhar said, reaching over for the *puris*.

"There's always room at my table, *beta*, and always enough to eat, and I do hope all of you will keep dropping in even after Jayant leaves.

At those words, the cuckoo clock in Jyoti's head drummed yet another line into the painful chant. Once Jayant left, there wouldn't any more of these noisy, happy weekends of heated discussions and hearty meals. And no Sridhar.

Chapter 6

The young men vowed they couldn't eat another morsel, but they kept reaching out for whatever was on the table until every serving dish was empty. Savitri smiled and packed them off to the basement. "Just don't get in my way." She hustled them out, when they offered to clean up. "Here, take a jug of water and some glasses, and leave me alone for a while. That's an order."

Then she went to Jyoti, who was putting the food in bowls on the counter for Krish and Sharad. *Jyoti looked so utterly beautiful and so utterly alone, perhaps because of being surrounded by boys*, she thought. She remembered her own teenage years, with a houseful of sisters and girl-cousins and aunts and great aunts. Her heart must have ached, she supposed, for the mother she had lost when she was two years old, but she honestly could not remember aching. There were so many mothers around her, and so many sisters. Here Jyoti had no one to turn to except her mother, and Savitri had as good as slapped her away yesterday. *Oh, if I could just tuck you back into my womb, my darling, all safe and warm.* She reached across, ran her hand down Jyoti's face and blew her a kiss Indian style. "I can manage on my own, sweetheart, you run off to your books. You've spent a lot of time already. Thank you for stepping in, *beti*, I was so sure they were coming for dinner; else I wouldn't have chatted so long at the mall. One runs into so many people one knows and it is nice to stop awhile and keep in touch. I wish I had more time to visit friends at home. Poor Usha,

Poornima is in the hospital again, her eyesight is affected, poor child. Then I met Maru; she raised my spirits with her laughter and tidbits of news. But tell me, what happened here? I am so glad Jayant invited this new boy. Is he well settled? Anything we can do to help?"

"No, he's well taken care of. He's part of the fold among all the Patels and Shahs and other gujjus."

"*Beti*, don't use such slangs. Run along, no, don't start on the dishes yet." But Jyoti continued stacking the plates ready for washing. She felt calmer, with Savitri back to her normal self. That little gesture of tenderness took her back to another space another time, of women, now faceless but whose touches she could remember, loud smacks with their *paan*-red lips touching their own fingers after running them down her cheeks or up her chin.

"Oh, Mom, you know we mean well and all these words are just friendly nicknames — mallus, gujjus, tam-brams.... Do you think I should transfer these to a smaller bowl so we can scrub the pans? If Dad and Krish haven't come yet, I'm sure they've gone to McDonald's already. Oh, I hear them. Here they are."

The door opened, but it was Vithal, coming from the basement. Sounds of table tennis came up before he shut the door. He came and put his hand on Savitri's shoulder and hugged her. She hugged him back. "Where have you been, *beta*? You never seem to come by nowadays. We are so close to the university, you can come for lunch or dinner any time. You still have a key for this house, right??"

Vithal smiled but said nothing.

"*Beta*, you haven't dropped out?" she said, perturbed.

"No, but only because I missed the deadline for voluntary withdrawals."

"Vithal, complete that degree, just a few weeks of work and it will be over. You told me at Christmas you were doing really well in all your courses."

Vithal smiled pleasantly. "Don't worry, *kaku*, a bachelor's degree is a just a scrap of paper nowadays, how does it matter?"

"The degree itself doesn't, but completing something you've started does. Let's make a deal. You write the exams no matter what and I'll ..."

"Exams and courses aren't the problem, *kaku*, I can get a degree like that." He snapped his fingers.

"Donna? How's Donna?"

Vithal sounded distant, "Oh, she's okay, I guess. I don't know. That's been off for some time."

"Something that's been on for three years can't be turned off that easily!"

"Wasn't easy."

"I can't believe Donna would break it off. I know her. She's devoted to you."

"She didn't."

"This is worse. Why would you? Donna is one in a million."

"Yeah, but I am a dime a dozen. A habitual dropout, a drag. And she's halfway to being a doctor."

"Stop belittling yourself. You have the Midas touch. But you refuse to touch anything. You can make a success of anything you take up, but you refuse to give anything and anyone a chance. Maybe you aren't into university programmes. Why don't you go back to Red River and finish your diploma? You've taken so many courses there."

"And become a cruddy electrician? Or finish my masonry course, maybe? Or the plumbing, why not the plumbing? Plumbers make more than doctors, we are told."

"It isn't the money and it isn't what you do but how you do it. It will make no difference to us, Donna included, as long as you apply yourself consistently to something you enjoy doing."

"I believe it, *kaku*. I'm sure you'll love me as much even if you wished I'd chosen to touch something else with my

Midas touch. Donna too. She'll love me, sure, and so would any children we might have, so would they all, all honourable men. But I have neither wit nor words ..."

"Please, Vithal, you are not being fair to any of us or to yourself."

"I am dead serious, kaku. Everything will be hunky-dory on the surface, but deep down, way way down she'd have that core of disappointment. Years ago, we were kids and I was better than her in everything. Let's face it, there is an imbalance between white collar and blue collar jobs. I mean, everyone has some basic expectations, especially professional women."

"In personal relationships that one makes with one's eyes open, one ..."

"Are our eyes open? We might still be wearing the tinted glasses of our first love, and of course at first everything will be okay, but then she'll go zooming ahead with her profession, and no, I can't see it working. She'll just give up on me after a while."

"Donna is like us, very Hindu in her values, more so than many of us."

"I don't doubt it. She'd never divorce me, and we'd be a great couple from the outside. I do like to dress well, and I know how to open a bottle of champagne and mix drinks just right. But the core, at the core something will be missing. A woman, even a Hindu-like woman, perhaps especially a Hindu-like woman, expects her man to be up there, a demigod. They will sympathize with other men's weaknesses but their own man? Oh no, he has to be a kind of Titan, up there."

"Get up there, Vithal, you can climb to the top of any ladder you want. Why don't you do something new? Why does everyone have to be a doctor or engineer? Join politics. It is high time we had some of our people up that ladder. Isn't that what your Desh Hall friends also say?"

Vithal had been looking out the window. In a low voice, he said, "I don't go there any more." He turned, and with his eyes on Jyoti's back as she washed at the sink, he said slowly, "You can do all those controversial way-out things only when you are basically happy. If I get into a violent situation — and at Desh Hall that comes naturally — even if I do just what I have always been doing, rebel and tilt at the system, that is, if something were to go wrong somewhere, everyone would promptly trace it to a broken affair or a broken home or whatever."

Savitri, who was about to put a bowl in the refrigerator, placed it on the counter with some trepidation. Carefully she said, "Veejala was to have lunch with me at school yesterday, but didn't turn up. On Monday, she phoned to postpone that lunch to yesterday; this time she didn't even phone. I thought something might have come up, something routine, I hoped."

She waited for Vithal to pick it up. He remained quiet. Then he walked towards the door. "She needs you," he said softly, "I guess we all do." He went down to the basement, shutting the door behind him.

Jyoti slowly, fearfully said, "What does that mean, Mom? What's happening?"

"He's always been a moody boy, so it is difficult to say. If only he could get a grip on himself ... how could he do that, breakup with Donna? It is just too depressing. How was he before lunch? I am worried for him."

"He was jolly. Talking nonstop, with more gusto, if anything, because he had a captive audience in that new guy from Delhi. You know his usual rhetoric, about 'we have the same rights as any of those pissed-off whites' and that 'we'll build a temple on the Red and Assiniboine, etc.,' all that stuff we've heard a hundred times."

"Yes, but every time I hear them, I am so moved I could cry even though I don't think or feel the same way as he does. Some day, I hope, Vithal and all of you will realize that we have already built that temple, because we carry our gods within and with us wherever we go."

While Jyoti started drying the dishes, Savitri put away the food. It was so late that there was no doubt Krish and Sharad had lunched somewhere. *Veejala*, Savitri thought, taking up on what Vithal had said; *so there was something happening*. Veejala was not one to phone for lunch appointments; she just dropped in at odd times any time it suited her. Well, she would find out soon enough.

Jyoti, too, was thinking of Veejala. Vithal had clearly wanted to talk about something. Maybe she should have left him alone with Mom. She needs you, he had said. "Mom, what is going on with Auntie Vee?" Savitri noticed the quiver in her voice because she knew the strong bonds between the two. Filigree; her mind dwelled on that image, filigree threads of silver and gold spun back and forth between them, each so slender and the cord so strong. *The spray of Veejala's torrential life-swirls had perforce soaked even her own children*, Savitri thought, *giving an edge of insecurity to Jyoti because of their mutual affection; how much more must be the suffering and insecurity of Vithal and Priti, who had been in the eddies of the whirlpool all their life, and poor Anant, who was drawn into the vortex from time to time.*

Savitri laughed it off reassuringly. "Veejal has always been a rebel, sweetheart. Where else do you think Vithal got that streak? But she's basically level-headed, believe me, and that is why I have faith in Vithal, too. Have I told you about how she sold an heirloom ring to take aviation courses?"

"No, never. Really?"

"It was soon after Dad and I got married. There was pandemonium such as I'd never seen in my parents' family. Later on, I came to know it was a regular feature of life at the Bhaves', but I was scared silly at the time. She wanted to take flying lessons, and of course the family had said no. So she sold the ring — I never saw it, but it was a diamond ring and, more than the material worth, it had been given by Peshwa

Balaji Rao, and that is why all hell broke loose, as you'd say. Oh, she's done some crazy things."

"So what happened? Did she get to fly?"

"She was halfway through the course by the time anyone knew about the ring, and you know how it is; your dad's uncle, who was the head of the family, dreaded any kind of scandal. By the time the ring had was bought back quietly, for twice its worth, needless to say, she managed to complete the course, quite impervious to the storm around her."

"More power to her. Maybe if you told Vithal the story, he'd finish his courses. Oh, that Aunt Vee, she's something else, isn't she? Always on the go, gorgeous every which way: looks, confidence."

"She makes it extremely difficult for one to excuse her actions, but I've always found it even more difficult not to."

"But she is a sloppy housekeeper, that's for sure. Poor Vithal hasn't had a good meal in ages. The *puris* and *raita* were his idea."

"I am glad of that. But he could cook in his own house too, you know."

"Uncle and he can't be in the same room for more than five minutes, I guess. I wouldn't be surprised if he never goes upstairs, just uses the back door to go to his digs in the basement. But still and all, that's no reason for Auntie Vee not to cook Indian food once in a while."

"Indian food takes up so much time and effort. Veejal was never much of a housewife. Back home she was used to returning from school, college, tennis, swimming, etc., to find a hot dinner ready, clothes washed and ironed, the house spic and span. I don't think she'll ever adjust to that side of life here."

"She's been here a lot longer than you, Mom."

Savitri said in a reminiscing voice, "That flat they had in Delhi when they returned from the States for what we thought would be forever: fabulous gadgets we had seen only in imported magazines till then — electric range, four-slice toaster, oven, washing machine and a fleet of servants on top of all that."

Jyoti found herself suddenly jealous. "C'mon, Mom, she has hired help here, too. If anything, you are the one who has a bad deal. You could have been the mistress of Grandad's mansion, Mom, once poor Uncle Rohan died. Instead you are working your fingers to the bone." She added with great intensity, "I hate to see you doing three full-time jobs, school and house and all the umpteen volunteering jobs you are into. Look at your hands. God how I hate this rat race."

"My hands will survive, sweetheart, but will our spirits? No matter how long one lives here, it is never long enough to forget either our old ways or our old comforts."

Jyoti laughed indulgently. "Mom, this is so funny. You've just finished saying we carry our temple within us, and now you say we can't ever fit in here. There's consistency for you."

Savitri joined her in laughter. "Is that inconsistent? You youngsters corner us at every turn. I don't know, Jyotishma, I used to think that if I could just take some time from housework and school to think, I could sort out all the questions, iron out all the inconsistencies, and figure out what life is all about." She paused, and then added, "But I am afraid to take time out, maybe. I am maybe afraid to know the answers. What if there is no pot of gold at the end of the rainbow? Maybe that is why we take up more chores than we can handle, why we make sure we never have enough leisure to think." She paused. "It works well most of the time, and life goes on without us having to figure things out, but those few times that we are faced with some brutal truth, we panic, we just can't cope and we lash out at each other."

She looked at Jyoti and Jyoti looked back. Though both stood still, their eyes moved imperceptibly, filigree threads of silver and gold spun back and forth between them, each so slender and the chord so strong. *Whose the understanding, whose the compassion? This is where in soaps they would embrace each other, the camera zeroing in on one face then the other*, Savitri thought as she put away things.

Savitri prepared the coffee pot and took out the fruit salad she had got ready in the morning. But it turned out that the young men left early. Jayant got a phone call and he announced he was off to join Jim and Brendan who were on their way to Jim's uncle's farm in St. Adolphe to sandbag the yard against possible flooding. The others insisted the mango milkshake had been more than a dessert, and soon the house was empty; Vithal slipped out unseen while the others were saying their bye-byes and thanks to Savitri.

Just as Savitri was about to close shop in the kitchen, the doorbell rang. It was Maru. She came in with a bag of almonds. She said she had gone to the Indian spice store after all, and figured she'd drop off the almonds that Savitri had talked about when they'd met that morning. Jyoti's antennae went up. Maru, Mrs. Khanna — she should never have let her guard down. Maru was one of the nicest friends anyone could have, as Savitri said many times, but the fact was Maru knew far too many people and heard far too much community gossip. Now that her sons were all grown up, she devoted even more time than before to her volunteer activities, all of which involved arm-twisting people to help her with a great many chores that just had to be done. She often dropped by unannounced, and stayed a few minutes, often without even taking off her coat, car key in hand, all set to leave. "I thought you might need the almonds for the dinner you're having tonight," she said, coming into the kitchen. Savitri welcomed her with enthusiasm, saying that Maru's timing was just right, since Jayant's friends had deprived her of her after-lunch cup of tea by leaving so suddenly. She explained about the confusion between lunch and dinner, and filled in on news about the new student, Danesh Joshi, from India. Maru, like most other women in the community, always invited newcomers to her parties.

Jyoti, on her guard, wanted to make sure she heard every word of what Maru had to say, to figure out if Mrs. Khanna had told her anything. She brought out a new tablecloth and set out cups and saucers. Savitri believed English tea tasted good only if served in cups and not in mugs.

"Yes, I met him the other day," Maru said.

"Sheesh, is there anyone you haven't met, Auntie Maru? Where did you run into him?"

"At Anuradha's a couple of weekends ago. Do you know her daughter, Ena? She got engaged to a very handsome chartered accountant from Scarborough. And there was the usual crowd, the food delicious as always with Gujarati gatherings. And the bride-to-be looked lovely as brides-to-be always do, and the groom-to-be looked a little sheepish as grooms-to-be tend to look, but you can't blame them, what with them being swamped by strangers. His sister and mother were there, of course, and they were very nice people. The boy's father passed on a few years ago, poor woman, but she has her children all over the continent, and so is okay, I'd think.

"All in all, everything was exactly predictable except for a little incident." Maru helped herself to a second cup of tea and said, "So what's with you folks, what have you been up to?" But Savitri had risen to the bait and prompted her to tell them about the "incident."

"After lunch I was sitting with a group of women on the carpet in the family room, with the *paan-dan* at the center. Santosh was making *paan-beeda* for anyone who wanted to have one, and she is such a good *beeda*-maker, mixes just the right amount of roasted fennel and sugar to give it that delectable melt-in-mouth texture. Duliya, Keerti's daughter, came in for something, and sure enough the women had to pick on her with the usual, 'You are next, Duliya, your turn next.'

"It is something all young women have to put up with, you know how it is, just a standard remark that married women make to unmarried young women especially at weddings and such occasions. You know about Duliya I guess, I am sure most of us have known for some time now about her. It is just that we don't talk about it, and as far as I know everyone has always been nice to her, even those who feel uncomfortable about her lifestyle, but Duliya for some peculiar reason decided she would come out of the closet right then and there, and said she was not one for all this crap of arranged marriages, and she proclaimed herself with the L word. Yes, she said it, 'I am a lesbian and don't need a man.' You should have been there to hear the deafening silence and the dismay on the faces of some of those women."

Maru smiled and reached for a saltine cracker. "Yes, it was an incident all right."

"So what happened?"

"I could sympathize with the women, especially those who didn't know about her orientation, but I could sympathize with Duliya too. I guess these unthinking assumptions of well-eaning women no doubt make her mad. Especially coming from those who think they could change her by suggesting their norm. She dropped her bombshell and left. But I think she would have become madder if she had stayed around to see what happened next.

"After that thunderous silence, the women went on as though Duliya had never come in, as though she had not said what she had said. It was quite mind-boggling, really, the way, the words had just gone into a black hole of silence, and then the conversation had gone as before."

Jyoti said, "And you didn't say anything, either?"

Maru turned to her. "Should I have?"

"Well, you are kinda sympathetic towards all wayward wenches, aren't you?"

"White boyfriends and all, eh?" she smiled.

"Yeah, and working at western Canada's great gay university and all."

"Fighting for legal rights is one thing, but indulging in

mere shock value is another, don't you think? It just was not the place and time, and I do insist that there is a place and a time for everything. Why do you young people have to make a public issue of your life choices? Sexuality is a private matter, all sexuality. We don't talk about sexuality, period. And that doesn't mean we are prudes or homophobes or whatever labels you want to slap on us."

"Heh, Auntie Maru," Jyoti said laughing, "maybe you aren't all that liberal, after all. I always thought you were an NDP supporter, but I guess you're a Progressive Conservative," she said, stressing the names to accentuate her wordplay with the political parties.

"There's no winning against these young people, eh, Savitri? Have you ever won any argument with your daughter? But then, I can't remember losing any argument with my mother, either, even though she was ahead of her generation. You know, some day I have to write about them, the women of my mother's generation, who keep knocking on my door every now and then like Poe's raven and won't let go, especially my aunts Chikkamma and Chittammai. Oh, what wonderful women they were! But I really should be going soon."

And away she went.

Chapter 7

Jayant put away his violin. After three hours of feverish work heaving sandbags in St. Adolphe, he had come home exhausted. He had turned to his violin for comfort. But it was no use. He couldn't get the right note. He wasn't surprised. Everything he touched turned to dust and ashes. Treachery had been his companion as far back as he could remember. Everyone to whom he felt close ended up by betraying him. He should be used to it by now; yet each time he was caught unprepared; each time it was a sudden rapier thrust. No, that was too dramatic, too romantic an image — only Romeos and Caesars got hit that way. He know of a commercial fish hook, a failproof hook that twisted itself ninety degrees into the fish, causing a long slow death; and a leg-hold trap which periodically sprang into (*jeesus*, he thought, *that was a sick pun*) headlines in the newspapers and television, spearheaded (*what would a shrink say about his word choice?*) by animal rights activists. These were his kin, the fish and fur-bearing creatures that got caught that way. The leg-hold trap immobilized the animal and slowly starved it to death. Was the skin on these animals as glossy as those of animals killed in one fell stroke? Wear a happy raccoon coat. Our cows die happy; they feel no pain; there's no adrenalin secretion that fouls up the meat. What about a kosher cut? That other sick image of long-drawn pain. When they first came to Canada, his mother had gone looking for vegetarian jello packets that did not contain gelatin; someone had told her she could get them at Jewish grocers.

They didn't have a car at the time, so she took a bus all the way to the north end, to a Jewish store past the Ukrainian Orthodox Church, and bought the jello packets; later they had found out that it was not that they did not contain gelatin, but that the horses had been blessed by a rabbi and been slowly bled to death, kosher style.

Anyone who suffers deserves to. If they are not men enough to stand up and fight for their rights, their goals, their principles, they deserve what they get. Spineless suckers.

He was quoting someone. He couldn't remember whom. He was always quoting others. He had no backbone, no ideas or ideals of his own. He deserved to bite into that hook and die a long slow death.

The throbbing at the left of his head was now spreading to the right. If he kept himself busy, he wouldn't feel the throbbing. If he relaxed, the ache in his neck would disappear. Or if he took the pills the commercials exhorted him to. He had no doubt at all about their efficacy. But with time one needed more and more of the same to get the same results. "If you want to get somewhere else, you must run at least twice as fast," said the Red Queen. He had gone through a phase of soft drugs. It was over, the teenage rites in high school locker rooms, trading drugs as he had earlier traded sports cards. He had gone through all the teen rites; once in a while there were parties and they got high; once in a while they went to Bogard's and danced all night. Once in a while they went to rock concerts followed by stoned-out nights. All civilizations had those rituals but some kept them under check with more rituals built around these rites.

He remembered *Sharad Poornima* nights, when the winter moon was full and the night usually clear, when the whole village would meet in an open area behind his family's ancestral house. A huge pot of milk would be boiled, a bonfire would be lit, folks would sit around the fire and sing songs and drink the milk. Grandad officiated at the opening; he was the first to taste the milk, and then he would hand out cups of milk to the children and older people of the village, reenacting age-old responsibilities of kings — like Dasaratha turning the first sod for the sowing of the crops — and then women would take over and serve everyone. After a few songs and dances, he and the whole family except for a few male members would leave. Later, after the village children went to bed, *bhang* was mixed into the milk and the merrymaking would continue all night. These festivals dotted the annual calendar, reaching a peak at the Holi festival in spring. Hinduism has a place for everyone and everything, one of Dad's favourite sermons.

If he had got into sex, Jayant thought, *he might have avoided drugs*. As though it had to be either or. And, if it had to be, he had simply taken one and Jyoti the other. No big deal, surely.

"Oh shit!" he said aloud. But expletives brought him no comfort.

He remembered the Filipino girl at the airport last month when he went to meet Dad returning from one of his business trips. The flight was twenty minutes late. Jayant walked to the end of the hall, watched two kids playing at the pinball machine, and walked back. He saw her then; it was difficult to miss her; she wore a dress of shocking-pink sateen, and she was sitting on a green chair. The colours alternated on the chairs, red-blue-red-blue on one side of the hall and yellow-green-yellow-green on the other. Her colour sense irritated him; if she had to wear shocking-pink, the least she could have done was to avoid a green seat. A second look told him she was rather pretty and elegant in her taste: *petite* and *chic*, her hair, jewellery and cut of dress showed designer goods. Against her Oriental features and complexion, even the pink looked okay.

"Oh shit shit shit shit!" If she had said it just once, he would not have believed he'd heard right; but there was no mistaking who had mouthed the word. She was almost the only one in that area. There was no mistaking the violence out of which the word exploded; that *petite* frame harboured some volcanic activity. "Damn!" she said next. "Damndamndamn." Between the two she obviously preferred the first, which she next repeated in a crescendo of frustration. She furiously riffled through her handbag for a tissue and fished out a crumpled purple one, with which she wiped her eyes reddened with weeping.

"Fuck!" She said it softly.

"CP Flight 85 to Edmonton and Vancouver, now boarding ..."

She got up and smiled. "That's some good news, at last," she said in a normal voice, and, picking up her tote bag, walked away.

So it worked for some people. But Jayant was not one of those. Not now, anyway. 'All those expletives, all the in-jargon....'

He picked up the violin and ran his bow lightly across the strings. He tried an old melody, the very first he had learned.

He remembered his grandmother, seated in the courtyard of their ancestral house on the familiar thick woven mat of silken straw. The courtyard was vast and rectangular, and seemed cut in two halves. The farther half had trees, a *bakul* tree that spread its branches over the far right wall, and there were flowering bushes of jasmine and *raat-ki-rani,* and a clump of banana trees. Along the far left wall was the vegetable patch from which the gardener brought in coriander leaves or mint and fresh okra or long beans every morning. There were trees along the wall — drumstick, *neem* and curry leaves; these were sources of endless wrangling between the servants and outsiders who tried to poach; the servants had no qualms taking what they wanted from the trees, but they guarded it from other poachers. At one end of the wall were three latrines of the old style, which no one used any more, except for the occasional visiting servant who used it only as a urinal. In the middle of the far wall was a door beyond which were latrines used by servants, and still farther the servants' quarters. The servants had their own well, beside which the *dhobi* had his stone for beating clean the clothes, his daily responsibility; the vats for the *bhatti* where he boiled the clothes, and various solutions for lye and starch, stood in his domain. The outer walls were crowned with bits of broken glass embedded in the cement, to prevent thieves from scaling into the courtyard.

The nearer half of the courtyard was flanked by the main house on one side, by storerooms and bathrooms on another and by the kitchen and dining room on the third. Here the ground had been plastered smooth with years of daily sprinkling of cow-dung water so that it was an even, mellow yellow, hard as a tennis court. At the centre was a planter of whitewashed brick for the tulsi plant, complete with little niches where the clay lamps and incense sticks could burn despite rain. And near it, under the shade of a parijata tree sat his grandmother with her violin.

It was a scene to which Jayant's spirit returned in quiet moments, and which he sought when storms came up. A scene where everything was exactly in place: Aji playing her violin every day just after her three o'clock tea.

At the time of his first visit back to his grandparents from Canada, Jayant was just fifteen, not young enough to admit openly that he wanted to sit by his grandmother, not old enough to take the initiative and speak to her. He was self-conscious of his Marathi, which had rusted in the three years away from India. Even though his parents spoke Marathi at home, he and Jyoti had switched to English, and his kid brother, Krish, didn't speak a word of Marathi. Jayant could not bring himself to enunciate once familiar words lest he make a fool of himself. So he lingered every afternoon, on the *charpai* or the nearby swing, a book in hand, Perry Mason,

John Dickson Carr, P.G. Wodehouse, names and authors he was reading for the first time at the rate of one a day. There were also stacks of yellowed comic books from the forties, of which he loved *Film Fun* the best, with its Laurel and Hardy cartoons on the first page and Bud Abbott and Lou Costello on the last, with a murder mystery and a ghost story in each issue. Now, as Aji played on her violin, he placed himself close enough to smell the potpourri that gave all the contents of her teak chest of drawers a subtle jasmine fragrance. But he was far enough away not to let on that he was listening.

Sometimes Aji sang as she played. She had a well-trained voice, and even his untrained ears discerned the felicity with which her voice moved like rippling water through the notes, the way she maneuvered her voice in the *alapanas* like water falling over rocks under shallow rapids.

One day, as he sat on the swing, biting into a green guava and pretending to read, she stopped playing after just a few minutes. He waited without turning his head, disappointed.

"Jayant."

"Yes, Aji."

"Come here. I've never heard you sing, *baba*."

He came over, lay on his stomach and raised himself, his elbows just inside the edge of her mat, cupping his face in his hands. "Aji, I don't know any good songs."

"Come, come, you know many English songs, right?"

"Oh, I'll never sing those; they sound so awful compared to yours." He laughed, embarrassed.

"When some say that, I know they just need some persuasion; but when others say it, I know they mean it."

"And which am I, Aji?" he said teasingly, holding out two fingers. She clasped both and then took his hands between hers. "Why, Jai *baba*, your palms are calloused. What have you been doing in Canada? Are you a woodcutter there?" She, too, knew how to tease.

"Aji, even woodcutters there have Palmolive soft hands."

He hummed the TV commercial tune. "We have machinery for everything." He imitated the sound and action of a chainsaw, shouted "Timber!" the way he'd seen in movies, and then proudly said, "I got all these here, from chopping wood. Ask Chhotu."

Chhotu was an old retainer, well over sixty and still ramrod straight and steady armed. He did odd jobs around the house and garden, including chopping wood for the wood stove on which bath water was warmed for the whole family. Chhotu had gone into a tizzy when the *vilayati baba* had first wanted to chop wood, but Jayant had cajoled him into yielding; Chhotu would teach him how, but only after absolving himself of responsibility by calling on all the gods to bear witness to the stubbornness of the young master. Some of the callouses were due to tree-climbing, an old pastime that Jayant had picked up eagerly within days of coming to Pune.

"Do you know where I would like your callouses to be? Here, here and here," she touched the inner tips of the fingers of his left hand, "like mine." She ran his fingers over hers and he could feel them just under the fine pale brown skin.

"When Savitri wrote to me that you were taking piano lessons, I told myself I would teach you to play the violin and leave my violin to you."

Jayant's eyes smiled brilliantly as he leaned forward. "Would you, really?" Because he had meant the bequest, he added quickly, "Teach me, I mean?"

Aji laughed, her small white teeth circled by the red tinge of *chunam* that spiced the *betel*-leaf roll she ate after lunch. "It is quite all right to mean both, *baba*, and I really would love to do both, teach you now and leave the violin for you when it is time for me to go. Can you believe that no one in our family — little Anu is my forty-eighth descendant, your uncle Balwant tells me — not one has taken to the violin? We have vocalists, dancers, tabla and sitar players but no violinists. Not one."

"You have one, now," Jayant said, and in the next three

months, whenever he was not in Bombay with Vithal, he picked up the rudiments of classical music on the violin.

Aji died two years later, July 19. It was a bright sunny day after a week of rains, Uncle Balwant had written, and she had not been ill, had just complained of a headache after tea and died at 3:20 in the courtyard. Had she been on her way to her violin, humming a raga she meant to play that afternoon? Had she left him her violin? He had not gone back since then. Perhaps he would know only when his grandfather died. Or maybe not even then.

His inheritance. Just outside old Pune, in the shadow of Shanwar Wada, the stronghold of the Peshwas, within sight of the Hill of Lakshmi whose slopes housed their family deity, Vithoba. His inheritance: trees that had stood there since the time a patriot had climbed the sheer face of the Moghul fortress with a rope tied to the tail of a giant lizard and earned for himself the name of Ghorpade; fields and villages that had increased gradually since the time Ram Shastri, to whom the family traced their lineage, had left Pune vowing never to return until the murder of Narayan Rao had been atoned with the ascension of Madhav Rao. Jayant remembered every detail of the proud family history that had been passed on to him through bedtime stories.

His inheritance. Foreclosed by his father.

How impatient his father had been to leave India! Jayant remembered the trips from Bombay to Delhi for their immigration formalities; the numerous trips to Pune to fill out forms for which only the family lawyer and munshi knew the details: What property had he inherited? What had he added? Moveable, immoveable? Income tax? Arrears? Did he have proof there were no arrears? Had he resigned his job? Had he proof his resignation had been accepted? Did he owe his employers money? Did he have proof he didn't? Would he repatriate the money he'd spend on airline tickets?

Forms, legal advice, bribes just to get people to do their job. In order to expedite the paperwork, his father had legally renounced all claims to ancestral and paternal property.

And now he was a real estate broker.

Betrayal, his lifelong companion.

Jyoti's words had twisted the hook into him. Jayant felt he would gladly run his sword through Pierre. That guy was slimy. There was something altogether suspect about his appearance; something phony about his symmetrical face that looked like a plastic surgeon's cast of Adonis; his hair a perpetual Brylcreem commercial, greaseless, blow dried, each hair bouncing back into place separately; his clothes that seemed taken out of glossy magazines; he earned good money though he was a college dropout, and he drove a Porsche. Except that he hadn't been driving lately. Jayant knew that his license had been suspended for three months, but didn't know just why; did Jyoti know? Three months ago he would have asked Pierre the most personal questions without hesitation but now he hated the guy so much he couldn't get past even the formalities of greeting. And at this moment he knew why; his instinct had alerted him to what Jyoti had told him.

Betrayal. His life was haunted by shadows. Pierre, whom he had loved, was a guttersnipe.

He remembered a boy named Billu, a year older than Jayant. He lived with Jayant's classmates, the twins, Abhinay and Avinash, to whom he was related in a distant way. Billu had come from the village, about the time they started school. His status in the family was tacitly understood to be that of a poor-relation, keeping the twins' room dusted and swept along with his own small room, cleaning their bicycles along with his, ironing their shirts along with his. But only along with his. Avi's father was an old time disciplinarian with a sense of justice. Billu had the same kind of clothes, shoes, bikes, furniture and food, as they. And he went to the same school, which cost money, as every boy at St. Francis Xavier knew as a matter of class consciousness.

Billu was an achiever. What roused Jayant's admiration was his defiance, his rebellious perseverance to excel at everything he did. Nothing came easily to him, especially math and English, but he had a tremendous will to succeed, pushing himself to the breaking point if need be to achieve his goal.

There had been a time when Jayant's ambition was to be like Billu. Although only a year older than them, Billu was big-bodied, having grown prodigiously after coming to live in the city. He could climb any tree, even the date palms that had no branches. His breath was limitless and his aim accurate, as anyone who played *kabaddi* or seven tiles with him knew. The final outcome of any game they played was often determined on that first toss. Whichever captain won the toss for choosing the first of the teammates usually lost the game. That came about because of unwritten class and loyalty codes. No matter how many other boys there were, the captains were always two of the three boys from the zamindar's family, Jayant, Abhinay and Avinash. Whichever captain won the toss would have loved to have named Billu as first choice, but loyalty demanded that he should choose the third of the master-trio. And so the captain who actually lost the toss ended up with Billu, and usually won the game.

And then had come the betrayal. Jayant had taken the bait, but had floated unawares for a whole week, the steel claw deceptively loose inside him. One day the boys had gone to the "last house" on the lane, to steal *jamun*, as usual. It was a sprawling house sitting on an acre of land with huge trees — jackfruit, mangoes, jamun, guavas — that were contracted out by the owner. To guard the fruit, the contractor hired a mean old man who lived in a shack in the orchard. He was a jealously alert watchman. It stood to reason that in their quest for adventure, the boys should steal from that garden and not from other neighbours' who wouldn't have minded them picking fruit for their eating pleasure. One day, the old man, with two young thugs to help him, caught the boys. The three had come upon the bys after Jayant and Avi had climbed the tree. The guards flogged them. Avi's father, to whom the three guards then led the youthful culprits, none of whom would ever have thought of revealing their manhandling, had roundly reprimanded the boys. It seemed only a coincidence that Billu had not been with them.

Billu was with them, however, when they went swimming the next weekend at Madhu-kund, a pond about a mile from home. As they dried themselves, they had compared notes and talked about forbidden things with the embarrassed glee of such talk. That evening Avi's father called them to his study. He was a man of few words. He told them that if he ever caught them talking about and doing the things they had discussed, he would have them circumcised — they could be like Muslims for life, because they did not deserve to be high-caste Hindus.

The pieces fell together. Billu had betrayed them not once but twice. Other pieces fell together as they recalled earlier jokes and pranks. And most galling of all, they had to continue to treat Billu as one of themselves because Avi's father never knew the real Billu. Jayant and the twins would never squeal. That was an inviolable code.

Betrayal. Jayant strummed listlessly on the violin with his fingers. Yes, of course he was jealous of Pierre. Not jealous in the psych textbook way that reduced everything to the physical, and to complexes neatly pigeonholed with freakish names. Jyoti was an extension of himself. It was a sacred inviolable bond that could be expressed only in symbols. Like the *rakhi* that girls tied round their brothers' wrists on Rakshabandhan day; like the Rajput wedding rite where the bridegroom rode to the bride's house on a mare, and was challenged by her brother to a symbolic duel, after which they embraced and went in together to the bride, who waited with roses to garland the groom. Through his childhood years, he had seen countless weddings. The panoply of rituals fascinated him for different reasons as he grew older. The flare lanterns, the drums and *shehnai* of the musicians, the dressed up mare — these had conjured up historical figures from the past. Later, he and the other boys always looked for the ludicrous aspects — the way the bridegroom's face sweated behind the strings of flowers hanging from his headgear, the way the mare left droppings along the path. Later still, at the weddings of his friends' sisters, he had felt choked with emotion at the scene, the way brother and bridegroom enacted the duel, and then embraced to a crescendo of trumpets and drums.

Jayant sipped at his pop. Some part of him was still resisting. Hogwash, it said, all this hype about rituals, but another part knew it was not rituals he was talking about. Love is not to be limited to a selfish thrust of one's own bloated ego. If only he could be sure that Pierre's soul was not just in his penis.

He had loved Pierre once, and not without cause, and therefore could love him again. Jyoti loved Pierre; and if she was not as radiant as she should be, it was because of them — he and Dad and Ma — their instinctive resistance to this alien seducer who had pulled away one of their own. They had withdrawn, each in their own way, from that core where all extensions came together like a spirograph drawing, intertwined, each inextricably a part of the other; so inextricably that though they had pulled their strands to themselves, the ends were still at the core, taut like high tension wires. He remembered the wires that ran along the railway track, humming with sounds almost but not quite beyond human hearing. They dipped at the centre between poles and then rose, dipped and rose, along the zillion miles of railroad, which they had travelled summer and winter through childhood years.

The shadows around him, undefined but familiar, moved to some inaudible theme song of the collective unconscious of all their lives. Jayant placed the violin carefully beside him.

The headlights of cars paused at the stop sign cast distinct shadows on the living room wall of the leaves, fruit and branches of the ornamental crabapple tree below the window. His memory, or need, from time to time cast silent inner shadows, defining one or two recognizable outlines that came alive with a face or a name: Ajoba's library, Aji's jasmine-scented saris, the stop sign across the street, Jyoti's denim jacket, the smell of camphor in the niche of the *tulsi* tree, the ridiculous oversized billboards on Pembina Highway advertising Stanfield briefs and Cougar boots.

He would do, with due grace and honour, what he had no doubt done with due grace and honour in a hundred past lives. When Pierre came on his white mare and plumed silk turban tasseled with red and white flowers, he would meet him with drawn sword, sheathe it, then anoint him with sacred vermilion and turmeric, and embrace him, with stars and moon and assembled guests as witness.

The dark night of the body was over. Jayant closed his eyes in gratitude.

Jayant must have fallen asleep on his knees, for Vithal was already in the basement when he raised his eyes. He must have been packing, for the large suitcase was half filled and the smaller suitcase almost empty.

Vithal was holding up a car compass. "I forgot to bring this to you this afternoon," he said, placing it on the table. "It's still functional, but I'd suggest you buy a new one. Worth the few extra bucks. This was real handy last summer when I was in the Laurentians. One hell of a maze once I got off the highway — not the parallel lines that run to eternity west of here."

Jayant felt relaxed and rested.

"Hey, buddy, why don't you come along with us? We

could have a ball. Yellowstone Park, Old Faithful and all. How about it?"

Vithal did not reply. He was bouncing a ball low on the table and bringing a bat slowly down on it. The sound of the drawn-out crunch was like a grating tampura drone as Jayant spoke on. "I've had some great hikes, but the greatest have always been when it was just us two. Remember the first wilderness hike we had back in '91? I was one raw hunk of a kid just off the boat; didn't even know how to tie a proper reef knot despite the usual scout camps back in Pune. You taught me more in those two weeks than I picked up in the previous four years. And then there was our summer in India in '93. You didn't spend much time in Ajoba's house, but I tagged along with you a couple of times when you went to Bombay.

"Remember the time we got lost near Mahalakshmi in Bombay? I've never figured out how we could have lost our way there. Tell me, every weekend you disappeared from Pune, you were at the races weren't you?" Vithal didn't reply. Jayant went on, "You're one hell of a guy, Vithal, and if it weren't for you being you, I'd never have got the guts to leave this asshole of a place now."

Vithal reached out for a carton of balls and slammed them with his bat one by one against the table as he spoke with startling vehemence. "Quit talking, fella. Running away, that's all everyone thinks of, run away, tuck your tail between your legs and scram the moment some problem comes up. But you, you want to hang on to someone even when you're running away. You've done nothing but hang on to apron strings all your life, and all the time ranting all that bullshit about parents being a pain in the butt. Deep inside, all you want is to suck your thumb and dream of Grandad's estate. You're pissed off, Jayant, you and your hang-ups; resenting your dad because he's not a super-scientist, yet you're emotionally tied to his coattail. Oh, man, isn't it time you were to someone the Olympian that he's been to you? That I've been to you? That every goddam person around you has been to you? instead of being an obnoxious leech with a thumb-sucking ego? All you can think of is running away. Run away like a coward. God, I'm sick of you, sick of the whole lot of runners-away."

Jayant sat there, looking up in pained bafflement, like a dog unexpectedly kicked by his master. He got up slowly from his crouched position on the floor, slowly collected Ping-Pong balls from the floor and couch where they'd flown, and mechanically dropped each with trembling fingers back into the carton. The chore composed him somewhat, but he still had a dazed expression.

Vithal, meanwhile, leaned his elbow against a wall, bat in hand, holding the side of his head with his closed fist. Then he sighed. It was a groan that shot through shatterproof glass, the cracks spreading like cobwebs along the length and breadth of the room.

After an eon of silence, Vithal said in a low voice, "I'm sorry, Jay, taking it out on you like that. I ... I have problems. I'm sorry."

Jayant knelt again by his suitcase, relieved, eager to accept his cousin's apology, pained to think how critical Vithal's problems must be to have made him hurt anyone that way. He, Jayant, had been wallowing in self-pity all along, oblivious of his cousin's sufferings. *Donna, it must be Donna, of course.*

"We're all made that way, I guess," he said, "a family of live volcanoes, except for Jyoti. I wish she ... did you know she ..." He stopped, shoved the suitcases under the table and rose. He threw the compass on the couch, picked up a bat and took out a ball. He pulled the table to the centre of the room, opened it and said, "Let's play, Vith."

Vithal came to the table and they started playing, a rhythmic, steady, defensive game.

"You're right, Jai, about getting away for a while. As you say, we're all too goddam alike. We look alike, we speak alike, we think and feel like each other. The whole lot of us. It's like being in a goddamn house of mirrors. Wherever you turn you're bumping into yourself, your own thoughts and guilts and loves and pains staring at you. That's why I'm glad about Jyoti and Pierre, that she's getting away from this pool of Narcissus. Pierre is good for her and for all of us, not a spaced-out freak like us but a normal kind of guy, to whom a buck is a buck, and a Porsche and tux suits mean a lot. Know what I'm getting at? I mean he's a guy who can put his soul into a fuck, no matter who the girl and where the place."

Jayant closed his eyes. Jyoti would be all right. Thank god for that. Thank god he had come to that same conclusion by himself and not through Vithal. Thank god he spoke and felt like Vithal because they were made that way and not because he was imitating Vithal. Thank god for everything.

"But I'm afraid for her," Vithal was saying. "Whether she can really let herself go, fall free. We're such an accursed family, we can be happy only with our own mirror images; we're like goddam Draculas carrying our casketful of earth with us. It's death to sleep on foreign soil and living death to sleep on our own. What's the matter with you, man? Missing every time."

"I can't," Jayant said, choking the words out, "how can I play when the whole bloody world is falling apart?"

"Cool it, man. Cool it and concentrate. Nothing is falling apart. We'll pull through. Get it? We'll pull through come hell or high water. Now give me that double spin of yours, I think I've found a way to return it."

They started a game. Jayant got tired of his spins and played straight shots. "Man, you think you've got problems, oh, man." Vithal zapped down Jayant's straight shots as he intoned his refrain. He whammed to victory, ending, "Wait till you hear mine. Oh, man, have I ever got a problem!"

He had been saying it much the same way as he strung out his usual curses. Jayant had pushed away Vithal's groan and apology into the deep, pulling a mental screen between him and that other world where the groan had sent the glass shattering into cobwebs but had been made whole as they played. *Donna*, he said to himself, *it must be Donna, but they'd pull through just as Vithal had said.*

Then Vithal said, "Ma is leaving us."

Jayant picked up the ball suddenly feeling panicky in the haze. "No," he said, "she can't do that.... That was all over long ago.... Everything's been all right a long time.... She can't do it," his voice broke. "What are you going to do? Oh, jeesus, what are we gonna do?"

"Play," Vithal said in a tight voice. "Pick up your paddle and play. Now."

They played.

Chapter 8

Jyoti parked the car on the "no parking" side of Kendall Road. She figured it shouldn't matter, because she just had to run in, pick up Priti and drive home. Aunt Vee had phoned the previous night to ask if Priti could stay the afternoon with them since she and Anant had to be at Pinawa all day; and if so, could someone please pick her up from the Mukherjis where she would be dropping Priti on their way that morning. Savitri had said yes to both and Jyoti had offered to get Priti around one o'clock, on her way back from the university.

Jyoti had spent the morning with her friend, Betty, in the Science Complex. They had reviewed a good portion of their polisci course for the finals, but when Betty left at noon, the silence had gotten to Jyoti and she had gone to the University Centre to look around. That place, too, was quiet as a tomb, so she got into the car and drove aimlessly down King's Drive, watching the river.

This year there would be no stately ice floes floating slowly northward. Instead, the flood was on its way. All of the city's resources had been mobilized. The river had crested in Fargo, very closely competing with the 1897 record of 11.9 metres. But Fargo had been spared, despite the winter's staggering 304 centimetres of snowfall. Would Winnipeg also escape? Jayant and Vithal had cut short the lunch festivities the previous afternoon when a phone call came from the Volunteer Coordinating Centre. Tremors of excitement rippled through the city with each new development. The presence of soldiers, who had taken over the construction of dikes in key areas, increased the sense of being under siege, but also increased the sense of excitement, of challenge, of togetherness.

Every local television channel was giving live coverage. Watching the ten o'clock news the previous evening, Sharad and Savitri reminisced about the Indo-Pakistani war of the 1960s, that Sharad remembered and Savitri claimed to remember, the way every town and village came alive at the time, with crowds at railway stations, cheering the *jawans* on their way to the front. It was war, but a war that had to be fought, a war that had to be won. "Oh, we'll win it, for sure," Jayant said, flexing his biceps that had heaved sandbags all afternoon. Jyoti had been cynical, commenting on the inappropriateness of her parents' war analogies.

Now, as she drove aimlessly along the river, circling the campus, Jyoti was struck by another war analogy. Why hadn't Hudson's Bay Company built a fort here, instead of at Selkirk? With the river on three sides, it would have been pretty invulnerable. But, she thought, the British were invulnerable anyway, with their ammunition and knowhow, against which the natives didn't have a chance. If they had built a fort here, the natives might have attacked by night in their silent canoes. More than the battles, she wanted to know what life had been like for the pioneers and for the natives. Maybe she should switch to an anthropology major; joining the archaeology summer group might be quite something. Perhaps Dad's excitement over Indian history, his picturesque retelling over the years, had rubbed off on her after all. Maybe she could do some cutting-edge work. Following recent data on the corn grown by the Blackduck tribes, one might be able to trace links between Manitoba and the Navajos, who were said to have migrated from Minnesota to New Mexico a mere century and a half ago; Manitoba, Minnesota — the First Nations did not recognize borders. Surely there was something waiting to be discovered. Even more fascinating, the pottery of the Blackduck and Laurel people reminded her of the shards unearthed in Mohenjo Daro. So much was waiting to be discovered. She could join the University of Winnipeg team that had dug up artifacts near The Forks.

That sure would solve some problems; did she really want to get married at twenty-one?

Face it, she told herself, *this was yet another dream of escape from her present life. She wasn't going to think about any of this, remember? Not until exams were over.* Just as well it was close to one o'clock, and she could concentrate on getting Priti on time.

She drove to the Mukherjis. Romona, who was about the same age as Priti, opened the door after fumbling with latches and keys; she pushed aside the stool on which she had stood to look through the peephole.

"Is Priti here? Everything is so quiet!" Maybe the two had fallen out, and Priti was wrapped up in a book, as happened whenever she was upset.

"She never came, didn't you know? Mamma had to go to the temple today and so she phoned Auntie Veejala last night to come in the afternoon, but Auntie said she couldn't and so 'Priti is going to sleep over next weekend, that's a promise,' Mamma said, it is going to be such fun, even better than playing in the morning.

So Aunt Vee had changed her plans, but hadn't told them about it. So like Aunt Vee.

"Won't you come in, Jyoti *didi*, and sit down for a while? Dad's gone out for five minutes, just to the corner store. Come *didi*, please, I want to show you my science project. We're going to the symposium early next month! I still have to rewrite some of this, come come."

Jyoti allowed herself to be dragged to the girl's room, and she duly admired the neat work Romona and her partner Bea had done on black holes.

The doorbell rang. Both went to the door. "Look first, see

who it is," Romona repeated the injunction that no doubt had been dinned into her.

Jyoti opened the door.

"Collecting pledges for the school band," said one of the two boys at the door.

"Nobody's home," Romona said. "You'll have to come later."

"Nobody's home," the boy mimicked to his companion. "What you see ain't people, them's ghosts," and both laughed wickedly as they turned away. Jyoti closed the storm door and was about to shut the inner door when she heard the boy shout, "Paki! Paki house!"

A shiver ran down her spine. She turned to Romona. "What did he say?" The girl nodded yes. "Did he say Paki?" Romona nodded again. Jyoti opened the door and walked out in her socks. One of the boys had just thrown a ball of muddy snow at the front window. The other was about to follow, but saw Jyoti come out, so he pretended to clean his gloves with the snow. Jyoti caught the boy by his coat collar and dragged him into the house.

"Did you say something?" she asked.

"Nothin'. I didn' say nuthin'," he mumbled sullenly.

"I heard someone shout Paki. It couldn't have been you, could it?"

"Wasn't us."

"Now, who could it have been, do you think? Eh?"

He struggled to shake himself free. She unzipped his parka so she could get a better hold of him. The other boy stood on the sidewalk, wondering what he should do. Jyoti shut the door, stood with her back to it, and turned the boy so he had to face her. Then she loosened her grip, but still held his sweater. "You're itching to grow up to be a barbarian, eh? This is a great place, a great country, but snot-faced kids like you are stinking it up." She lifted his chin so he had to look at her. "We are getting a bit tired of uncivilized pigs like you. Yeah, let me tell you, our older boys are getting a wee bit impatient with nerds like you, and they have formed a clean up brigade. Do you know I have only to make a phone call to get them out to take care of you? They might not move in today or tomorrow but you can bet they'll move in on you when you're not looking; and when they're done with you, even your mothers won't recognize you, and they'll throw what remains of you in the garbage bin in your back lane. You wouldn't like that, would you?"

Her voice was cold, knife-edged. The boy stood as though she was still pinning him down.

From her pocketbook, she whipped out a colour clipping of a California quartet with trendy spiked hair and bikers' jackets. The picture had happened to be on the back of a newspaper item she had cut out for her sociology term paper, but she knew the photo was just right for what she wanted now. She waved it in front of him. "Just to give you fair warning, this is them. How come you haven't heard of them, eh? This is from a Toronto paper, just in case you want a copy. Yeah, Toronto knows them more than we do, eh? Maybe it's time to introduce them to you. Doesn't take long to get to here from the Maples. Just check this out with any pal you might have in the North End. If they're anything like you, he might even have personal experience with these guys. They act quick and they leave no trails."

The boy backed into the divider next to the door.

"Well, you seem to need a lot of time to figure out what needs to be said, eh?" He sullenly kept quiet. "Say it," she said, "starts with an S, and it's not your favourite four-letter word either."

"I'm sorry," he muttered.

Jyoti opened the door. "Can I take it you'll give your friend my message? I don't mind spending a few minutes more, if it would help twerps like you to see the light. I guess you aren't so dumb that you'd forget it too soon; be sure you tell him about the garbage bin, too. I should tell them that the BFIs are bigger and easier to throw skunks into. That's where you belong, you skunk."

She pushed him out, closed the storm door, and watched him stumble toward to his companion. She was trembling inside with a deep sense of power that frightened her.

Romona was looking at her, her round eyes made rounder with awe and admiration. "Oh, *didi*," she said, "did you look at his face? He was so scared he'd have peed in his pants if you'd slapped him."

Jyoti ran her fingers through the girl's hair. Romona wore her hair like most everyone her age, parted at the middle, feathered at the sides. She looked like every other nine-year-old, in blue jeans, with an open-laced shoe design on the hip pocket, a plaid collared shirt ... exactly like everyone her age, born here and unaware of any other place, let alone any other country.

"Have you ever peed in your pants?" she asked.

Romona laughed. "No, I've sometimes felt like it, but of course never really done it. Oh, my, no!"

"When? When have you felt like it?"

"You know," (like Krish she used that phrase with a stress on "you") "these Junior Highs who hang out at the 7-Eleven, they make swear signs," she half gestured with her middle finger, "but ..." she giggled with embarrassment.

"Do they call you 'Paki'?"

"Not when I'm with Bea and the rest. We always walk home together. Gee, it must be nice to be a boy, or at least have a brother."

Romona had two younger sisters.

"You don't have to be a boy to be tough, and since you're the oldest, you'd better start being big brother in this house, okay?"

"Oh, gee," Romona said, "he was so scared he'd have peed in his pants."

“Tell me, have you talked about this with your Dad or Mom?”

Romona was suddenly very defensive; “Like, what should I say? Gee, they might get kind of ... I dunno.”

Jyoti said, “You must, Romona, you’ve got to tell them.”

“Maybe you will, *didi*? Daddy will be back soon. I think he just goes to have a cigarette because Mamma doesn’t like him smoking at home. He’ll be home soon.”

Jyoti almost laughed at the girl’s artlessness and perceptiveness. Kids knew so much of what went on at home. She didn’t really want to meet Mr. Mukherji, a big man with a big paunch, balding but trying every hairstyle possible to hide his bald spots. He was nice enough, but Jyoti got along better with Mrs. Mukherji, a hardworking happy woman who volunteered almost every weekend with the cooking at the temple.

“Listen, Rommi, I’ll talk to your Mom soon, but if you talk to Dad or Mom will you please give me a ring so I’ll know what to say when I meet them? I have to go now.” She did not want to leave the girl alone. She waited until she saw Mr. Mukherji’s car turn into the driveway, then walked quickly to make her getaway without having to meet him.

Jyoti released the hand brake and shifted into gear. She waved to Romona, who was at the window, and slowly drove away, her mind in turmoil. The incident deeply disturbed her. It was her first encounter with overt racism. Oh, she had heard of it of course; with Vithal telling her of such incidents, there was no doubting that racism existed. She had read of it and discussed it in her sociology courses, but this was her first encounter with it face-to-face. She had always thought that Vithal exaggerated, but now she felt differently. She couldn’t even begin to sort out the feelings that had rushed through her when she heard that shout, “Paki, Paki house,” the uncontrollable spasm of fear and shock at the word “Paki” flung at her.

There was something about the encounter that frightened her far more than the actual incident warranted. Her first fear now was for Romona. Had she only further jeopardized Romona's walks home from school? The boys were probably the same age as Krish, but they were big and they were bullies. But like many bullies, they were cowards, too, else her response would not have worked. It had worked, and that was even more frightening, that Vithal should be right. She had acted exactly as Vithal would have her act, and it had worked. They had even fallen for her bluff. She felt a surge of power and was immediately angry with herself, with Vithal, with the father of this girl, who had to have his smoke, with the mother, who had gone to the temple for her weekly prayer meeting — oh, jeesus, did one have to beat on drums and chant songs? Now she was thinking like Jayant.

Racism. This was the black hole we should be alert to. What good was it for these kids to earn all the science awards in the world? "Easy, take it easy," Arun always said. "It is just a matter of time," Sridhar had said. "Just wait a couple of generations and there'd be a lot more white-brown kids who will solve the problem for us." Her own, for example. They would be beautiful. They always are, these children of two races, black and white, Japanese and white, Indian and white. Just wait a couple of ... Jyoti caught herself short as other thoughts spilled over. Pierre, was he the man? But how could she doubt it, why this nagging fear? Would Pierre ever understand what and how you feel when you have the word "Paki" flung at you? No, she wouldn't go into that; but that stream of thought flooded in anyway; it refused to be contained in its separate sluice, and the iron gate lifted to let the stream gush out. Sridhar, the vein on his forehead thudding blue. She had never thought him capable of passion, he was so taciturn and clownish. *Time was all of Winnipeg was brighter because of you ... but now*. No, she wouldn't think of his words etched on her mind. But the floodgates were open and the words flowed over her just the same, the ripping hands, passions and persecutions she had never thought him capable of having.

One thing at a time, and the only thing right now was to get the exams out of the way, the cursed political science especially; the first exam was always the worst.

Jyoti found she had driven past home; now she was being like Aunt Vee. What would Aunt Vee do in Jyoti's situation? Lovely, confident Veejala, selfish overbearing Veejala? Everyone had more than one face, oh god, and all the faces were part of oneself.

Priti, where was Priti? What if those boys waylaid Priti one of these days? Priti, poor kid, where was she? Jyoti broke into a cold sweat. She turned the car and drove home. Priti was there, playing carrom with Jayant.

"Pierre called," Jayant said as soon she entered. "I've jotted down his number on an envelope on the refrigerator. He'll be there till six tonight."

"Oh," Jyoti said, not wanting to talk, but Jayant's voice followed her into the kitchen, forcing her back to the living room. "We had a nice chat. That guy's okay, Jyo, I'm glad for you."

She was too tired to figure out if Jayant's was a rehearsed speech, his way of apologizing. One thing at a time. Polisci exam tomorrow morning. No Pierre, no Vithal, no Jayant, no snot-faced kid shouting "Paki." But how could she clear her mind of them, those junior high boys she had never seen who made obscene gestures to nine-year-old girls? No, she wouldn't think of anything, no throbbing veins or angry hands or even Jayant's attempt at apologizing. She remembered the look between her mother and herself the day before. She went to her room, closed the door and lay on her bed, conjuring her mother's undemanding arms around her.

Jayant heard her shut the door. *Poor sis*, he thought, *what an unholy rush everyone is in*. Why did he have to leave just when she was sinking under the weight of her own worries? And now Aunt Vee with her box of dynamite.

The total helplessness of the previous evening had left him, but there was a new weight. No one else knew about Aunt Vee's crazy decisions yet. Just as well no one was home; else he'd have blurted it out. Poor Priti, with parents as zany as hers, it was just as well she had his family around. After Priti had put away the carrom board, he made her do her homework. He sat back in the recliner, glad for the respite. His whole body ached from the strain of sandbagging. While he had no doubt that the city would beat the flood, figures being rattled off in the media were mind-boggling. Four hundred square miles had been flooded eighteen years before, in 1979, and the lake that formed had been fourteen miles across. This year, the lake was expected to be twenty-five miles across. Jeesus.

"I'm finished," Priti said, closing her scribbler. "Can we play something else?"

"Sure," he said, "your piano lesson."

"No, please pretty please, no." She tried to get out of it. "I can't get this new piece. I just can't, I hate it."

"You will practise your piano lesson," he said sternly.

"It's so boring. Why do I have to? Why?"

"Because."

"Because it's good for us, like carrots? Yuk."

"Because your mother wants you to be good at the piano."

"Mother knows best? Not my Mommy."

Jayant yanked her to her feet. "Stop that, Priti, that's quite enough of your impudence. Now move your ass and get to the piano. Git." He dragged her to the piano, pushed her on to the stool and opened the book. "Which one is it?"

"It is not in this book," she said, "lemme go. I'll practise it at home."

He looked into her school bag and found it. "What page?" He turned page by page. "This? This?" till she nodded her head. He fixed the page open and said, "Now play."

She sat still, stubbornly closing her fists.

"Get up." She rose, thinking he had given in. He turned her around and slapped her face lightly. Her eyes distended in disbelief, then filled with tears.

"I hate you. I hate you!" She tried to fight loose. He shoved her back on the stool and stood behind her, his hands holding her shoulders down.

"Play."

She started playing. He removed his hands. "No hanky panky, you practise till you get it right." He picked up the sports section of the newspaper and went to the sofa, tucking three cushions as pillow. The back of his neck ached and he could feel his blood pounding against his forehead. He placed the newspaper on his face and closed his eyes.

Poor kid, what a life, zany parents, devil may care brother, and so he had slapped her? Poor kid, he'd make up for it. Was this year's Ice Capades over?

Jayant remembered sitting on the floor in his grandmother's room. It was a large room next to her bedroom, bare except for various musical instruments belonging to different members of the family. The floor was of black granite, Cuddappah marble, shiny smooth and cool.

She was teaching him the basic scales. "Again," she said, for the hundredth time. "Hold each note to a count of two and hold the second "ga" to a count of four before you go on to the next ... Sa re ga re ga; ga ma pa ma pa."

"Why can't we start on the song? Aji, it isn't as though I'm going to be here forever. I'll never learn even one song at this rate. And you say you will give me the violin only after I learn to sing!"

"You will get it, *baba*, just keep your temper and try. We must start with twenty minutes of drill every day; after that I'll spend as much time as you want on that song. I'll stay here all morning, if you wish. But scales first."

She was firm. He could wheedle all kinds of favours out of her, but she would not yield on this.

After he had learnt the first verse of the song he tried to beg off the drill, but no, she wouldn't budge. She agreed that the daily drill of basic scales was the most frustrating part of music. She didn't know of anyone who had liked that part of their training; but then she didn't know of any good musician who had bypassed that step. Yes, it was maddening, but Jayant was much better off than her, as she had told him. As a child, she had to get up a whole hour earlier than her brothers so she could have her music lesson before going to school. She hated it, having to repeat the scales endlessly. For the first six months, her master — oh, the way he'd take his snuff — had not taught her even a line of any song, just scales, up down, up down, backwards, forwards, one beat, two beats, three, three beats, two beats one. Her whole musical training — vocal and violin — had been one long torture between ages six to fourteen, when she'd been married off.

For thirty-five years after that she had not touched the violin; there had been no time at all; but then her children grew, got married; her daughters-in-law took over the running of the house; she had more time and more, far more worries, to be sure, because in a joint family there were always interpersonal problems — rivalry, overlapping rights and responsibilities, a diversity of temperaments and moods. Every day was a mini crisis, but at least she was not directly responsible for the feeding and homework of all the little children around her. It was then that she had taken up the violin again, and after that she'd hardly had a day these last fifteen years when she didn't spend at least a half hour on her violin.

"Music is something that will never let you down, Jayant *baba*," she said. "It is like moving away from this time-ridden world. It is like forever holding your first born at your breast, a little baby that always remains one, a gift you hold in trust in perpetuity, forever in your arms and still to be enjoyed."

Priti was singing in a low but intense voice, her fingers banging on keys without any effort to translate her tune to her fingers or keyboard. "Jes you wait, Enry Iggins. Ja yant, jes you wait."

Jayant briefly considered his options from behind the newspaper. He decided not to do anything. Priti sang her way to pinning him against the wall. "Fire!" she shouted gleefully. Then she went back to her lesson.

Jayant read about Tiger Woods' feats in Augusta, Georgia. Tiger was poised today to overturn Jack Nicklaus' 72-hole record of a 17- at the Masters. The guy was hardly twenty-one. The stunts some people pulled off just out of their cribs. What did Jayant have to show for his nineteen years? It was time to get off his butt and go on that trip. He was half tempted to get up and switch on the TV to check on Tiger, but he couldn't let Priti off the hook.

"I got that right, didn't I? I got it right, just right," Priti was yodelling. She was her usual cheerful self, no resentment whatsoever.

"Play it again."

"But I got it!"

"Three times running, that's the rule."

"Okay, listen." She played the line again, and again, and again.

"The whole piece, Pix, not just one blooming line.

"But that's the most difficult one. You get that you get it all." Her resilience, glory be; that kid had tantrums, she cried easily, but, jeesus, she had spunk.

Chapter 9

It was Wednesday afternoon. Savitri was home after a teachers' meeting. Among other matters, they had discussed Pete Kozolski, and everyone agreed he should be punished in a way that would hit home; he would have to forfeit the television hour for the next four weeks, and do something else instead during that time. Savitri offered to take their annual inventory of library books a little earlier this year to put Pete to work, an offer that was readily accepted; it was so sweet of her, they said, to give up the fun of television hour, a participatory session that required the children to listen to and observe the details of *The Muppet Show* and *Mon Ami* more closely; such a delightful learning experience.

Savitri had smiled to herself at the punishment. Pete did not like their television hour. At home he did little else than watch television when his mother was away. His mother was a sorter at the main post office, and often worked the afternoon shift, returning home late evening. They lived on the second floor of a house and the landlady took care of him much of the time; given Pete's hyperactivity, the easiest way was to let him watch television in his own apartment with the door open, and check on him from time to time. Pete made his own lunch and dinner on days that his mother had not got around to making his lunch sandwich or was late returning. He watched a lot of television since his mother was often too tired or too busy preparing dinner to bother with him. He knew all the prime time series, could give a commentary of ball games, and more recently had got hooked on PBS. Savitri liked to think she was instrumental in sparking this interest in him.

There had been a special bond between them from the first day of classes. While the other children had followed her every instruction, Pete had flouted every one of them, testing her with a sly acumen that had temporarily thrown her off balance. But she took control by lunch hour and he knew that she knew he was trying to see how far he could push her. It had been a subtle combat of wits for the next few days, after which she won him over. Mainly she put him to work after school, making him help her with chores and talking to him of nothing in particular. His boisterous hyperactivity was not an act, and yet a core of loneliness surfaced in him once she got past his rebelliousness.

By Remembrance Day, he had put aside his suspicions about her motives. “Is it good for me?” had always been his first question, and his second, “Is it going to be fun?” She said it was neither good nor bad, for she had right-away seen his questioning to be a trap. But it had taken her just a little longer not to fall into the trap of saying it was fun. His eyes narrowed with suspicion every time someone said, “Now, boys and girls, this is going to be fun.”

One Friday afternoon, he had complained about there being no hockey game coverage that Saturday because it was a home game. Savitri’s first thought was to offer to take him to the arena, but she resisted. “I guess you’ll just have to settle for Channel 3 instead,” she said. “*Julius Caesar* is on at 2 o’clock.”

“Is it fun?”

“No,” she said, ”but it is interesting, she had loved it as a child, had loved the long speeches made by Brutus and Mark Antony and the crowds of people and all that. Others might find it quite boring, really — who wants to see old places and old historical tales of wars? — but she loved it, so why should she care if others didn’t?”

He latched onto PBS then, and talked incessantly to her every day for the half hour she spent at her desk after school. He caught on to operas, though he had more fun mimicking the lead singers who sang soulfully at burning castles instead of getting in and saving their girl or child or whoever was trapped in there. He didn't like ballets, they put him to sleep, all those sleepy movements and fluffy pouffes. But he seemed to love Shakespeare. She couldn't believe it. She wouldn't tell him, of course, that she herself really couldn't sit through a whole PBS play except for *Julius Caesar*.

"Do you follow what they are saying?" she asked.

"No," he replied, "not usually but they looked good and sounded good." When they said something, even if he couldn't understand the words, he knew what they meant, like how Mark Antony was a real cunning guy the way he was playing up to the crowd.

Savitri was thrilled. She repeated it at dinner. Vithal, who had happened to be there, said it was the pedagogue in her, that possessive passion in teachers to grab and shape their students in their own image. She herself preferred to think of pleasanter parallels, of a sculptor moulding his clay, a "would we not shatter it to bits and then remould it closer to our heart's desire" kind of thing. "As long as you remould them at school and not at home," they said.

So Pete had been punished into forfeiting television hour, she thought, sipping her tea, and she was pleased in a childish way, as though she had fooled someone into granting her a favour.

Readjusting her thoughts to the home front, she wondered why Veejala was so impatient on the phone about not getting to meet her. Tuesday had just been too busy, and she had neglected to return Veejala's call. Why couldn't Vee call at home in the evening instead of at school? It was awkward getting messages from the secretary in her mail slot. This morning the secretary had given her a message during the morning recess and when Savitri had called, Veejala had impatiently said, "Talk about an awful sense of timing, Savit, I've been waiting two days to speak to you and you call just as I'm leaving for class. I'll call you later."

Savitri poured herself another cup of tea just as Sharad came in. His face was flushed and his eyes swollen. When he was angry, his eyes had a way of puffing up, as though he had been crying for hours. He sat down heavily without removing his parka, boots or gloves.

"What is this about Veejal?" he said. "Why didn't you tell me all these days?"

"What happened?"

"You mean you don't know, or are you putting me on? You women are just so damn secretive."

So no one was dying. Thank god. "Tell me. Is she okay? What happened? I had a message, too, and when I called her she hung up saying she was on her way to class, and would call me back. Here, have some tea and relax."

"No, I don't want any. I'm shaking and shivering all over. It's a wonder I managed to drive home without an accident." He wiped his forehead with a white cotton handkerchief.

He breathed deeply as though to control himself. "When I came back to the office an hour ago, there was a message asking me to call her back. Marie said the call came in around ten in the morning."

"You've had a long day."

"Yes, Mrs. Pringle's deal came through at last, and I was stuck helping her with the forms. The way the market is, with nothing moving, it should be cause enough to celebrate, but now, with this news ..." He wiped his face again.

Savitri waited patiently. He continued, "I called her back, and she was as cool as cool can be. Said she had resigned her job and was going back home. That she wanted to tell me herself so I wouldn't have to hear it from someone else. That was all, no reason, no nothing. And I couldn't very well ask any questions, you know how our cubicles are. So I rushed through my work and came home. Who's she going with? Do you know him?"

Savitri looked at her husband; the news had taken her by surprise, but an affair certainly had not occurred to her. "Why do you assume she's going with someone? Did she say something, anything that makes you think so?"

"Why else would a woman leave her husband and children?" he asked, impatient at her slowness. "And the way you are taking it, I'm sure you know a lot more of what has been happening. For godssake tell me, what's been happening? And at her age, too! Gods help us. She's crazy."

Now he was more hurt than angry. How could she do this, without telling them anything at all? Why did they choose this god-forsaken eternal winter of a hole except so they could foster a sense of family even though so far from home? Just to be near her so they'd have each other to turn to in times of need. But she never came, never asked for help.

He had taken his gloves off and unzipped his parka and now sat with his head in his hands, and his elbows on the table. "She always came to me," he said softly, "not to Mukund or to Balwant but always to me. Whether it was to take a sliver from her finger or to help her with arithmetic, always she knew she could trust me. Even when she was grown and in college, it was me she confided in. Any boy Father considered for her, she wanted me to meet him first. 'Bhau, never mind looks, never mind money, make sure, make absolutely sure he won't stand in the way of my studies,' she'd say each time. She relied on me and I carried out her trust. Anant is so ..." he searched for words, "so brilliant, so modest, so tolerant of her every quirk … For godssake, what do you women want in a man?"

Savitri watched him in pained silence, resisting rebuking him for the way he generalized. She looked at the puddle his boots had formed on the tiled floor, watched the grey in his hair that she had never noticed before.

"So, who is he?" he yelled suddenly.

"There isn't any man in all this."

"Did she tell you that? Did you ask her?"

"No, no to both." She made a gesture of exasperation. "How little you know your sister!"

"How little we know anyone," he said bitterly. "Veejala, my little sister who wouldn't choose her Diwali sari without consulting me, leaves her husband and home for some idiotic loon."

"Stop jumping to conclusions. She isn't that kind of a person. She just wants to get away from this stupid university, probably. Her department is full of people as old as the stars they keep peering at. Maybe she just wants to spend some time in India."

"Going home for a holiday is fine," he said, cooling down a little, "we can always take care of Pixie." He paused. "But why didn't she come down and tell us in person instead of exploding a bomb over the phone? She did mention about being in Pune at Christmas the other night but," he was upset again, "how can anyone be so imprudent as to give up a job? With all these cutbacks and retrenchments, doesn't she know she can never get it back?" He got up and started pacing up and down, his boots plopping and spreading out the puddle. "She could have taken leave. They'd be only too glad to let her go on loss of salary. I could have told her that if she'd given me so much as a hint that she was contemplating something so drastic. Did she talk it over with Anant?"

"I have no idea, but I think she would have."

"That poor man has the patience of a saint, gods bless him. Unless," he clutched his head in sudden apprehension, "Anant hasn't been ..." he said questioningly.

Savitri was angry at him and at the same time wanted to laugh at his discomfort at speculating about possible infidelity in a male. He was so impossibly, naively chauvinist in his viewpoint. She said, "Anant, of all people? Anant! I wonder if you aren't a wee bit Old World or is it totally New World, that you can think only of illicit relationships as the root of all troubles. I don't know what Veejala's problem is. We know she does crazy things, but her sense of morality is even more puritanical than mine, the morality she sets up for herself, I mean. She doesn't care a whit what other people think, but she cares a lot about what she thinks. I have to be able to live with myself, is what she always says, if you've ever bothered to listen. Why don't we just wait?" She did not mean it that way, but she had effectively confirmed what he thought, that women stick up for each other and keep secrets from men.

He walked off in a huff, took off his boots and coat, took the newspaper and slumped down in his recliner in the living room.

Wishing to move away from combat zone, Savitri went into the kitchen and said, "What's news of the flood?"

"Nothing to add to last night's bulletin," he replied, "but the outbreak of German measles in southwest Manitoba is spreading. I wonder what's happening to Turnbull Drive."

"Poor people, they are always the worst hit."

"They jolly well knew it when they bought their plots for a song, so they shouldn't complain now. Everyone here wants to eat his cake and have it too."

While Savitri looked into the refrigerator to consider what vegetables she could cook for dinner, she heard him shout, "Oh no no!" Savitri placed the broccoli bunch on the table and called back, "Are you okay?"

"Come, see this! No wonder she was in such a rush to tell us."

"What's up?"

"Photograph and all, oh no!"

Savitri went to him and looked over his shoulder. There it was, with banner headlines, "Prof Quits 'U of Backwoods Manitoba'" She glanced through it, taking in the gist. "Dr. Veejala Moghe, Associate Professor in the Department of

Astronomy ... resigned her faculty position ... claims this is a backwood where nothing of significance has been done or can be done in her department ... plans to spend the summer at Pasadena Observatory at the University of California before leaving for her native India.... Asked if conditions were any better in India, she said even if they were not, she would feel better wasting her life in her native country than in these backwoods ... 'This place doesn't exist on any academic map ... but my name just might if I get away.' Dr. Moghe has published extensively in her field and is a Fellow of the Royal Astronomical Society.... Asked if she felt her work was not recognized here and if so why, she replied she had never pushed herself politically, but had hoped the department would be expanded.... When asked if she felt any sex-discrimination in her discipline ... said, 'It could be I am the wrong colour as well.'"

"If she wanted to go," Sharad groaned, "why couldn't she just go quietly instead of drawing us all in?"

Savitri sat on the carpet with the newspaper section, spread it out and read the whole story over again, smiling appreciatively. *Vithal would love it*, she thought, *and this would be hot news at their temple and weekend parties*. So that's why Veejala had been so impatient, and why she had been in the back of Savitri's consciousness.

But as Savitri set about getting dinner ready, the sense of jubilation she had felt a few minutes ago vapoured away. Savitri felt sad thinking about it. Why did things always have to be just a little out of reach? Would things have been different if she had been at home last Wednesday when Veejala had dropped by or if she had called her back yesterday?

Chapter 10

Savitri hummed a *Meera bhajan* as she set the table for two. Veejala had phoned early that morning asking if they could have lunch together somewhere near her school, and Savitri promptly decided she would do whatever it took to be at home for Veejala. She lied to her that she had a very long lunch break that day because of some group activity designed for two sections together, and so they could meet at home. She went to school early, and arranged for a teacher's aid to take over her classes after half past ten o'clock, and for a substitute to come for the afternoon. She rushed home to get some lunch ready before noon.

After the first wave of appreciation, Savitri had started having mixed feelings about Veejala's decisions, misgivings about the way she had acted towards her employers and media, and her family. She had spontaneously told Sharad that Veejala would of course have consulted Anant before her headlong dive, but on reconsideration, she knew it didn't have to be so. Not too long ago, Veejala had talked about the way Anant and she led their lives. They spent hours discussing their social schedule, which parties to attend and which not. As she explained, one had to be careful to spread oneself around, never to accept twice in a row, never to decline twice in a row. They also discussed at length when to have parties and whom to invite. What with so many people not getting along with so many other people, only Anant had the patience to keep up with the falling-outs and reconciliations, so Veejala made sure to go over the guest list with him in great detail before she sent the invitations. Anant helped plan the menus, for he was the one who remembered what had been served not only at the parties they hosted but at recent parties at which they were guests. Yes, they spent enjoyable hours on such matters, but on such professional matters as which conferences to attend or which students to choose as their assistants, for years they had only told each other of their decisions after the fact. They rarely discussed their children, especially Vithal because that was too painful.

Savitri took the*kadhi* out of the refrigerator. She had made it on Tuesday. It was her habit not to keep any cooked food for more than a day but to serve it the next day as is or with some "recycling" as the children called it, and to throw out whatever was left on the second day. She had forgotten about the *kadhi* the previous day, in the hullaballoo of Veejala's news, which had been duly reported on local television channels as well. But on Tuesday, when she had prepared it, she had remembered Veejala, who loved the dish and never bothered herself to make it because the buttermilk curdled every time she tried. Savitri had hoped aloud several times during dinner that she wished Veejala would drop by. Now, as she poured the *kadhi* into a Corningware bowl from the Tupperware container in which it was stored, Savitri could not but hum another old song, "*Dane dane per likha hai khanewale ka naam, lenewale karod denewala ek Ram.*" (On every grain is written the name of the one who will eat it; those who receive are many, but there is only one giver, Ram.) The *kadhi* had Veejala's name on it, she mused, which was why it had not been eaten up the previous day.

Savitri mused on the workings of destiny, if such it was. Veejala, who had lived almost as long outside India as in, who in appearance, dress, accent, food habits, outlook and every variable one could think of, was at home in the western world, was returning to India, whereas they would continue here, with their old ways, old values, old everything. But why not? India had moved on, would move on, and people such as Sharad would be left behind no matter where they were. Life was easier here than there.

Destiny. *There's a divinity that shapes our ends, rough hew them how you may*. Her older sister, Mrinal, had always paused after "rough" and said the lines meant that fate always dealt a bad hand, especially to women, and no matter how you hewed it, it was always rough. Even long after she had carved her own optimistic formula for looking at life, she had believed that it was Shakespeare who had placed the comma after "rough", and not Mrinal.

What should she say to Veejala? She did not know, but the moment would no doubt bring its own answers. So she spent the time on little details that Veejala liked — the table set aesthetically with good china and cutlery. She brought out her lace tablecloth, hand-crocheted in fine silk cotton by refugee Sindhi women who fifty years ago had flooded into their little town on the west coast, in the nightmare aftermath of partition and independence, and whose cause her aunts had espoused at a time when local feelings ran high against these unwanted intruders with another culture, another language. As part of her trousseau, her grandmother had given her a whole cupboard of laces and embroideries done by these refugees, but this was the only piece Savitri had brought to Canada.

Those women had such patience and skill, she thought, remembering what her aunts had told her. Their fingers moved so quickly, their embroidery needles were so fine, the sand dust from the desert in their eyes grown lacklustre and dim with the long hours of work in the deepening twilight after the day's work at the cooking, the cleaning, the feeding of children and menfolk, stitch stitch stitch, in poverty, hunger and dirt, and still with a voice of dolorous pitch, would that their cries could reach the rich, they sang the song of the shirt. Savitri sighed. Maybe Mrinal had a point about the fate a woman is born into.

She spread the tablecloth and felt its silken sheen. This had been custom-made; her grandmother had personally provided the woman with the silk-cotton reels. Those women had so little sense of colour coordination or finesse in their patterns; she could vividly recall the jarring combination of blues and greens that they had invariably used, and their casual switch from white to off-white to light brown within the same crocheted bedspread or tablecloth. That final touch of harmony, alignment she had called it the other day. Coordination? Synchronization? Or was the word synchronicity?

Yet, was it so necessary, this coordination of disparate items according to set preconceptions? The lace tablecloth, so fine it called for coloured candles on tall elegant holders, was out of place in the noonday glare that streamed in through the window; and yet it had a beauty of its own, regardless of any accessories. Interior decorators would insist on accessories being coordinated, but if interior decorators were to have their way with placing members of society according to their own preconceived notions of harmony and coordination, Veejalas would be blackballed and Pete Kozolskis phased out of existence.

She scolded herself for exaggerating. It was time to set things on the stove.

Veejala arrived a few minutes after twelve. She threw her heavy fur-collared leather coat on the living room sofa with a sigh.

"Well, we won't need that much longer," she said, "but as long as the snow is around, I feel I need it, even if so many are walking around in shirt sleeves. Mm," she said as she embraced Savitri, "I love the sandalwood smell in your clothes."

"It's a wonder you can smell it through your Chanel No. 5," Savitri said, withdrawing herself and immediately regretting doing so.

“Oh, Chanel No. 5 is old hat. This is Nina Ricci *l’Air du Temps*. Not as good as ...”

“Come to the table, Veejala, the soup will get cold by the time you finish your catalogue of cosmetics and perfumes.”

“Sorry I’m late. Everyone and his dog seem to be going home today. Took me five minutes to get out of the parking lot. Mm, I see you have good food, but not quite the welcome mat. Hope you haven’t been waiting long.”

Savitri injected more enthusiasm into her voice. “That’s okay, I’ve taken the afternoon off.”

“You have? At such short notice? I thought your old Mr. Grierson didn’t like anyone getting a headache without three days’ notice.”

“He doesn’t know. Bev will manage to get a sub. Anyway, I deserve a break. I haven’t called in sick or taken leave all year, not since Krish cracked his forehead in the gym last October and had to be rushed to Emergency.”

“You make me feel as though I am dying or something, that you’ve taken half a day off for my emergency.”

Savitri set bowls of soup on the table, setting Veejala’s at Sharad’s usual place, on the longer side, and hers at her usual place, facing the window. She plugged in the coffee pot. “Some people think it is,” she said unsmilingly.

Veejala sat down. “Sharad? Poor Bhau, I suppose he’s frantic with anxiety?”

“He was at first. But now he’s too angry to be anxious.”

“Ohhh,” Veejala said exaggeratedly, “I was hoping he’d be worried sick.”

“I wish you’d figure out some day that people like to feel needed. For some people, the best gift you can give is to ask them for help.”

“I ask of you all the time! ‘Please pick up Priti. Please help me set up for this party. Please may I borrow this that the other.’”

"Oh shoo, you know what I mean. Sharad is hurt that you didn't ask him or come to him."

"Oh shoo, as you say, it only messes up issues to endlessly discuss them. I can see Bhau wanting to be told, and I did. It is the zamindar in him. It is such irony that he should be stuck in this hole. He should be back in Pune, presiding over the family in our ancestral Wada: Zamindar, dispenser of ancestral wealth, friend of the lessee peasant, godfather to all the village brats who want a college education." Veejala pushed away the soup, half eaten. "No offence, Savi, but the garlic stinks — even if you say there's only a smidgen. What I need is whisky neat, but I don't suppose you have any in this abstemious household. I have this horrendous headache coming; hasn't come yet but I know it's coming."

"Shall I brew you some masala tea?"

"You should be there too, Savi, flopping your shapely bum in a nine-yard sari: Annapoorna, generous mistress of the manor brewing masala tea for sore throats and aching hearts."

"If anyone needs to be there, it is you, Veejala. You could puff away at a cigarette and stomp around in shorts or a bikini, and you'd have got the rebel out of your system for a while. Here you have to kill yourself to prove a point because nothing short of a bombshell will get people to acknowledge your presence."

They looked at each other across the table, both hurt, both troubled. Then Veejala said, "Why are we being so crabby to each other?"

Swallowing her tears, Savitri said, "Because."

Veejala leaned forward. "Don't you know why I did it? Don't you understand?"

Savitri shook her head.

Veejala played with her diamond ring, twisting it off her fingers. Softly she said, "I'd hoped you would, at least you."

"There are many things about you that I don't understand, Vee, but that has never come between us."

"And this has?"

Savitri's answer was even less audible. "No, it hasn't. Perhaps it should, but it hasn't."

"It should because you don't approve?"

"I don't know, Veejal, I've always held that when an essentially moral person does something that is considered immoral, there is likely to be some moral reason behind it."

"But in this you don't see it."

"I don't know. I just don't know what to make of it. What can I say except the usual things, that at least for the children's sake ..."

"The children don't need me, a child grows as a flower grows."

"But the flower grows better when there's sunshine and there aren't weeds around it." She shook her head, dissatisfied with herself. "It is hard not to fall into clichés."

"Because this is a cliché situation? A woman walking out on her husband?"

Savitri shook her head, "I don't know."

They sat in silence, Savitri having her soup, Veejala playing with the handle of her empty coffee cup. Seeing which Savitri brought the coffee pot from the counter to the table. Then Veejala leaned her elbows on the table and pressed her forehead with her hands. Savitri looked at her. Sharad had sat in that very place in that very posture less than twenty-four hours ago. How alike they looked. Their fingers were slim and long with short stubby nails, the ring finger almost as long as the middle finger; Jayant's was, too. Strange that she should suddenly notice this oddness only after living with them more than twenty years. 'How little we know anyone,' Sharad had said bitterly. True, but one did not need to know another to love, to feel, to respond.

Hands reaching out for help, to help, the same hands. But by the time one figured out whose hands they were and why they were there, whose the need, whose the reassurance, it was too late to do anything, always too late. Ramses, with what bitterness Jyoti had said it. *My darling child, the still core of sadness in your eyes.* Jayant, ah, but he was looking so much better yesterday than he had last weekend, or was it only in contrast to the others? Hands that reached out now asking, now giving.

Savitri wanted to touch Veejala's hands, those long slim fingers with stubby nails lacquered over with nail polish, to hold them to her heart, do all those exaggerated sentimental things people did in Hindi movies. *My sister, my dear dear sister.*

"The children," Veejala was saying slowly, "they are not really ours. They are their own, and all too soon they realize that. When Vithal went off that summer, that first time, I missed him, oh how I missed him, and yet when he came back, everything was changed. He was his own world, set in his ways, self contained, the umbilical cord severed. Everything seemed the same, but it wasn't."

"Like when we leave our parental home after getting married," Savitri said.

Veejala considered it. "Yes, maybe that's how our mothers felt when we got married. I remember my first visit, my first Diwali, for Bhai Dooj, after I was married. Oh, I was so happy to be back, it was like rolling back into the niche where I belonged. My room had been kept just the same way, right down to the *kathputli* doll dangling from the ceiling at the base of the bed. Maybe it wasn't so to Mother. Come to think of it, I was pampered and indulged, her honoured guest, not her child anymore. That's how I felt about Vithal, how I feel about him, as though he is a transient who will suddenly decide to leave one day and never come back. A pain, an excruciating pain where the cord has been pulled off, not just cut but uprooted from deep deep in the guts, something final."

She paused, short of breath. "No, it is not the children I will miss or worry about ... I have always been somewhat of a magpie, as you know only too well.... It's Anant. Already I feel as though I have left half my self behind ..."

"Then it is wrong for you to go. Listen to your instinct."

"It is done already, Savi. Things build up, the moment comes and then it is over. The cord, once severed, cannot be joined again."

"That's with one's children, Vee, not with one's husband. The bond is not an umbilical cord that is useless after birth, but a lifeline."

"Oh, Savitri." Veejala stretched her hand and cupped Savitri's face against her palm comfortingly, reversing their places in a single gesture. And Savitri, grateful for the support, covered the hand that held her.

Gently Veejala said, "It is a half that is perhaps best left behind."

"It is the suddenness of it all," Savitri said, "even I didn't know it was coming. One could see the problems, of course, the incompatibilities and expectations that lesser intellects would not have. But then every marriage, every job has some of those. And we haven't had more than a bearable share. So why?"

"That's not it, Savi, not it at all. But don't ask me what it is. I don't know. It's my turn to say that."

Savitri looked fondly at her. "Maybe you're still too much of a spoilt brat."

"Or maybe it is my last desperate attempt to do something worthwhile, instead of being tied down to a bloodless rat race. We came here because we had been continents apart for two years, and we needed to stay put for a while, and this was the only place that offered us both a place, and we didn't know just how god-forsakenly mediocre it is. We have been here longer than we have been in any one place, and it is time to go. Oh, I know just what Sharad will say: sixty-five thousand dollars a year and no sweat to speak of. A distinguished scientist for husband and two lovely children. A two-hundred thousand dollar house and the whole works. We have already made our reputation, so why not relax and do other things now? They also serve who only stand and wait, he'll say.... But when I look through that telescope and see the stars, when I watch the shimmering dance of the Borealis, I feel I have to have one last crack at real scholarship, real research." She paused. "'Leave everything and follow me,' he said, and straightaway Simon who was called Peter left everything and followed him."

She continued with more energy. Did she really have it in her to do anything worthwhile? She wasn't sure. But she had had so much at one time that surely it couldn't all have vapoured away. Just a smidgen of spinach, Priti had said, a teensy weensy smidgen of spinach. "Just what was the significance of all those stories that insisted on a smidgen of something? Jesus and the loaves and fish, Krishna and Panchali, Krishna and Sudama, Gopala and what was the story? not Panchali's *akshaya patra* but the other one about Gopala the Cowherd, remember the one in Sister Nivedita's *Cradle Tales*? Tell me the story."

Savitri thought, *How like Priti she sounds! Imperative and cajoling at the same time*. Just the way she would to Priti and Krish, she narrated it now — the story of a poor widow with a son she had named Gopala, after Krishna. The school was on the other side of a dark grove of trees and little Gopala was afraid, but his mother prayed to Krishna and then told her son that his older brother, Gopala the flute-playing cowherd, would take him through the grove. Krishna played on his flute and related stories as daily he walked the boy to school and back through the woods. One day, the teacher asked every pupil to bring something from home for a potluck party, and the poor widow didn't have anything. She told her son to ask his brother while they walked through the woods, and Krishna gave the boy a little bowl of sweet *dahi*, and when the teacher poured it into a bigger bowl, the little bowl filled up again and again and again and everyone enjoyed the sweetest yogurt they had ever tasted.

"So, what do you think is the point?"

"That we need only one acorn to have an oak tree. We've been blessed with so many, Vee, even if we could nurture just one ..."

"Couldn't the story just as well mean that if there's nothing left, no matter what you do, it is a dead-end street? That is what I am afraid of, that my brain has atrophied beyond repair, not even a smidgen left. But at other times, I feel the world is still there for the taking.

The sun shone on the left side of Veejala's face and arms, flashing off her diamond ring to dance on the ceiling, which reflected it back onto her coffee; her eyes were looking at a star-studded sky in which new worlds opened door beyond door. Savitri could have kneeled down that moment and kissed the hem of the other's garment. *My sister, my dear dear sister*. Veejala moved her hand and the dancing borealis on the ceiling disappeared, but her eyes were still seeing door beyond door.

The phone rang, and Savitri answered. "... I am feeling better, thanks, Bev ... did you try Cindy, she is usually home Thursdays... yes, Mr.Grierson ... I'm feeling a little bit better, thanks ... well, they're working on their project for the first hour and I suppose I could come out for the last hour ... no, I'm sorry there's no way I can get myself out till I've given the aspirin time to act ... yes, I'll be there at two."

"Sucker, every time a sucker, Savitri. I know, you have to go, I heard. You are so unrelentingly sweet."

"So unrelentingly stupid, is all. I have no scruples about the ethics of fibbing, Vee. Anyone who is a mother knows that, but I just don't have the training in chess, of preparing for all kinds of permutations."

"I didn't think you did too badly with your funereal tone and aspirins."

Savitri laughed. "Those are just fibs. What I don't know how to do is tell lies, real cool lies; it is as essential as knowing how to fall the right way in hockey or skating."

"If you've realized there is a need, you are halfway to being there. Keep it up."

Savitri got up. "Let's have lunch. Look what I have for you!" She brought out the *kadhi* and *saag* and *chapattis,* and told her the story of how the *kadhi* had been destined for her.

"And how is your bright-eyed darling, the teacher's pet?"

Savitri talked about Pete and the chocolate-covered laxatives, his punishment and Mark Antony. The year had been worthwhile because of what she had done for Pete.

"I know what you mean," Veejala said, "just one student who understands even one idea worth picking up makes every three-hour honours seminar justified. I am glad you're okay, Savi. Whenever I give an evening or summer course, I have several grade school teachers and you can spot them rightaway, especially those who teach grades one, two or three. They have this saccharine sweet way of talking. Well, you've escaped that, the force be with you."

It was a mixed compliment as Veejala's usually were. But Savitri was not offended.

At some point, Veejala looked at her watch and said, "You'd better get back to your sheep, it is half-past one."

"After that hard-won skirmish, I couldn't possibly reach there a minute before two." To prove her point, Savitri took a clean cup and poured herself another cup of coffee. But it was like a parking meter ticking away. She soon got up and went to have a quick wash.

"Take your time, Vee, rest for a while, sorry I have to rush," she said, leaving by the back door.

"Do you have to go?"

It was only when she was backing the car out of the garage that she really heard and saw Veejala's words and face, Do you *have* to go? Savitri, her mind already at school, and moreover expecting something sarcastic from Veejala, about her conscientiousness and/or fear of Mr. Grierson, had decoded her message wrongly. For a moment, Savitri thought of parking the car and going back into the house, but the moment passed. With a sigh, she backed down the driveway and went on her way, disturbed that Veejala, who had sat like Pallas Athene, the sun shining on her profile while diamonds flashed overhead, should have ended with a plea to which she had not responded, preoccupied with her own petty worries about the principal and her classes.

Veejala continued to sit at the table, leaning her head against her hands. *I am not young*, she thought, *I can't concentrate even an hour on anything I read. My eyes are half gone. And I haven't churned out even my usual quota of papers these two years. Am I throwing away a pearl of great price for something glowing in the dark that could well be a leopard's eye staring at the kill?*

Veejala folded her arms on the table and laid her head on them. In kindergarten, at the Jesus and Mary Convent School with its gray arched windows, they had had to sleep after lunch in that posture. How comfortable it was, and how she had rebelled against it almost every single day, with Sister Cecilia threatening that the eternal fires of hell awaited her for her disobedience. It was good to feel the sun on one's face, its red glow darting behind one's eyelids. Lines from some past life came to her:

> I could lie down like a tired child,
> And weep away this life of care
> That I have borne and yet must bear,
> Till death like sleep might steal on me,
> And I might feel in the warm air
> My cheek grow cold and hear the sea
> Breathe o'er my dying brain its last monotony.

Juhu beach. The Bhave family had a house overlooking Juhu beach, at which they had spent many weekends, taking the *Deccan Queen* from Pune, being met at the station by a liveried chauffeur in one of those huge humpbacked Chevrolets ... fine sand under one's feet that became heavy clods when they ran along the sea that splashed and sprayed fine salt that they loved to lick off their lips their hands, and far away the lighthouse turning, turning, the beacon brighter on one side than on the other, why was that? Was it real or an optical illusion?

She woke at the sound of a door opening. It was Jyoti. She looked at her watch. It was only 2:25 but she felt she had slept a long drugged sleep.

Jyoti came in. In a guarded tone she said, "Hullo Auntie."

"Hello, Jyo!"

"Been here long? Had lunch?"

"Yes, thanks, delicious *kadhi* and *chapatties*, I am not used to such lunches, I'm zonked out. How about you? Had lunch?"

"Sort of — a salad — Mom home?"

"She left a few minutes ago. I have to be going, too. I have a special seminar coming up in an hour or so. One of my students is from Morris and he said he might have to canoe out of his house when the crest hits them. I have two more makeup seminars next week, as well."

"What a drag." Jyoti helped herself to a can of pop from the refrigerator.

Veejala poured herself some cold coffee. "How are things going for you? How's Pierre?"

Distantly Jyoti replied, "He's all right. Thanks."

"None of my business, in other words."

Jyoti had her back to Veejala as she opened a cupboard for a glass. "It's your business, Auntie, just as it's mine to ask you what is happening with you. But we've lost the ability to ask and answer."

After a moment's pause, Veejala said, "We are lucky as long as we have one or two people with whom we can still talk."

"*If*. But everything burns up in your hand. You feel really close to someone and then, bang slam, the door shuts on your face."

Veejala waited. Jyoti brought an apple and her drink, and sat with her back to the window."

"Care for some apple?" Jyoti quartered hers and cut out the centre. "Or would you rather have a whole one?" She got up and brought out another Golden Delicious, plate and knife." Veejala pared it carefully, drawing the peel in one long spiral. Jyoti bit into her apple. She wanted to talk to her aunt about Pierre planning to set up house in Regina, house and business and all, without consulting her. Did couples discuss in advance such issues as a matter of course? Had Veejala talked her trip over with Anant and Vithal? Jyoti, judging by her parents' reaction, decided that her aunt had not. And if she hadn't, what was wrong with Pierre deciding on his own? Anyway, no, she couldn't talk about Pierre to Aunt Vee. No, she didn't have anyone to talk to. "Bang slam the door shuts on your face," she repeated.

"Pierre's okay." Veejala said.

The temptation was great to tell Veejala all about her problems with Pierre, but she resisted it.

"And how is our half-starved genius from Madras taking Pierre?"

"Who?"

"Come, Jyo, you know whom I mean."

"Well ... actually it is him I was thinking of about ... I mean I used to be able to talk to him no holds barred but now ..."

"I know you are sometimes rather dumb, dear niece of mine, but you aren't that dumb that you don't know he is head over heels in love with you."

"I could talk to him, I really could."

"One can never talk no holds barred with anyone that close to oneself."

"He isn't that close. I mean, you know how he exaggerates and flirts and ..."

"And quotes far-out poetry. I love his crazy versatility. That young man can go a long way if he'd only concentrate. He'll get over you once you are out of reach, Jyo, so tell me how are things going for you? Is there anything to tell, and if there is, how are you planning to handle your father?"

Jyoti kept quiet, chewing on her apple. Then she said, "It's too confusing, right now. Let's talk about you, Auntie Vee."

"What makes you think my life is any less confusing?"

Jyoti sat up. "But you've taken action! One can't come to that point without having resolved all confusions."

"It could be," Veejala said smiling, "let's be academic for the nonce. It could be that one takes action thinking one has resolved the problem, but then finds oneself still confused. Hasn't that happened to you? After you first made love, for instance?"

Jyoti flushed angrily. "Mom has ..."

"Nothing of the kind, Savi hasn't told me anything."

Sarcastically Jyoti said, "Just a shot in the dark, eh?"

"And you were dumb enough to give yourself away."

"A shot in the dark," Jyoti repeated, to show she didn't believe it. "It shows in my eyes, eh? The sparkle of stars and all that."

"More in one's hips, I believe, after a while." Veejala could match hit for hit.

Jyoti sat silent, with sullen defiance on her face.

"Mine was a shot in the dark," Veejala said casually, "but those grandmothers and aunts back home had an acute sixth sense or something. They always knew just looking at you if you were having your period or were pregnant or having an extramarital affair. In my days, we didn't have premarital flings, there just wasn't any opportunity, but they would have seen that too; an amazing sense of observation, I suppose, the ability to read body language. I wish I had picked up some of their tidbits of knowledge. I remember the orange seller who came to our door once in Trombay.We had rented a flat for Sharad when he took up his first job, and I turned her away because we had enough oranges. My Aunt Ranjana, who was with us, saw her back as she walked away and recognized she was a *hijrah*. Amazing."

Jyoti wanted to know more about eunuchs, a subject that had always intrigued her, but Veejala was already leaving the past behind with a shrug. "I am remembering too many things today. Sign of old age, right?" Veejala looked at her with an amused smile. "I simply assumed you were no virgin, Jyoti. It is the tight-lipped type that gives in; the so-called flirts who let themselves be patted and stroked by all and sundry hold on to their virginity a lot longer."

Jyoti hated herself for letting tears fill her eyes at this unexpected jab. Two minutes earlier she would have been ready for her aunt's usual sarcasms, but all that digression into old-wives tales had thrown her off-guard. She should get up and walk away, tears or no tears. Let her aunt figure out what she will; she would just get up and leave the room.

She sat, tears welling up faster than she could swallow them.

Veejala briefly glanced at her and looked away. Her niece was so lovely, so vulnerable and lovely and so hurt. "That was mean of me, Jyoti, I am sorry. And ashamed. I guess I'm used to sparring with your mother. You're just a kid, a hurt little kid. I am on your side, Jyo, I mean it. I'll bat for you against your dad, count on me. And it is a beautiful experience, quite quite ravishing, shall we say?"

She stood behind Jyoti and kissed her on her hair and hands much the same way she would have comforted Priti at age three, kissing away the hurt of a fall. She realized that was what she was doing, and burst out laughing. "Look, Jyoti, I am terrible at comforting or apologizing. All I know is how to work at the planetarium, and maybe I am not much good at that any longer. Look, I have faith in you, in your common sense. I think I know how you feel. Yes, it will be confusing for a while, and the gossip will be hard to take. Tongues have started wagging already, and it will be hard on all of you especially because Sharad and Savi are so well known, such pillars of the community and all that. People will say you are a fool, and that your parents especially are to blame, to go for an alien foreigner when you can have one of our own clean-cut, conscientious boys. Now, if Pierre were a physician or even an academic, they just might forgive and forget your choice, but Pierre doesn't have a degree of any kind, leave alone an M.D. or Ph.D. So, yes, there will be a lot of hassle, not for you directly but for what you'll be putting your parents through. But ignore them, my love. If this were India you'd have the same gossip against Sridhar, the alien southerner among our own sweet Maharashtrian boys. So just ignore them and marry anyone you choose. If you want to marry at all, that is."

Veejala placed one last kiss on the top of the young woman's head before moving back to her chair. "Sharad would kill me if he heard me say this, Jyo, but it is as sound a piece of advice as one needs for living in this age in this country: jump into bed as many times as you wish with as many different people as you wish, with condoms of course, but don't jump into matrimony. We, people like your parents and I, my generation, born and brought up in another age, another culture, know that marriage is for keeps and we are willing to accept a million eccentricities and needs in each other; but you kids who grow up here are so rigid in your expectations, so lax in your commitment, you throw in the towel the minute something goes wrong. If we hadn't the background we have, your uncle and I would have been divorced a dozen times in these twenty years; both of us have been outrageously irresponsible; I've done the craziest things when we had money, and he's been the reason why we never had any money; we were students for the first million years of our married life! Why do you think it took me fifteen years to get my degree? Because I had to work all the time while he kept changing his department, his courses, his thesis topic, and so losing out on assistantships. You know only about back home and about our degrees and awards since then but about little else. We've worked at all kinds of jobs — library, dishwashing, parking lot attendant, waitressing — anything we could get when we needed money; of course we never worked if we had enough for the month, for the week even. In those days, students had it easy in the minimum wage market. Now they are being crowded out by adults in line for the same jobs. I noticed our newsboy is fifty years old if a day. Last Christmas I called him up so I could put a face to the person for I was leaving a gift certificate for in the mailbox, and I hear this old man's voice. In my day, if you were young you could be poor forever but never starve."

Jyoti forgot her own problems at this incredible revelation. "You mean you were poor?"

"As a churchmouse."

"But why? I mean with all that money back home, and ..."

"There were reasons, my love, there are always reasons for every blessed thing. But that's not the point. The point is those were great times. We were both A+ students. And both of us were crazy. One has to be a little crazy if one is to achieve anything.... My first conference paper, back in '81, was quite something. I kind of came out full-grown like Aphrodite rising from the foam, a rather pregnant Aphrodite at that. No gradual climb to the top for the likes of us, no, sir.... Pasadena, that's why I'm going there. Because that's where I started. It was a very exclusive conference of the top experts. I was the only graduate student among the presenters. I was shaking like leaves hit by the summer loo winds when I started, but I had a really good theoretical base about my ideas on the activities in Virgo, my favourite constellation, naturally, being as I am one. Though the experimental data had huge gaps, it still made quite an impact. The question hour continued forever, it seemed, and it was late afternoon before I could get away. I rushed up to our hotel room and threw up." She gestured with her arms. "There was Vithal open-mouthed and just finished with one round of bawling — Anant had frantically tried babysitting him all day — and me doubled over the washbasin, and who should knock but Professor Jake Steiner, come to congratulate me! Steiner in person, and me puking in the bathroom. Nineteen eighty-one, wonderful, sad '81.

"You lost the baby right then?"

"No, two weeks later, back home in Michigan, thank god. You needn't look so commiserating, Jyo, I couldn't have cared less at the time. Success was so heady, so absobloominutely great, it seemed a fair shake — recognition in exchange for a five-month-old fetus. I got more than sixty requests for a copy of my paper that year; people who weren't there heard about it and asked me for a copy; it got an award in its category that year, pretty restrictive category and so no big deal if you think about it, best paper by a beginning scientist under 30 years, etc., etc., but sixty-five requests, you know how at the beginning of one's career we keep note of such details ..." Veejala started twisting her ring off and slipping it on again. "You have to pay a price for everything and I didn't regret it at the time; it was a fair and square bargain. A pound of fame for a pound of flesh. But what's left of it now? Which is why I have to do what I have to do to show that something gold can stay." She rose and looked out the window.

She had said it thoughtfully, sadly, but Jyoti was excited. "Pasadena, London, Ahmedabad, it sounds so exciting, and ..." she added more hesitantly, "it's reassuring to know you're not breaking up with Uncle Anant for ... just for the breaking up."

"You would like to be really really sure of that, wouldn't

you?" Jyoti nodded yes, half eager, half afraid. Veejala drew the girl's head to her breast. "We're all in one goddawful mess, my love, but still lucky; we have one or two to hold on to.... And now I'm going to rest for a few minutes in Savi's ever ready guestroom."

She went out of the kitchen. Jyoti sat munching the apple pieces Veejala had left almost untouched. They had been neatly pared. Without the skin they tasted unfamiliarly sweet to Jyoti. As she dwelt on the new stories of her aunt's life, an idea formed back of her mind. She would go away with Aunt Vee; away from everything so she could get a proper perspective.

The doorbell rang. She went to the front and opened the door. There was a red sports car on the street, with someone in the driver's seat who made no effort to get out. The bell rang again. She rushed to the back door. It was Pierre. *At last, at last he was here*. She let him in. "Oh, how I've missed you, Pierre darling, mmm." He enclosed her in his coat and kissed her. "Mm, my angel." Through the familiar smell of his mouth spray she could smell whiskey, and was irritated. Whiskey at three in the afternoon? He wanted her to come out with him. "So who's in the car?" she asked, putting two and two together. It was Gord, someone from Regina. He would drop them off at Pierre's apartment. Pierre had to meet some people that evening, and he was returning to Regina the next day. This was a real quickie trip to spend a few hours with her. He promised he'd drop her back by dinnertime.

No, she said, she couldn't come out now. They wrangled on the landing to the basement. Wasn't he returning for the weekend? They could be together all weekend but not now. No, he might not be able to come before Monday. That was okay, she'd be totally free by Monday noon, all exams over, free as a bird. Oh, come, he was starved. He had lived on fantasies for more than a week; please. No, not today, please Pierre, don't pester me.

He flared up. "Pester you! Is it unnatural for anyone to want a date with one's fiancée one hadn't seen for more than a week?"

"I've missed you, missed you so much. If you didn't have to go ... if you had never gone, maybe ..."

"Maybe what?"

Jyoti didn't know what. She clung to him silently for a few moments. He relaxed, confident she was preparing to yield. But Jyoti's voice was quietly firm when she spoke. She would not go with him now.

Later tonight then? He could pick her up after nine.

No, it's not for long, he'll be back Monday, please be back Monday.

"What's the matter?"

She leaned against him. "Why can't we be like this forever, close, comfortably comfortingly warm?"

"Oh come, I'll make you warm, cosily comfortably warm." He nibbled at her ear.

"No, please, no."

He withdrew angrily. "Why? Just give me one beastly reason why."

"I could give you half a dozen reasons, Pierre, all true: I'm working this evening at the University Centre standing in for a friend who has a summer job interview; I still have another exam to go; I've promised Mom I'll run some errands. All true, darling, but ..."

"But what? What've you been trying to say all week over the phone about sorting things out? What things?"

"Things. You and me. I need time."

"Damn it," he yelled. "How can you be so cool, so rational?" Physically intimidated, she stepped up the stairs, backing into the kitchen. He followed her and filled the doorway.

"Don't do that." She pushed his encircling arms away.

"Damn you, Jyoti. One day I'll get to your inner kernel of

snootiness. I swear I'll tear my way into that silence and hear you scream with lust and pain. Damn you, you bitch, standing there as though nothing moves you, but I know you, I know how you lust inside. You're a cauldron of emotions sealed four times over, but I swear I'll break you, you ..." He went out the kitchen door, slamming it behind him. Jyoti closed the screen door first, watched him turn towards the front of the house, and then she closed the door and went back to the kitchen.

She stood by the window watching the snowflakes just starting to fall. Veejala came to the kitchen, coat in hand.

Jyoti smiled self-consciously. "I was hoping you wouldn't have heard," she said, wondering how she could joke about it.

"Quite an earthquake, wasn't it?" Veejal helped herself to a glass of water. "I grant you aren't the average-kid-next-door, Jyoti but this ... oof. What in you brings out such violence? I am academically interested in your seismographic map. The Richter scale would have registered a 7.5, I'd say."

"What do you think I should be feeling, academically speaking, as you say?"

"Hm," Veejala played the game, continuing in the same half-serious half-amused vein that Jyoti had adopted, "I think you should be thrilled to pieces to have aroused such passion in someone."

Suddenly despondent, Jyoti said, "Maybe I am nothing. Just a blank wall or mirror. Each one sees himself, but not me. I am nothing in myself; maybe that's why I arouse such violence."

"You are not talking any sense, my love. Go sleep it off."

Jyoti looked at her for help. "I'm so confused. Why do the same words that make me feel so warm one day make me feel so distant the next day?" Veejala looked discreetly at her watch. It was 3:05. She placed her coat on the back of a chair. The poor child was pale, so upset and distraught. "We are far too serious about everything. Why don't we just laugh, roll around in the muddy snow, build a snow castle. Just sing."

Jyoti caught her sleeve. "May I come with you to India? Please. I've always wanted to. I haven't been back even once."

Veejala patted her hand. "I heard the cyclone pass through, remember?" More quietly she said, "To tell you the truth, Jyoti, I have regretted that miscarriage. It was a girl. She was there already, all of her, my daughter, not just a fetus. She'd have been sixteen now. I've burnt with envy a million times, my love, seeing you and Savitri together, these last few years that you've been such a lovely young woman. By the time Priti grows up, I'd be all washed out. Yes, I'd love to have you by my side, my dear, and the only reason I haven't is that I want it so badly. Which is why I can't take you with me."

"Come again. I lost you."

"Never mind. Forget all that, Jyoti. You have some mega problems and you'd better face up to them; you can't run away from them, not with me anyway. Never run away. I'll let you in on another secret, my love. For several years, ever since I knew this was a dead-end street with no future for me, I've wanted to quit and strike out as I'm doing now, but things weren't quite right between Anant and myself. If I'd left then, I'd have felt guilty all the time that I was running away from something that I perhaps didn't want, rather than going towards something that I want with all my soul. Now that we are happy with each other, I can go."

"Do you really have to? Vithal needs you."

"Most others would say Priti needs me, but you ... you know me better."

"Vithal, I said Vithal as an excuse. I need you. Please." Jyoti laid her face on the soft fur collar of the coat Veejala had put on as she spoke. Veejala embraced her. "We are all in one godawful mess, my darling, but we'll survive," she said lightly. Her hands were warm and undemanding as she stroked the girl's hair. Jyoti was glad she had at last the courage or cowardice to tell someone she needed that she needed her. It had been so simple, really; one just had to say it straightforwardly: I need you, Jayant; I need you, Mom: I need you ... Pierre, she said to herself, refusing to name the other.

Veejala could feel peace enveloping the girl. A strange aura surrounded them, surely there was something mystical in the way she was transmitting peace to someone when she herself did not have it. Poor child, under that proud sullen veneer was a confused child ready to cradle her face in her arms on the table, crying crying for something she could not describe or define.

> But what am I?
> An infant crying in the night,
> An infant crying for the light,
> And with no language but a cry.

It was peaceful here, like a river in the plains. A river made sense, a fountain didn't. Anant liked to watch the Memorial Boulevard fountains on summer evenings. But it made her want to scream, the regularity with which the jets rose and fell, up down around unendingly. She wished the streams would stop, and the water flow or stand still of its own accord, not be pumped up endlessly into a regular pattern. It was worse at the beach if one made the mistake of watching the water instead of running along the sand. The breakers never ceased; did the waters never tire of lashing the sand? There was peace in the river, flow and stasis; there was peace in a mountain as there never could be in an ocean.

Her phobia made no sense, especially in an astronomer. How could there be peace in her own special domain, in the planets that moved endlessly in their orbits? Besides, there was so much explosive activity up there that no one but an astronomer could imagine it. Perhaps she would never be able to find out what she sought, in people, or in her work. She had not followed up on her paper on M87, that galaxy 50 million light years away which perhaps held a key to black holes. To think, those holes might have sucked in the weight of three billion suns in a contracted space no bigger than our solar system.

I don't know how polar bears keep their fur through summers," she said, coming down from the mountain, "but I just might get a heatstroke if I don't run outside in thirty seconds." Jyoti pretended to snore as she nuzzled closer.

"But since you are my favourite niece, you can now drive me all the way to the farther door of the chemistry block and pick me up at the same spot at 5:45. In all the rush to go to Brussels last summer, I forgot to apply in time for my parking spot and ended up with Lot B."

"Behind the library?"

"Yes, miles away."

"Stuck with a rotten timetable, too. No wonder you're quitting your job. I mean, a parking spot in Lot B and timeslots 4 and 15, that's cruelty to animals."

"Impudent, impudent," Veejala slapped her lightly on her cheek. "I am rather late as is. Are you planning to come out in your shirtsleeves?"

"Just cancel the class. The students would love you for it."

"When two of your students drive fifty or more kilometres each way to attend your seminar, it becomes a burden of a rare kind; I've spent more hours preparing for these seminars than on the rest of my teaching and committee work put together."

"What a crying shame that a professor has to actually spend time preparing for classes. The students are good, did you say?"

"No one gets to stay in my class unless they are good," she replied with easy arrogance.

"Good students even in these backwoods of Canada?"

Veejala laughed. "Touché. I am getting late, chauffeur."

"Slave driver."

Jyoti grabbed her Norwegian handknit cardigan, slipped into her rainboots and followed her to the car. She adjusted the leather seats and mirrors and rolled in smooth luxury towards the University.

"So how come you still have classes?"

"We are above petty rules and regulations, m'dear," she said, assuming a British accent.

They turned into King's Drive. In her normal voice, she added, "I scheduled two extra graduate seminars this term. One of the students is rather exceptional, not homegrown Manitoban, let me add, and the extra time is well spent. I hope to have him work with me this summer."

"At Pasadena?"

"Don't sound so envious. Yes, it is one way to repay Jake Steiner. When someone stands you a cup of coffee, don't keep count and pay for his coffee next time around; pay for someone else's."

"You don't need to look at your watch so often Auntie Vee, five minutes fifty-five seconds is all it takes." Jyoti stopped at the walkway near the door.

"Drive home, or wherever you want to, Jyoti, I do appreciate the favour. Please, come back at 5:40, though."

Chapter 11

Her problems crowded her mind as Jyoti pulled out of the parking lot after dropping off her aunt. If this Gord or whoever had not been there with his red sports car, she might have been more responsive, less rude to Pierre. It had just been bad timing, not his fault that she wanted to be alone for a while chewing on her apple and thinking of what Aunt Vee had said. If he had asked her to walk to the plaza or the University Centre, she'd have agreed rightaway. But that was dumb, she chided herself even as she thought it, who'd want to walk in this weather, love or no? The sidewalks were slushy and the snow black with mud and exhaust wastes. Pierre did not care to walk even in the best of weather, Besides, as he made clear, his ten days of abstinence was what was uppermost in his mind. Jyoti wished she had gone with him. She missed him, missed his lovemaking; she thought of his body ... its hungers, its seductive smooth beauty as it reared itself up. Jyoti sighed. She was plainly stupid, she scolded herself, penalizing him for his wrong timing instead of going with him or agreeing to a late evening date. Yes, she should have sent him off after agreeing to meet him later. That way she would have got to be with both Aunt Vee and him. Maybe now she could drive down to his apartment. What if he was with — no, she couldn't possibly not trust him.

She drove around to Lot B and parked the car. She might as visit the library. On the other hand, Pierre might phone, to apologize, to ask her again to join him wherever he was going to be after the appointment with whomever he was meeting at six. And this time she would not refuse, and he would massage away all the tension in her neck and shoulder, would plant wet kisses all the way down her spine and turn her over and do likewise all the way.... She had become an addict. If six months had made her an addict, was it any wonder he had been so angry at being thwarted? Jyoti had never once asked him about his earlier girlfriends. He had told her there had never been anyone but her since they started dating, and never would be and she believed him. They had never talked about his past, but that did not mean she had not thought about it from time to time. But no, it was not important; nothing counted except the present and the future.

Quite aimlessly, but by habit, she wandered into the anthropology section. Was it habit or was it because of some subconscious desire, knowing she had run into Sridhar a couple of times in that section during the last year? No, it would be awful to run into Sridhar now. She went to the floor above. She remembered what she'd wanted to review. She should have brought her books with her, the ones to be returned and the ones she needed to review for the exam tomorrow, but in talking to Veejala she had become even more disconcerted than she had with Pierre. Aunt Vee had such an overpowering personality, she thought, already aching with nostalgia for those moments by the back door that already seemed a long long time ago. Once the exams were over, everything would fall into place. She had bumbled her way through polisci and sociology. Two down, two to go. If she could get through anthro, English would be no sweat. Kiss. What was she going to do about the concert? She'd not mentioned it in her daily phone calls, subconsciously postponing possible unpleasantness, rationalizing it would be easier handled in person. Worries were crowding in again.

She walked to the shelves grown familiar over the year and picked out the volumes she needed. As she moved towards the carrels, she saw a black-haired head at a farther carrel. Reflexively, she moved forward to see if it was anyone she knew. Why did she do that with every black-haired person, why does it always have to be we-they? Sridhar had said. Why do you identify yourself with all brown faces? he had asked Jayant. She shook him out of her head. She shook Jayant too out of her head. Black hair; Pierre's hair was black and Dad loved him for it. She wouldn't think of them. And no, it didn't matter diddly who that black-haired student was. Jyoti sat at a carrell and opened a book, drawing out some crumpled, folded blank sheets of paper she usually carried in her pocket. "Paki house." It was an us/them thing and not because she wanted it that way. For the first time in her seven years in Canada, she had confronted racism head on — if it was racism — and had won the first round, if that was a win. No, she wouldn't think of it.

She assiduously took notes from the two chapters most useful for the exam; it was easy once you got the hang of how to impress a given instructor. A bibliography a mile long, Rick had said about his professor; never take sides, Laura had said of her philosophy professor. The name of the game was to find out each one's quirk and satiate it.

Jyoti's attention span ran out in half an hour. She decided she would checkout the books and cram at home sometime between then and tomorrow. What if Pierre had called already and given up on calling for the day?

At the checkout counter she met Parimal. Rajen had introduced her a year ago as a newcomer, the daughter of a visiting post-doc in his department. Jyoti had told him she would help orient the girl, but had never got around to visiting them till after they were well settled. After that first visit she had forgotten them altogether until September, when Parimal had joined the university. Once or twice they had had lunch together and they periodically waved with enthusiasm across the hallways. A vague sense of guilt prompted Jyoti to be extra cordial every time they ran into each other.

Parimal checked out what seemed to be a dozen fat volumes. After greeting her, Jyoti asked if it wasn't rather late to be reading all those. "Never too late," Parimal answered happily, "the nearer to the exam you read anything, the shorter the time you need to keep them in your head. I always study everything during the last week before exams. I have a good memory, a good short-term memory."

"Swallowing and regurgitating doesn't work in this system."

"That's one of the myths people here like to perpetuate," Parimal said as they walked into the lobby. "All you need do is to throw a façade of argument over the whole stuff. If you have an argument format, some professors will swallow anything you regurgitate, pardon the cud analogy."

One of Parimal's books fell and Jyoti picked it up for her, apologizing, "Oh, I'm sorry I never thought to help, here let me carry some of them."

"Quite okay, Jyoti, I've been toting books piled up taller than myself all my life." Jyoti remembered the number of texts and scribblers she had to carry in India even in grade two, and of course those schools had no lockers where one could keep anything overnight.

"How do you carry them on the bus?"

"Not on my head, don't worry, though maybe I should introduce the basket idea. Why not? It just might catch on, like the backpack."

"I could give you a ride, if you're leaving for home now."

"Let's go." Parimal set off towards the main door.

"The car is there." Jyoti moved towards the rear doors of the library.

"My, this is a fancy car," Parimal said as Jyoti opened her door and released the power lock on the other door. Parimal was in no hurry to get in. She walked around the car, running her hands over the name on the side, Lincoln Continental.

"I have it just for the afternoon," Jyoti admitted, suddenly reluctant to mention Aunt Veejala.

"I know why it's so familiar, I've seen Dr. Moghe driving this. Your aunt, isn't she? That's one gutsy lady."

How quickly she's picked up an accent and the jargon, Jyoti thought. It doesn't take long. But that didn't stop people from shouting, "Paki house."

Jyoti drove along Chancellor Drive.

"Not so fast, you have to turn here," Parimal said.

Jyoti turned as directed, and drove towards the house number Parimal gave.

"You've moved?"

"Yeah, someone on sabbatical wanted to rent it out and we jumped at the chance of having a house."

"Clearing the snow and all?"

"Surjit is a help. He's my cousin. Please do come in, Jyoti and have a cup of tea. My mother would love to see you. Oh, I forgot, she goes to work Thursday afternoons. But come in anyway, do."

"I'd love to, Parimal, but I have an exam tomorrow, and ..." As she stopped in front of the house to let Parimal off, she recognized the faded blue Biscayne on the driveway and her heart raced. "... I don't want to be a bother to you," she said lamely.

"Not to worry, please do come in for a little while, it is your first time to this house, you can't say no to sweetening your mouth with a little something," said Parimal in Hindi.

Jyoti drove into the driveway and parked behind Sridhar's car, unaccountably excited as she manoeuvered so her front bumper lightly touched the back bumper of his car.

Parimal opened the side door through the open garage. "It looks as though Surjit has some friends over," she said. "Let's go to my room."

She led Jyoti through the kitchen to her bedroom. Jyoti shook her head to herself: so typical to segregate her female friends from her cousin's male friends.

"I didn't know you had a cousin," Jyoti said, to make conversation.

"Yes, he came over last September as a graduate student. He was to have come two years ago, but there was no one to post him the six thousand dollars minimum bank balance Immigration require of visa students who come on their own."

"They do?"

"Yes, didn't you know? It's not necessary if you come with an assistantship, but Surjit didn't get one. Mind you, some departments don't give admission unless they have funds for an assistantship as well. So he's lucky."

"It doesn't seem fair," Jyoti said. "Visa students aren't allowed to earn money at other jobs either, someone said. It isn't fair."

"I don't know. Depends on which side of the table you're on. Immigration thinks visa students ..."

Visa students — another of those terms she had often heard without registering its implications.

"Excuse me while I go change my pants, they're wet at the cuffs." Parimal took a fresh pair from her closet and went to the bathroom. Jyoti smiled. She herself would have had no hesitation changing in front of another girl. Oh well, Parimal would outgrow her inhibitions soon enough if she stayed a little longer.

She opened the door that Parimal had shut; the young men's voices came from the living room. Her ears were honed only for one voice.

"The matrilineal system isn't exclusive to Kerala," Sridhar was saying, "you find it all over the world; in Canada, for example, the Tsimshians of Damelahamid had a matrilineal setup."

"The Tsimshi what?"

"They were — are — a group of Pacific Coast Indians."

"Good lord, Sridhar, where do you pick up such weird details?"

"Here and there. I wander through the library when I want a break. Today, for example, I came across a rather interesting volume of translations from Papuan songs. I'm sure they'd sound neat put to music:

He hiki ke hui me ko'u lahui me ka weli 'ole
'A'ohe maka'u no'u iho, me a kia'i pa'a ole ia

It means:

I mingle with my people without fear.
My safety is no concern, I require no bodyguards.
Mine is the boast that a pearl of great price has fallen
  to me from above,
Mine is the loyalty of my people."

"You are crazy, *yaa*r, storing up such useless details in your grey cells. Look, you've got to maximize on computer time, you know, not clutter it up with irrelevancies."

They laughed, Sridhar as loud as any.

"Okay, I'll tell you some relevant details I found in the anthropology section today. Did you know there are 146 dialects of Hindi recorded in Fiji Islands?"

"The less educated a people, the greater is the variation of dialects," said someone. Someone else disagreed. Sridhar did not respond. Jyoti wanted to run out to the living room and see him.

The doorbell rang. Someone came in, saying, "Don't take the Arlington Bridge today, guys, it's a death trap."

"It is always a death trap," said someone else, "such a monstrous humpback. Why don't they redo it the way the midtown bridge over Donald was redone?"

Sridhar said, "The Arlington Bridge is an historic treasure. It was built in 1911 on a design originally planned for spanning the Nile."

Parimal came out of the bathroom. "I wonder if I shouldn't make tea for everyone," she said.

"I have to be going," Jyoti said, "I have to pick up my aunt."

"Please, you must eat something."

Jyoti knew Parimal would be hurt if she didn't eat a bite of something. How sweet they were, she thought, with their traditional codes of hospitality, not just in what they offered but the way they offered it; "must sweeten your mouth," the language so floral, so touchingly ornate. Parimal brought some *burfees* and *laddus*. Jyoti helped herself to a piece of each and fled.

Back in the car, she marvelled at her behaviour and reaction. The sight of the faded blue Biscayne had drawn her like a magnet into the house. Like those magnetic cranes at the docks, she thought, what power they had, to haul huge vats of cargo and pipes. If she didn't keep a tight rein on herself, she'd be chasing him all over the city. *I'd go to sleep touching the tips of your fingers*. No, she wouldn't think of it. *I'd be thrilled to pieces, to use Pixie's turn of phrase, to have aroused such passion in someone.*

Pierre, Pierre, Pierre, she chanted the mantra. He was a known quantity, but Sridhar had become the great unknown, a U.F.O. suddenly darkening the sky. Pierre, Regina, video stores, these were known qualities, whereas who knew anything about this unpredictable ill-dressed man except that he had a divine voice? He had parents back in an alien place and a great many siblings, brothers who probably depended on him to find a suitable job, sisters who needed him to find a husband and a dowry. She longed to be surrounded forever and a day with the comfort of familiar places and people. Regina, what kind of place is it, that lunch stop on the way to Calgary and the

Rockies? But what did it matter? With Jayant and Aunt Vee gone, it was time for her to go. It would be good to get away, start in a new place, away from — no she wouldn't even think his name.

She switched on the radio. "The fate of Manitoba river lots will depend on how much force the Red River picks up as the crest moves towards North Dakota. Showers and thunderstorms in the northern part of the state have increased the possibility of higher levels.

"Fargo, which will get the crest tomorrow, expects little damage to the city. The crest will be at a maximum of about 53 feet when it reaches Grand Forks on Saturday. The dikes are not expected to hold up in Grand Forks but Duff's Ditch is expected to hold and save Winnipeg. Provincial flood spokesman Larry Whitney says there is no reason to panic. The Red River floodway can handle the increased flow, and diking and sandbagging operations are going ahead of schedule."

She switched to another station. "St. Norbert residents are outraged at the city's levy of a $1.10 fee per sandbag. The forty-pound sandbags are available to the public for the first time, but many residents think that some flooding could have been prevented had they been made available sooner."

She switched to another station. A list of locations at which volunteers were urgently needed was being read and repeated. The addresses spanned the entire city, not just Turnbull Drive — threatened with flood in past years — but Elmwood, West Kildonan, Kingston Row.... The list went on and on.

She switched to another station. "Sandbags will be available at the city's six district offices during office hours. After office hours, residents in need of emergency measures are advised to contact . . ." and the locations and phone numbers were repeated several times.

She continued listening to the flood news, unable to switch

to a music station. If you allowed yourself to listen long enough to something, anything, it hooked you.

Ergo, she shouldn't ever allow her mind to replay that voice again. *Time was all of Winnipeg was brighter because of you.* No, click it off. *Dammit, I wish I could hate and have done with* you.... She was being mesmerized.

Pierre, Pierre, Pierre. He'll call, he has to call, please please make him call.

She drove homeward. This time next week Jayant would be gone. Next month Aunt Vee would be gone. Three months from now she'd be gone. *We're all in one godawful mess, my darling, but we'll survive.*

At home, Savitri had all four burners turned on, and Jayant was in his work clothes, drinking from a jug of orange juice. The kitchen radio was on as was the television.

"Hi, Jayant, had a mud bath?"

"Hi, sis, how did your exam go? Mom, I really have to rush off, I'll have a bite of anything there is, don't bother."

"Where are you sandbagging today, Kingston Row?"

"I'm on my way to Dugald. Remember Nick Courteau who was in my grade in junior high? He was working with us this morning and he said he's going to Dugald to help his uncle move furniture out of the basement. A couple of his uncle's neighbours could do with some help too. I said I'd go help. We might be a little late coming back, Mom."

He hastily ate a plate his mother filled up, and was gone like an arrow. "I didn't know he was sandbagging today, too. Where'd he go yesterday?"

"Close by, on St. Mary's. The threat of flood would be a blessing in disguise if it doesn't do too much damage. The junior high kids are so excited about doing something that has such visible effects. They have been out all day in St. Norbert, and the grade fives and sixes are hoping to join tomorrow if we can get enough parent volunteers. My children are so disappointed they aren't old enough to go out. Poor little tykes.

We're going to bake some cupcakes and make sandwiches for our older kids tomorrow, so we don't feel left out of all the action. The boys don't think much of baking, but they will before we are through tomorrow. There is so much energy and enthusiasm, it is heartwarming."

"Remember the bus strike a couple of years ago, how everyone was so friendly to everyone else, giving and taking rides."

"Sad isn't it, that there has to be such a disaster before people will come together ... on the other hand, it is comforting to know that people do help out at such times. Just think how terrible it would be if we got so hardened that even disasters didn't make us human again."

"I've got to go. Aunt Vee wanted me to drive her to and from class. See you in a few minutes."

"Be sure to bring Veejal in for a snack of hot *chapatties*. I could pack something for the others as well."

"Mom, you indulge her way too much."

"Oh, come," Savitri said in her placid, conciliatory tone which made Jyoti continue, "You know what? If we hadn't come to Winnipeg, maybe she'd have become more responsible."

"You have to make allowances for people, *beti*, else you'll stifle their strengths. Veejala is extremely talented, Jyotishma. This phrase everyone is using now, 'the force be with you,' is an old old one. It is Shakti, we say. The goddess chooses a few of us above others."

"Democracy, Mom, we are all equals."

"Not in talents. It takes Veejala half a day to cook a simple meal; I've been home less than half an hour," she spread her hands at the four lidded pots on the stove and counter, "it is as atrocious a waste of energy for her to be cooking as it is for me to be typing or doing mathematical calculations. Blake says somewhere, 'One law for the lion and the ox is oppression.' Pete, for instance ..." Blake, Tsimshians, Tulsidas ... Jyoti felt ignorant everytime anyone flung quotations at her. She hammered the salt-cellar like a gavel on the table and said, "Listen, Mom, I shall try not to be jealous of Aunt Vee, but you say another word about Pete Kozolski and I'll scream the house down."

Savitri stopped stirring the vegetables on the skillet, and looked at her, spatula held up in the air. "Oh, I never thought of that," she cried with genuine concern. "Oh, my baby Krish! He's had ten out of ten in every subject three weeks in a row and I've done nothing to at all for him. Let me whip up some chocolate fudge for my sweetheart." Jyoti left as her mother started another burst of activity.

Chapter 12

A knock sounded on Jyoti's door. Jyoti pulled the quilt up to her ears and curled sideways, facing the wall. She heard the door open. Her mother came in and leaned over her, placing her hand on Jyoti's forehead and neck to feel if she was running a fever. From the smell of sandalwood, Jyoti guessed her mother was wearing one of the pure silk saris kept in the chest of drawers, distinct from the Downy-fragrant synthetic silks that hung in her closet. Jyoti remembered that she had promised to iron some of her silk saris this weekend. Several parties were coming up during the next few days.

"It is almost noon," her mother said softly. "Krishna and Dad and I are going to the Khoslas for lunch. Jayant is out sandbagging. On Scotia Street, I think. Do you need anything? Are you okay?"

I need you. Ma, I need you. "I'm okay," Jyoti mumbled. Savitri ran her hand over Jyoti's forehead again, pushing her hair back. "This room gets too warm during the change of seasons; you've been sweating; shall I leave the door open?" Jyoti mumbled again, and her mother took it to mean yes because that's what she herself wanted. The room was way too hot. Had the heat vent been accessible instead of being on the other side of the bed, Savitri would have closed it.

"I don't know about Dad and Krish, but I won't be there too long because I do want to visit poor Mrs. Cianflone at Misericordia. So we are taking both cars. I wish you'd visit her too, Jyoti, she took such good care of all of you, especially of Krish. Poor woman."

Jyoti heard them leave.

So it was noon already. Last night, or rather this morning, she'd thought she'd never fall asleep, but she had, and soundly too. If only one didn't ever have to wake up. What was she going to do? Oh god, what should she do, what could she do?

She had started being deceitful even before tying the knot. She had heard and read of it, of course, of women pretending to enjoy themselves just so their men would feel satisfied, flattered, or generous with their money, or just get off their back. But she had never thought she herself would ever start on deceit.

Pierre had phoned the previous morning. She had been deliriously relieved that he had postponed his trip back to Regina, and made it clear that she wanted him and soon. He had picked her up after her exam and they had gone to his apartment. There was no doubt about it; she loved the sex. They had dinner at Swallows and then drove across town to a disco. The strobe lights gave her a headache within minutes of entering but she pretended to enjoy the place. They returned to his apartment and she was happy to be with him, away from the crowd, away from herself.

Perhaps it was the physical tiredness of her studies, perhaps the rollercoaster of a week, perhaps she was so satisfied with the afternoon, but all she wanted was to sleep. It felt just so right, to nuzzle against the curve of his armpit and go to sleep, cheek against the fuzz of his chest hairs. Yes, he knew it all, just one more exam to finish, just one more week before Jayant took off, just one more week before the bank finalized the loan deal, just one more of everything, darling, and she knew what he meant as he gently ran his fingers around her nipple spiralling outward. She cringed at his wet kisses, but then decided the sooner she could be done with it, the sooner she could sleep. She pretended she was getting totally carried away, made all the gestures and sounds appropriate to the dissimulation. She did something he had always wanted her to do, lick him all the way from neck downwards to his balls; a dog can do it on its own, she thought, remembering the dogs on the streets of Pune smelling and licking themselves and their mates, circling around themselves and each other, licking licking licking. And then he had mounted her and jabbed into her in one great thrust.

Deceit, it was plain bald deceit, and she had resorted to it already.

Far more depressing and frightening was the fact that Pierre had been taken in. This had been the best time ever, he swore, absolutely undoubtedly they were made for each other and for making love. She had said yes yes yes, she had lost count of the number of home runs they had scored, as he called it. Oh they were made for each other.

It was the ease, the success with which she had feigned that frightened her now as she lay in the silent house contemplating the glass-walled corridors of time ahead, infinite mirages conjured up by parallel mirrors that extended into eternity.

Wouldn't he have known? Surely he must have known that she wasn't really there. Had he really been taken in or was he also dissimulating? If he was, wouldn't she have known? Had he known but ascribed it to exams, tiredness, wrong time of the month just to spare her, or maybe to spare himself from facing up to the fact that he didn't turn her on. But hadn't he? Denying that would be to lie through her teeth.

She tossed and turned, threw off the blanket and a minute later pulled it on again, shivering. She honestly did not know what she had or had not felt. She had been trying too hard to forget herself, surrender herself to the passion of the moment, and so perhaps had missed the moment. Once Narada was extremely upset, and Lord Vishnu asked him why his favourite *bhakta* was out of sorts. Narada said that he was disturbed by the Lord's partiality for a particular devotee, who was so steeped in mundane responsibilities that he spent only a few minutes on prayer. Why should that man be dearer to him than a renunciate such as Narada who spent every hour of every day on meditation of the Lord? Lord Vishnu said he would get the answer after he carried a pot of oil on his head all day without spilling a drop. And Narada had been so engrossed in not spilling a drop that he did not think of god even once that day. Jyoti remembered her father's story, but in her drugged state couldn't figure out why it had surfaced. She buried her face in the pillow. Odours of his secretions, her sweat, emanated from her and the pillow.

She had resorted to deceit and had won, just as the other day she had resorted to violence and won.

She remembered the first time she had been in a room of mirrors. It was a travelling fair in Pune, in one of the tents, a cramped little room where they allowed only two persons at a time. She and Jayant paid their money and went in. She had been delighted to see herself in endless succession, pirouetting in her pink organza dress with fine lace at the collar and skirt, dancing in the eternal now.

But here in Winnipeg the glass-walled corridors of time stretched ahead, they were all crowded in the small aisle, the organ peeling forth, the canvas flapping in the wind, tapered candles throwing shadows and reflections in volcanic abandon, she and Pierre and Jayant and Mom and Aunt Vee and that other she refused to recognize.

Had he been there all the time? She could not remember, would not remember. She had cast her die, she had made her bed and would lie in it. *I thought thy bride bed to have decked, sweet maid, and not have strewed thy grave.* That would not ring a bell with Pierre; which was in his favour; she wanted to get away from the stranglehold of her family, with their crosswords and quotations, Shakespeare and Kalidasa, mythologies Greek, Judaeo-Christian and Egyptian, all garbled into an enormous mess that leaked one into the other like the plastic bags of pickles that people smuggled in every time they returned from India. From where had Pierre got the "cauldron sealed four times over?" Surely not on his own.*Playboy* bunny language? What would she know, who was as illiterate about it as he was about crosswords and quotations? And the other, whom she pushed back into the far recesses of her consciousness with his 146 dialects of Hindi in Fiji. Who cared? Get real, get real baby. Get real indeed. If she only knew what "real" meant.

"What a pickle I'm in and my hair stinks," she said aloud to dispel the gloom with the magic broom of banality.

She got out of bed. If she was going to to swap everything to be a ruddy run-of-the-mill housewife with a four-bedroom house and an insatiable husband, she might as well be good at it, and tidy up the house and iron her mother's saris as she had said she would. When all is said and done, a four-bedroom house with a sunken living room and a husband who could deliver the goods anytime of the day or night was not to be sneezed at, no, sir; most women should consider themselves lucky to have one or the other. Rajen would like that turn of phrase.

She went into the shower and sang loudly and long. "Let us sing pray forth we beseech thee o lord, let us pray o lord, let us pray pour forth we beseech thee o lord thy grace into our hearts that we to whom the something of christ thy son was made known by the message of an angel ..." She tried it several times but that was as far she had ever got, even at the Convent of the Sacred Heart, where the nuns made them repeat the angelus every noon hour. Jesus, always with that martyred face, his white robe open to show a red heart with five drops of blood spurting, like Pierre's noodle, which dripped even when it was lax. Was that how it was with everyone? How would she know, as illiterate in everything that counted as...? She couldn't even think of an appropriate simile. Why had she taken an English course? Who cares. "Let us sing."

She continued to sing her way through brunch; the therapy

worked, almost. Napoleon, she'd heard Jayant say, could do five things at the same time, but she was glad she wasn't similarly endowed. When she sang aloud, she couldn't think, and that was wonderful. All those naive people who endlessly chanted the million names of God may or may not reach heaven or salvation in any afterlife, but they sure shut out a great many things. Poor Mrs. Cianflone, whose name had triggered the angelus chant that she had never ever figured out, even though she got the scripture prize the year they left for Canada. How comforting it must be to repeat a thousand Hail Marys on that rosary of hers while all those cancerous cells inside her were nibbling away at all those non-cancerous cells and making them cancerous. So, let us sing.

Jyoti decided to out-housekeep Mrs. Cianflone, god bless her; she would not only iron her mother's silks but wash her mother's nylon and chiffon saris that were neatly stacked in a laundry basket. Let us sing.

She poured pure soap flakes into the washing machine, thinking they really should change to another with a different fragrance so that one didn't have to be reminded of diapers all the time; she waited for the water to start whisking, so the flakes wouldn't clump together, before throwing in the saris. Gentle cycle, cold water. Let us sing.

She was conscious that her odd behaviour echoed the oddness she was feeling, a disoriented empty-headedness that bothered her, but the singing worked, almost, to drive away the bat-like shadows that flitted in the periphery of her mind. She ironed two saris in quick succession. The basement was getting dark already; what a cloudy day! For a few minutes she continued to iron, fancying herself a nightingale that pressed its throat against the thorn so it could pour its melody into the encompassing night. Yea, let us sing. But nightingales didn't have to iron clothes, nor John Keats neither, and she went to the corner to switch on the lights. Newspaper sections lay scattered on the floor. She avoided stepping on any of them;

hearing her great aunt back in their ancestral house chiding, "All printed words are goddess Saraswati's domain. Never step on paper if you want her blessings." She noted that it was last Saturday's paper, just one day's paper. She remembered how that same great aunt would bargain with the vendor to whom she sold old newspapers, who next sold them to grocery stores, who turned the pages into neat cones which they filled with flour or lentils or whatever it was that the buyer wanted. How fast those little boys in the grocery stores were, and how adroitly they clambered over sacks to reach the higher shelves where smaller items, like toothpastes and face creams, were stacked!

While trying to stack the newspaper a little more neatly, she came across a full-page advertisement with plenty of white space and "no small print" as it blared its sales pitch. The white space was doodled over with geometric designs. In the top left quarter of the page, written diagonally across in calligraphic characters was a verse:

> In vain I hoped that at Niri Mund you would
> grace my house as it was never graced before;
> I hoped in vain that at Niri Mund, together
> we'd enjoy our ancient household chores.
> (*A Wreath of Funeral Songs from Tribal India*)

Jyoti's fingers quivered with an urgent need to run her fingertips over the paper from which the words floated out at her, the way a blind man runs his fingers over a face he wants to remember forever. It left her limp, almost moaning aloud with a pain that was not pain. Nay, let us sing.

With missionary zeal she started ironing the saris. Then she decided to sort them into those that needed to be pressed and those that didn't have a pressing need to be pressed (Krish would love that atrocious pun). At the end of it there were still too many that needed ironing. Meanwhile the washing machine called. She walked to the laundry room and took care of the softener liquid before the extra rinse cycle that her mother insisted for her nylon saris, maybe to get rid of the diaper smell of pure soap.

Coming back to the rec room, she took out her mother's wedding sari — the one Savitri had worn at a recent wedding reception — and draped it partly over herself, feeling the rich brocade, the pure gold strands crisscrossing to form a cascade of sheer gold. Would she get to wear this for her wedding? Would she wear a sari at all? How would it look in a church or at St. Vital Park — their two options. Assiniboine Park didn't allow weddings, what a drag. She rubbed her cheek on the silk. This sari would bring her luck, and she'd need as much as she possibly could of that commodity.... She had stopped singing, and that would never do. Come, let us sing.

She switched on the basement radio, an old model that crackled its age. "The walls came tumbling down in Grand Forks," the newscaster said, clearly enjoying the phrase. "The Red had crested well over the predicted 53 feet. Ever since the evacuation sirens had started blaring at 4:19 pm the day before, area after area had fallen. First to go was Lincoln Drive, then the Golf Course, and then the southern part of Grand Forks had got isolated. Grand Forks Mayor, Patricia Owen, had invoked her powers to proclaim compulsory evacuation." Several people who were interviewed described how they had time only to turn off the main electric switch, grab their precious belongings and walk to the shelters. A policeman spoke about a reluctant family they had to force out. Jyoti switched to a Winnipeg station. Everyone was optimistic. "Duff's Ditch would hold. The rural municipality of Ritchot had used 800,000 sandbags. St. Adolphe had just added two feet to its permanent ring dike. City Streets spokesperson McDonald assured callers that they would promptly look into any situation where a property owner thought his property was lower than their immediate neighbours'. Minister Frank Pitura had asked Ottawa to send in more army personnel. One hundred soldiers had been flown in to work in the Richer area." But everything was under control. Duff's Ditch would hold. "Premier Filmon had asked the federal government to pick up the bill, but Lloyd Axworthy would not give him a firm answer. Though no rain is forecast for the next week, the city would take no chances.... It is ten minutes past two, and this is CJOB in Winnipeg."

Just as she finished hanging the washed synthetics on the line, her mother came in. Hearing her on the basement steps, Jyoti switched off the radio and trilled out, "Hello, mama mia. How are you, my darling mama?" As she came into the room, Savitri answered in the same tone, "I'm fine, my loveliest, onliest daughter," but her eyes searched Jyoti's face for the deeper roots of this cheerfulness.

"So, how was the party, Mom?"

Savitri answered at some length, with a great many tidbits to liven up the narrative. The food was excellent as usual and the house was crowded as usual, with at least fifteen couples and a dozen children. She had come away just as they started the movie, a Hindi movie rented from the grocery store. The Khoslas had bought a 48-inch television and a DVD player. All the old movies were being remade into DVD format. She'd loved to have stayed, for it was a beautiful film starring Waheeda Rahman, her favourite, and the title song had been on the top of Binaca Hit Parade for months, as old Mrs. Singh said, in the 1960s. Or was it the 1950s? Mrs. Singh could not remember. As Savitri folded a sari for ironing, she sang it. "*Chaudhvin ka chand ho, ya aftab ho, jo bhi ho tum khuda ki kasam lajawab ho.*" Ah, those Lucknowi lyrics and love songs knew how to exaggerate! Wouldn't Jyoti love for someone to sing her that line. "Whether you are the full moon or the bright sun, whatever you are, by god, you are incomparable!"

Jyoti shrugged. "Mom, you are such a double-dyed romantic. So, why didn't you stay?"

"I don't have the time for all that."

"Mom, you should do what you want to do without always following chore schedules."

Savitri smiled as she answered. It wasn't a chore; she really did want to visit Mrs. Cianflone much more than she wanted to see the movie, and she had dropped in only to see if Jyoti might feel like going with her. Yes, maybe some day they could rent it that movie, even though she had seen it half a dozen times if once ... like *Gone with the Wind* or *The Ten Commandments*, a hit no matter how often it was shown or seen. But today she must visit Mrs. Cianflone.

Video machines are the toys of the future, DVDs are state of the art, status symbol and all that, Pierre had said. Let us sing.

Savitri took the iron from Jyoti, and asked her to pull the sari slowly as she ran the iron over it, so that between them the job would be finished faster. She went on to give news about the people she had met. Farida and her husband were moving to Florida; all the doctors who could do so, were, just as the newspaper had said. Vimal was planning to get her parents over this summer. Suresh and Mary Ann were expecting their second baby in October. Poor Neera had decided to return to India, her husband's affair has been going on for so long everyone had assumed she was going to live with it, and so were surprised.

"But that's crazy," Jyoti remonstrated, "what would she do in India?"

"What is she doing here, after all?"

"She has her job and friends."

"Her family in India are reasonably well-off, and besides, the children are young enough to adjust to relocation."

"So much gossip! Surely they would have said something about Aunt Vee and me too!"

Savitri paused in her ironing. "No, they didn't, but as soon as I left they probably did." She laughed.

"How do you feel about Pierre, Mom?" She asked the question bluntly; there was no other way.

"Your dad is very fond of him."

"I know that," Jyoti said impatiently, "How about you?"

Savitri looked briefly at her daughter. "I think he is a fine young man, Jyoti. He has a lot of energy, enthusiasm, ambition; he is a hard worker, and he loves you."

"But?"

"No buts."

"Oh, there always is, there has to be."

"I have no reservations about him, Jyoti. Why do you?"

Jyoti was taken aback. How could her mother know she had reservations? She reacted typically, by taking the offensive; she said something that she had never consciously considered. "Would it be okay with you if I moved in with him?"

"Is that any different from getting married? When you hold a man in your arms, in love not in lust, you are bound to him whether you are legally married or not."

It was not what Jyoti wanted to hear. There must be some way of shocking her. "There must be an awful lot of bigamists in this world."

"I suppose so, even if you subtracted all those with only lust, I guess there would be quite a few. Only Rama, as far as we know, practised monogamy in spirit and in letter, and even he didn't prescribe it as a general rule. Through his own actions, he told us what was ideal, but he knew we are human."

Jyoti pounced on the chance to twist the argument, "That suits us fine, because we don't think we can be faithful to each other, this lifelong bond till death do us part and all that." Jyoti was pushing her to see how far she could be pushed. Savitri's thoughts went to Pete Kozolski, whose mother seemed to have taken a new boyfriend. She refocused as she pulled the ironed sari off the table and folded it.

"Don't think I haven't recognized your contempt for us who have been faithful all our lives, Jyoti. Your contempt hurts, even though I know it comes from some form of idealism — that love is free, not to be bound — I, too, believe it, that love is free, not to be bound." She took the next sari to the table and spoke slowly, "Love, the state of being in love, especially the first time ever, makes one beautiful, so breathtakingly beautiful. My cousin, Kanta, she was staying with us, going to college ... that was my first experience of what being in love can do. It was second-hand as first experiences often are ... it was one of my best teen years, because when someone is in love, she can give and receive affection so purely, so spontaneously, that the happiness keeps spreading in concentric circles drawing more and more people into itself ... oh, she was beautiful."

"Aunt Kanta beautiful?"

"She was, that year she was exquisitely beautiful."

"What happened then?

"What happens to so many girls. There was a big hullaballoo, and she was married off to a rich widower with several children who lived so far away his family couldn't have heard any of gossip. Kanta has been spending her life milking cows and supervising the measuring of the harvest. But ..." Savitri's eyes shone with remembrance, "she had it, Jyoti, even if only for a few months, she had the real thing. That is why I feel so much for you, your sadness."

Again, Jyoti felt caught off guard. The fight had suddenly gone out of her; she was tired, too tired to swallow the tears that came. Softly she said, "It's not the real thing, is that what it means?"

Savitri answered after a pause, "If I were sure of that, I would tell you so. I would have told you so already, if I were sure it wasn't the real thing."

"I have to believe it is, Mom. This is my first love," her voice broke, but she could not bear the pity in her mother's eyes. She stopped until she took control of herself. She pointed to a crease in the sari and said in a normal voice, "I think you missed this part. It needs to be redone."

Savitri took the cue. Half-jokingly she said, "Never consummate your first love and you'll have it all your life. Mother Mary Zacharias used to tell us that at the end-of-the-year counselling sessions, as she called them. Her motives were different, but the dictum is a rather nice one, don't you think? Never consummate your first love."

Jyoti asked with studied casualness, "Did you have one, Mom?"

Savitri laughed. "Now, now, my loveliest onliest daughter, how am I supposed to answer that? If I say I didn't, I'd plummet down in your esteem," she pointed her thumb downward.

"And if you say you did?"

"I'd plummet down sometime later, and some shrink somewhere would blame me for all your problems."

Jyoti did not want to laugh it off. With sudden intensity, she said, "We need to know, Mom, we've got to know more about our parents. We never do. I've sometimes wondered, in what senseless moment of upward kicking of legs and flailing arms I was conceived."

In a voice kept matter-of-fact with effort, Savitri said, "Would it help if I said you were conceived in the springtime of my love, in a floodtide of desire? It is true, but how does it help? As for knowing about one's parents, we don't reach out with facts but with feelings. My grandparents, who brought me up, I can now see were so different from each other. But when I was a child, a girl, even a young woman, I naturally and blindly believed they were an open book to one another, that they kept no secrets anywhere between them..."

Jyoti had knelt to release the sari length from under the ironing table where it had accidentally got caught. She looked up and said, "But that's how I see you and Dad!"

Savitri laid the iron on its rest and placed both her hands

on her daughter's head; then, holding the girl's face between her hands bent down to kiss her on the forehead, combining the ancient rite of blessing with the universal gesture of love.

"All is not lost, my munchkin. May you be as happy as I have been."

Chapter 13

Jayant came home just as Jyoti and Savitri were about to leave for the hospital. His pants were soaking wet to the knees and his shirt wet at the waist, his galoshes and parka having been made useless by carelessness and rain. He was tired and looked it. Savitri fussed over him, insisting that he change into dry clothes right away. But he sat at the dining table, grumbling at the inefficiency of people. They had run out of sandbags. "Jeesus, you'd have thought someone would coordinate volunteers so the sandbags were filled faster than they were used. And you wouldn't believe the number of sightseers gawking at the workers and at the floodway, in the way of the trucks."

Savitri brought him a change of clothes and dried his hair with one of the thin towels from India that she used for herself. She made him a hot cup of soup and saw to it that he finished it. The wet clothes slopped in a corner of the kitchen and as she was about to pick them up, he stopped her. "Mom, I have to go down anyway, you forgot to get me a pair of briefs, and I've still got them on under these, which by the way are my dress jeans, if you don't mind." Knowing she'd hover over him till he did, he went down and changed.

Savitri told him where they were going. Dad and Krishna would probably stay on at the Khoslas for dinner — they always did that, what with all the food and company. She and Jyoti would be back by dinnertime, maybe. Jayant said he would be gone by seven o'clock, which was when they hoped to get fresh truckloads of sandbags.

As Savitri drove along Pembina Highway, Jyoti played with the car radio. "I'm trying to get some station that has music instead of news. Flood flood flood, there's got to be something else happening somewhere."

"How can you get tired of the flood coverage, Jyoti?" Savitri said, "There's so much happening, so many human interest stories."

"Remember one of the early stories of yours, Ma? About the first blizzard you ever saw, and how your new friend, Tom, was trudging through the snowstorm and the police cruiser picked him up thinking he was stranded, and he directed them to the Liquor Commission, which is where he was headed so he'd have enough booze in case they were snowed in? I can imagine the look on the cops' faces."

"Well, that too, but I was thinking of stories of courage and sacrifice, like that woman last night near Fargo."

"What did she do?"

"Three months pregnant, she was driving home last night with her three-year-old daughter when she ran into a flood of water across the road where a creek had overrun. This morning they found the car, which had been washed away, but she must have got out of the window, dragged the child out, and headed towards a farmhouse."

"Really? Gosh, I'm glad it ended all right."

"No, it didn't. Soaked to the skin, she must have carried her child for a whole mile in sub-zero temperature. Two hundred yards from the farmhouse light, she probably ran into another rush of water and stepped back. She must have fallen or lain down to rest for a minute, and never got up again. A helicopter found her and her little one just a while ago."

Jyoti turned off the radio and sat still.

Savitri said, "Walking a mile with little one in her arms, and then dying two-hundred yards from safety. So heart wrenching, but you know, if it weren't for the child, she would have given up much earlier. One might say she merely prolonged the agony, but to me there is something inspiring, something that reassures us about the strength of love. She was a petite woman, they say, but she got strength from somewhere, to walk with the wind whipping over her, holding her little girl to her heart to give her her own warmth and give her, too, a sense of security ..."

Savitri stopped, then continued, "I remember a poem by Kamala Das, who used to be one of my favourites. It is half hysterical, as many of her poems are, but so powerful:

> when i was ill, my three year old son was brought to me amma he said leave this hospital come home with me even if i had died that week i would have walked as a ghost to my home and him.

Jayant was stretched on the living room sofa when the phone rang. Priti's voice came shrilly over the wire. "Jai? Oh Jai, thank God you're home." Panic and relief came through clearly in her voice. Jayant's expression instantly grew soft with concern and tenderness, but he kept his voice self-consciously normal, "Hi, Pixie Trix, whassa mattah ? Are you being chased by the big bad wolf? Need big Brave Jai to rescue you?"

"Oh, Jai, can you pick us up? We're stranded."

Jeesus, that Aunt Vee had left Priti at some friends' house as usual, he supposed. "Sure, where are you?"

"At Polo Park."

He almost jumped, "At Polo Park? What do you mean 'we'? Who's with you?"

"Laura. Laura and me. Mommy was supposed to pick us up, but she hasn't come."

Under his breath, Jayant said, "Jeesus, it's past six."

“It’s 6:15 and she hasn’t come yet. Most of the stores are closed and the people are leaving.”

Jayant angrily thought, *How irresponsible can one get. She doesn’t deserve to have kids*. He said soothingly, “Chin up Trixie, just where are you, near Sears or Eaton’s?”

“Near Sears, Mom told us to be near the Locks and Keys booth. Why hasn’t she come?” She was sniffling. “There’s nobody here except an old man who asked us for coffee money.”

Jayant swore under his breath. “Listen carefully. Stand by the door close to the cinema. There will be people coming for the movie soon, so don’t worry about being alone. I’ll be there in twenty minutes, but first tell me, has Laura phoned home?”

“No, should she? We’re supposed to be doing our project at home, and her dad will pick her up at seven.”

“Good, she doesn’t need to phone. I will.”

“But Mommy ...”

Jayant spoke soothingly, “Come come, Pixie, maybe she’s had a flat tire or something. Don’t worry. I’ll be there in twenty minutes. Stay between the double doors, not inside the mall, not outside, but between the double doors, and wait. What is the time on your watch?”

“Laura has one.”

“Take a good look at the time now, else you’ll think after five minutes that you’ve already been waiting an hour. So, remember, I can’t reach there before 6:40. And another thing, even if your Mom turns up before I come, get her to wait for me, and don’t take a ride with anyone even if you know them, because I can’t be chasing you all over town. Ready or not, here I come.”

“Should I hang up now?’

“KO, Pixie Trix, see you in twenty minutes.”

He banged down the receiver, checked that he had his car keys and rushed out without a coat. He came back a minute later, dialled Laura's parents, and said the girls were running a little late and he would drop her off a little after seven.

An hour later, as they neared home, he said, "How about a hot cup of chocolate before you go," but Laura declined, saying her mother wouldn't like her drinking anything just before dinner. So they decided to drop her off first.

Priti and Laura, whose chattering voices had not ceased from the moment they got into the car, now spent a few minutes discussing the project they were supposed to have worked on.

Back home, Priti burst out crying. The hot chocolate Jayant had whipped up spilled as she rocked the table with her sobs. "What am I going to do? What can I do?"

"What's eating my petite princess?"

"Three times this week I was late for school. And today she forgot altogether."

"Just a rough patch, Trix. Your mother has a lot of things on her mind right now. Take it easy."

"Three days! You don't know Miss Grindlay. Takes a ratch even for no reason. And if there is a reason," she sobbed, "you know the school rules, we just have to be there on time or else."

"I thought you liked this school. Your mom was praising it so much. She said you loved it."

"Now I know why she put me there. It has a residence. That's why. So she can dump me there and not worry when there's no home left."

Angrily Jayant started to say, "Bull" but, controlling himself, ended, "y for you. You silly goose, you have two very good homes, and next year while your mom is away, you'll stay here, naturally. And I'll drive you to school every day from now to the end of term. Howzzat?"

Priti took it up as a game. "Promise by the hair on your chinny chin chin?"

"Promise."

"Cross your heart and hope to die?"

"Cross my heart and hope to die. Absolutely."

Priti sipped at the chocolate, back to her normal cheerful self. "Just a teensy-weensy problem, Jai. You are leaving next week."

"Can't. Have to cancel all plans. I've promised by the hair on my chinny chin, etc., etc." He pulled at his chin.

"That's very nice of you," Priti said in an adult way. "But you have places to go, fortunes to make." Just a little whinily, she added, "I'll take the bus. It's a drag. I have to get up much earlier because the connecting bus always takes a long time, and there's no shelter. And Mommy doesn't like me to stand in the wind so she says she'd take me," she got more and more plaintive as she spoke, "so I get up late and she gets up late and she thinks we have to be there by nine but it isn't because we have to be there at 8:45. We just have to."

Jayant patted her shoulder. "Eight o'clock every morning from Monday to the end of June, or is it middle of June? Whatever. And if you aren't ready, oh boy! You'll get it from me, never mind Miss Grindlay."

"Grouchley," Priti whispered.

"No, not even when whispering. Miss Grindlay is her name and I'll make you write it a hundred times if you say anything else."

"But you're all set to go on your trip."

"I am not. But let's keep this a secret for now, okay?"

He ran his fingers through his hair, and turned his back to her as he needlessly opened the faucet. He thought, *I'll stay. If there's a christly chance for me to do something for someone, I'd gladly stay here to the end of time. Jeesus, how dispensable we are. I'd stay put even if that stupid parakeet of yours needed me to clean its cage every day. How much more readily would I stay for you.*

He turned to her, "What a glutton you are! Didn't leave

even a drop for me," he turned the saucepan upside down and took it to the sink.

Chapter 14

The phone was ringing when Jyoti entered the house.

"Hello."

"Hullo, Jyoti, how was the exam?"

"Hi Shri!" Jyoti was happily surprised. "Who cares how it was? It's over, the last exam, the last spike, over, yippee. I'd have danced all the way back if the sidewalks weren't so sloshy; what awful weather."

"I've seen worse."

"What do you care? You run about in your Biscayne. Wait a sec while I take off my coat. I've just come in."

"I know. I saw you."

"Saw me? Where?"

"As you turned off University Crescent."

"And you didn't think of giving me a ride? Boy, some folks can be mean."

"Would you have accepted?" To cover his hesitancy, he added, "To some folks used to driving a Lincoln Continental, a '76 Biscayne might be too infra-dig."

Jyoti, who had not missed the question behind the question, said, "What were you doing around here this time of day?"

"Following you, what else would I be doing?"

Jyoti's colour rose even though his tone had been bantering as usual. She wanted to give a suitable repartee, but her lips trembled, and she said nothing.

"You didn't think all those chance encounters over the last

year were accidental, did you? You didn't think I lived in the anthro section of the library for love of anthropology, did you?"

She got back to form. "Hey, that's called stalking; we have laws against that, you know."

"Whew, I'd have quite a stockpile of black marks by now, and I can't afford that, what with the way my stocks went crashing down the other day."

She didn't reply.

More hesitantly, he said, "I made an ass of myself ... just some suicidal streak in me ... I suppose that's the end? I've got to get it from the horse's mouth, what? From Arab steed to dhobi's ass ..."

"Speak Canadian, like, Lincoln Continental to '76 Biscayne."

"Golden Boy to Newt-on Red."

"Kiss to Drainer Cent."

"Give up, that's too Canajian, eh, for me."

"Don't give up, it ain't too hard to go from eh to zed to zee."

"Oh, you dirty Yank. Zee indeed."

"Touché, you caught me on the wrong foot."

"Finger in the pie."

"Head over heels. Thorn in my side."

"Ha ha ha," she sniffed, "your wit is so sidesplitting."

There was a long pause, and Jyoti was afraid he would hang up. She could see him gripping the receiver, his right hand doodling geometric designs, *In vain I hoped that at Niri Mund you would grace my house as it was never graced before,* the words had such a sad lilt she tore herself away from them to say something, anything. What if he just hung up? She said, "What's up, I can't believe you've run out of quips."

"No, no, I was just checking if I had my first aid kit for sewing split sides."

Another pause. She had to think of something, anything so

he wouldn't hang up. But the haunting lilt was making her cry. *I hoped in vain that at Niri Mund together we'd enjoy ancient household chores.*

"Listen, Jyoti, I've got to say this and have done with it." The echoes were deafening, no no,*I wish I could hate you and have done with you*. But it was just his manner of speaking. "Listen, the other day when I started spouting my great declamation, there was a moment when I could have stopped myself ... but I went on, thinking it would do me good to get it out of my system ... what an ass I was ... you didn't look at me once all that afternoon ... and I've got the message, but I want to say I am sorry, that's all I want to say and I know we can't meet on the same footing anymore ... can we?" She could hardly hear the last few words because of the lilt in her ears, *I hoped in vain that at Niri Mund....*

"No," she said, softly. *That you would grace my house as it never was graced before, I hoped in vain that in Niri Mund together we'd enjoy ancient household chores*. Tears flowed down her cheeks.

He sighed, and then tried to be flippant. "Quoth the raven, 'Nevermore'. Well that's that."

"I ... you ... I think," she stuttered, hoping he could hear; what if no sound was coming from her throat, what if he were to hang up thinking that was the end! Please don't, please make him not hang up, please. "Not on that footing but maybe, maybe," she'd got it, "seeing as you are so simian in your wordobatics, you could get a good hand grip on ... help me out, Thesaurus."

"Jyoti!" he was incredulous, overjoyed. "Oh, Jyoti! You mean we might with a bit of coordinated amnesia talk again, meet again?"

"Maybe ... I ... I hope so."

"May I come over now?"

"Hey, hey," she said, her eyes clear by now, "not so fast. I just want to unjam the keys, that's all. I'm not typing out messages or receiving any, okay? Just putting on a new cartridge, wiping the mouse so it moves instead of jamming, just opening some clogged lines of communication, is all."

"I'll fix it, Jyoti. You know I'm a real good handyman with all makes of mechanical equipment; your computer is in good hands, or your telephone or drain, whatever your mixed metaphor fresh from your English exam. I can fix it. Just don't hang up yet."

Jyoti laughed into the phone. With her free hand she disconnected the line but stood cradling the receiver, running her fingers over the mouthpiece, playing on the touch-tone keys a song of the sky.

Jyoti lay on the living room sofa. Thoughts crowded in again, pushing out the free fall feeling. Tic tac toe, round I go, if I miss I take this. "I have no reservations at all about Pierre. Why do you?" her mother had said. Because she felt bound hand and foot. Her mother was right; Jyoti felt irrevocably bound to Pierre. She didn't want to be, bound yes, irrevocably no, she was not ready for the finality of it. In love, not in lust, her mother had said. The line was thin, very thin between the two, the cry of fulfilment was an animal cry of relief; she could not believe it came from them, that the unreal disembodied voice that sometimes filled the bed, the room, was hers, was his.

I have no reservation. Why do you? On the other hand, was her mother sincere when she said that? Perhaps she had said it to push Jyoti towards Pierre, knowing how far they had gone. In every Hindi movie where a woman was raped or had a lover, she never got to marry and live happily ever after; she was either killed off, or the rapist married her and beat her up again and again, or if the film was avant-garde, she disappeared and surfaced at another place, as a prostitute or a kept woman. No unwed woman who had ever slept voluntarily or by force with a man ever got to sleep with any other lover, period. That was the norm. She was being unfair. Any mother would want her daughter to marry the man with whom she was having an affair, she thought. But Savitri wasn't any mother. Her ideas were way different from everyone else's mother. Did she really mean that monogamy was only a social practicality, not natural or necessarily an absolute? It didn't make any sense, saying that in one breath and in the next upholding fidelity. Her mother spoke above her head. She couldn't be bothered with trying to decode. But what she had said about Aunt Kanta was something else. Button-nosed, button-mouthed, pudgy little Aunt Kanta, whom she had seen at family weddings trailing her half-dozen country-clad kids, certainly didn't look that type. And in the 1960s too! When everyone was so old-fashioned and straight-laced.

Her own children would probably say that of her and the 1990s.

Her children, what children?

I hoped in vain that at Niri Mund we'd together enjoy ancient household chores. It was the "ancient" that pulled her, that feeling of being connected to a past, but it was a chimera; her household was here, in Canada, not among people and places she did not know, had left behind. From *A Wreath of Tribal Funeral Songs.* Jyoti shivered. Someone was walking over her grave. *I thought thy bride bed to have decked, sweet maid, and not have strewed thy grave.* She shivered again. Say three Hail Marys, was the standard prescription she'd been given by the pious nuns. Why did some of these adjectives go with some of these nouns? *Pious* nuns, *sacred* heart, an open red apple under the white gown, spurting five drops of blood, at the head of every classroom and corridor. Were the nuns at peace, walking up and down the length of the red-clay quadrangle behind the slate-gray buildings of the nunnery, secretly rolling the beads of their rosaries, as though titillated at the touch?

Rosaries. Mrs. Cianflone. On the wall above the foot of

each bed at the hospital was a crucifix, discreetly placed there by the Gray Nuns who once ran the place, and who were probably all dead. Who would ever want to be a nun in Canada? Mother Teresa knew where the pickings were good and that is why she went to India and not here. What pluck they must have had, braving wind and sea to come to this prairie to tend to pregnant pioneer women trundling along in covered wagons under these endless skies; and those pregnant women, god, what ever sustained them? The nuns at least had their martyred Jesus with his open heart spurting five drops of blood, but these women had only their all too human men carousing and working themselves and their wives to death. She had read about the journals written by pioneer women; for lack of paper, they wrote along the margins and then literally between the lines of old account books, and figuratively too for us to decode, mentioning somewhere they had morning sickness, and then five months later, buried in the daily accounts of flour bought and skins traded, mention of a small sum for a tiny coffin. What pluck, what suffering. Jyoti could not forget the sight of Mrs. Cianflone on the hospital bed, unseeingly watching the rented portable television that obscured the crucifix on the wall at the foot of the hospital bed. What was the symbolism there? Who cares? She was through with her English exam, with all her exams. Ophelia could float forever downstream and Lear could rave in the wind; she would ignore them. *I thought thy bride-bed to have deck'd, sweet maid*; she would ignore them, if she could.

She was free as a bird. Positive reinforcement, all she needed was a mantra. And it couldn't be a name.

A bird with twin weights suspended from its wings, Jyoti brooded. The simplest solution was to cut off those dead weights, both of them.

Mrs. Cianflone had.

Jyoti shuddered, a primeval shudder, to counter which she joked about it. You're in good company, Mrs. C. along with first ladies and all. It's quite the vogue, Mrs. C., like tuberculosis in the nineteenth century. People are writing books about it from every possible angle as a sure scoop. Keep your chin up, Mrs. C. even if you can't keep your boobs up. The great cancer fear is preempting even the great castration-fear syndrome.

Jyoti felt nauseated with her own sick humour. Poor Mrs. Cianflone, who had been their housekeeper for the first five years until they could do without one; who had been so patient, so conscientious she would flop through snowfalls and rainstorms in her loose camel-hair coat, a hand-me-down from some rich former employer twice her height; who had not learned to speak English fluently despite her twelve years in this country. Poor good woman, dying alone in a hospital bed with a crucifix hidden behind a portable television. "You been my family, Sabeeti," she had said. "God bless." She was forever thanking them — for giving her a chance to serve them? For giving her a chance to bring them cheap little trinkets for Christmas and their birthdays? Every few months, ever since Mrs. C. left their employment, Savitri had heaped food and sweaters and money on her for her nephews and nieces who lived in various places. Did they ever visit her? Probably not as often as Savitri did. Mom, god bless, for sure. *May you be as happy as I have been*, Mom had blessed her, but she didn't deserve to be happy; she was a callow creature who had two lovers and didn't want to give up either. *Count your blessings*, was one of Mrs. C.'s favourite phrases. God bless. She would visit Mrs. C. twice a week as long as she was at the hospital.

The doorbell rang. It was Donna.

"What a pleasant surprise! Come in Donna, it is ages, god, really, it is good to see you."

Donna came in with a large paper bag in hand. She slipped out of her shoes and walked to the kitchen. Placing the bag on the floor, she took off her coat and fluffed out her blond shoulder-length hair. She was a slim woman of twenty-three, just an inch taller than Jyoti. She was wearing clothes characteristic of her, a tailored skirt and blouse that gave her an efficient yet extremely attractive personality.

"How are you, Jyoti?" Donna was one of the few non-Indians who pronounced the soft "t" in Jyoti and Priti the way it should be without mangling the names to Joti and Pretty.

"I've just finished my last exam."

They talked about the drag of exams; at medical school one never got finished with exams. Donna told her about her current schedule. Jyoti wondered at Donna's sudden appearance. "That's all over long ago," Vithal had said a week ago.

They discussed the flood. Jyoti told Donna about Jayant's sandbagging and volunteering all week. Donna said she knew about it, that Jayant and she had always been in touch. He had been at her place yesterday.

"We had a long chat last night, and we decided to have a family celebration today. Oh, that reminds me, let me put this in place before it melts." She took out a pail of Dutch Maid ice cream from the paper bag and opened the freezer door on the refrigerator. "Almond mocha, my favourite flavour," she said. She crumpled and threw the white and purple bag in the garbage bin under the sink.

"We used to get some fantastic almond ice cream at the University Food Science place. It is a pity that closed down."

"Sure is, and they used to have a lot of almonds, too, mmm."

Jyoti wondered why they were making such inane conversation instead of talking about this family celebration. What did Jayant have to do with Donna? Strange thoughts went through her head.

"I was glad to hear that Jayant was going on this adventure-binge, and now I'm even gladder that he isn't."

He wasn't? Jyoti felt terribly alone and left out that he

should have told Donna before telling any of them, or had he told Dad and Mom and left out only her? She had thought they had cleared the clogged lines of communication between them, but maybe not.

"He was so cheerful yesterday," Donna went on in her quiet, serious voice, "as though he had at last found himself, you know ... a ... vocation? As though he now knew what he wanted, what he had to do. That's such a wonderful feeling... rushing along without a sense of direction and then, suddenly, to see a roadsign ... clear and luminescent on the green board ... *Jayant's Haven, Exit 2 km*, and you're home free."

What was she talking about? How could she know anything about Jayant? What was Jayant up to? He couldn't do this to Vithal.

Donna turned for the door. "I have to bring in a few more things," and away she went to her lemon-green Rabbit, returning with a cardboard carton. Out of it she took a big, covered casserole dish. "It would work out just right to start the oven soon after four o'clock. Jayant said we should have an early dinner. That would be 5:30, I assume." She was behaving as though she was in her own house, opening the refrigerator and cupboards, cleaning the counter so she could place there what she had brought.

It was at least three months since they had last met, and at least six months since Donna had visited their home. Jyoti became conscious of her resentment and tried to be rational. Four years ago, when Vithal first started seeing her, Donna was on the main campus, and had been a frequent visitor. Moreover, every summer, when the family had gone on their annual three-week vacation, another of Sharad's decrees about family bonding, Vithal had taken care of the house, and Donna's imprint was visible when they returned, kitchen cupboards and tables polished with lemon oil, months of newspapers taken away to for recycling.... Even so, Jyoti was uncomfortable with Donna's easy informality, as though she lived here.

"I've put in several kinds of cheese. I do hope it turns out well." Donna moved the casserole from the table to the counter, and took a salad bowl from its place in the cupboard above the sink. She chatted about how the oven in her new apartment had a mind of its own, like Jayant and Vithal. It was most unpredictable. She really should take time out to buy an oven thermometer.

Jayant and Vithal, the names tripped off her tongue as though she owned them. Even through her increasing resentment, Jyoti became aware of the irony; if she, Jyoti, wanted to play around with two men and not let go of either, why shouldn't Donna?

Hadn't there been some talk of Donna moving from her Langside apartment? Jyoti asked in a polite voice, to conceal her unease.

Yes, she had, end of November; now she was a little closer to the Health Sciences Centre, on the other side of Notre Dame; the place was comfy, though old; they liked it because it was roomier and bigger; now they could live without getting into each other's hair because they had taken one of the two rooms in the attic as well.

She used the plural in a most matter-of-fact way.

"Vithal?" Jyoti asked.

Donna blushed. "I'm sorry, I thought ... I mean ... well, you do know about us, don't you?" Then added, "We don't want to hide it or anything, but I mean ... well you know how inhibited Vithal is, and we don't want to hurt others' sensibilities, his parents, your parents ..."

Jyoti was embarrassed too. Of course, everyone in the family, the adults, had guessed but no one had ever referred directly to it. Now that Donna had, she could be at ease with her. Jyoti was also relieved to hear it was Vithal and not Jayant. How could she have ever thought it was?

With great sincerity, Jyoti said, "I'm glad to hear that, because ..." she hesitated, "Vithal was depressed, I mean, he looked like he was depressed, last Saturday, and I thought you had split."

Donna looked out the window. She gestured with her hands, "We get together and then move apart. It's one of those things. I don't know how to get our relationship off the seesaw. That's why I am so glad for Jayant. He knows what he wants to do. I keep hoping Vithal will reach that point."

She turned from the window and looked at Jyoti, and in her soft serious voice said, "Comes a time when you have to make a commitment to yourself and stick to it. I made mine two years ago when I started med school, set up on my own, and pledged myself to Vithal. The first two are working out well enough, and I am sure the third will too. But sometimes it seems ..." She stopped. "I just hope it won't be a long wait.

They were silent for a while. Donna kept looking out the window; Jyoti looked at her, wondering at the complexity of relationships and at Donna's uncomplicated approach. Make a commitment and stick to it. Exactly what her mother had said, but her mother was of another generation. Now she was back to her problem. Commit to whom? It was so even, she might just as well toss a coin. But Donna had said the commitment was to oneself, what did that mean?

Donna had a chiselled kind of beauty, a fineness of features, clear line of forehead, nose, lips and chin, that together in profile with a clear thin skin gave her a classiness one did not often see in students. Everything she said and did had a stamp of sincerity. Vithal was one lucky guy and he'd better realize it.

"Do you never get frustrated or angry, Donna?"

Donna, still looking out expectantly, smiled. Even her smile was chiselled, serious. "I'm afraid I don't have the time to get worked up. It takes me a long time to cool off so I can't really afford to get hot, and I don't. My studies take a lot out of me, I am not brilliant, like Vithal, who needs to read something once to have a photographic imprint of it into his brain. Yes, I do get rather frustrated, but one learns to get patient with so many patients around." She too had become infected with the family weakness for puns. "When the work piles up or I get to the end of my rope, I call up Jayant and we go cross-country skiing or sloshing through the trails. "

"Jayant?" Surely she meant Vithal.

"Vithal hates our great winter outdoors though he loves summers," Donna continued, "And Jayant ... I assume he enjoys it, I've never asked. He is so easy-going, so compliant, I guess I am simply exploiting his love for Vithal when I ask him to do all kinds of things big and small for me."

She was still at the window.

"Are you expecting someone, Donna?"

"Yes, Jayant certainly ... and Vithal I hope."

"Does Vith know you're here?"

"I ... I haven't seen him for three, almost four weeks, but I hope, I'm sure Jayant would have ... well."

"But why didn't you phone him? He was so terribly depressed."

It pained Donna, Jyoti could see that. Her usually sea-green eyes, made brilliant by her contact lenses, now became hooded. Jyoti realized she had overstepped her bounds. Donna had not asked about Pierre; she was not one of those who asked but waited for the other to open up. She had opened up to Jyoti, and Jyoti felt she had let her down even by that well-intentioned question. The gossamer threads of communications, one lapse and poof, it was gone. But Jyoti knew better than to make it worse with an apology.

"We have cucumbers in the fridge. Do you think we could add some to the salad? I see you've already prepared the lettuce and tomatoes." Jyoti took the plastic bags of lettuce and tomatoes from Donna's carton. Opening the oven to check that it was empty, Donna took out a skillet that was in it and put it in a cupboard.

"That would help. I forgot to pick up a cucumber. I don't know what else I forgot. Let's get to work. I've put the timer on to tell us when to switch on the oven."

"That was nice of you to come all the way to the airport," Anant said, as Veejala and he came down the escalator after seeing off his American colleague.

"I just got the impression at lunch that you didn't have much to say to him, so I came along to make small talk."

"Thanks for helping out. Len was a bit put out, naturally. I told him two weeks ago that my mind was made up, but he came anyway, thinking he could make me change my mind after I'd seen the details. Len is thorough, very thorough, a pleasure to work with."

Veejala noticed the genuine admiration in his voice. *So, it had not been easy*, she thought.

"But I like to have a lead time of twelve months, to plan and set up; things don't work out otherwise."

"Winter would be rather ideal, wouldn't it, considering he's already done the planning and I wouldn't be around to be treading on your toes." She was tactfully probing to find out if his reasons for declining were professional or personal.

They had come to the car. Anant unlocked Veejala's side of the car, opened the door for her, helped her with her seat belt, closed the door and went to his side of the car. Anant had a courtly way of attending to these little details of etiquette. The three years he had spent at Khadakvasla Military Academy before quitting in favour of university had left their mark on him. There was a correctness about his clothes, walk, talk, and logic. He belted himself and started the car. Veejala wished he had started the conversation after they were on the road so the tenor had not got lost in interruptions.

Anant patted her on her knee. He seldom looked at the

person he was speaking to; preoccupied with his own studied manner of expressing himself, he tended to concentrate on the horizon. But now he looked at Veejala, his brown-grey eyes smiling at her. He had that light complexion and grey eyes that made people here mistake him for a Caucasian though he was not atypical in appearance in Pune.

Anant, patient and correct always, waited for the engine to warm up.

"Len is impatient once he seizes upon an idea, and there are enough people who would jump at a chance to collaborate with him. I have my plate full."

"Keeping house?"

"You shouldn't worry about the house," he said, smoothly deflecting it from himself. "You should go ahead with your plans, get away from housework and, for heaven's sake, away from guilt feelings."

It was the first time he had directly talked about the personal aspects of her decision. They had discussed the professional aspects just before and soon after her resignation. He had urged her to continue at Pasadena rather than go to India; there were other places she could go to — Kitt Peak, U of Arizona, Mauna Kea, Whipple — where her work would fit in better. He had not been too happy about her decision to resign, but he was not worried about it the way Sharad was. There would be some delay if they wished to relocate, to find a place that could accommodate both of them, but it certainly was time to move on from here, so she shouldn't worry. Put first things first. Go to India if she felt she had to, with no burdens or baggage. Between him and Savitri, Priti would be well looked after.

"So, you are staying for personal reasons," she said.

"Get rid of your guilt feelings," he said.

"Few seem to think I have any," she tried to laugh it away.

Anant pulled the car out of the parking space and drove out of the parking lot.

In another hundred years, maybc, he said, women would get out of the bind, but now to be born a woman was to be born with all kinds of guilt complexes. The two of them had an even tougher time because of their hopping between cultures. Didn't she remember what she'd had to put up with in North Carolina when he was away in Europe for two years? Leaving her with a job, a house, a child, while their white colleagues and neighbours, well-intentioned to be sure, had assumed he had abandoned her? What a hilarious idea, she as an abandoned woman. She could expect another version of the same attitude if she went to Ahmedabad as she insisted on going; eyebrows would duly be raised that she had abandoned her family responsibilities. In India, it was perfectly acceptable for a man to leave his wife and children for years on end in pursuit of his job. His own father, in the Railways, had spent years at railway outposts while his family — he had fathered seven children in those twelve years of nomadic assignments — grew up in the city.

Veejala interrupted to say that conditions had changed in India. The women's workforce had grown prodigiously, and the sheer momentum of economics had changed many middle-class homes.

She realized that they were veering away from the personal to an academic discussion. It always happened that way. The security of the impersonal.

"Social norms exert a tremendous lot of pressure on one's psyche," he was saying.

"Yes," she said impatiently, "but when have we ever cared for society's norms?"

"We haven't," he replied patiently, "but these norms, these expectations, preconceptions and misconceptions though they were, had a way of exerting pressure, forming a malignant tumour that grew unfelt and burst unawares to poisoned the whole system, oozed toxins into the system, sapping it of vitality. The only way to counter is to be conscious of it and to consciously fight it. Which is why," he said, his hand once again on her knee, "I am warning you to consciously withstand guilt feelings."

Veejala looked at his hand on her knee. Did he know that it was his characteristic way of reaching out to help or for help, that he placed it there when something was worrying him or he thought was worrying her? Did he know that? And if he did, did he know that she knew? So delicate and deep it was, this manifestation of the link between them, that she had been careful never to bring it to the surface level by placing her hand on his.

"But you too, Anant, have to fight it, don't you? Refuse to feel guilty."

"I try to, yes, I try to."

"Then why stay in Winnipeg instead of taking up Len's offer?"

"It so happens," Anant replied, "that I love to stay home, want to be close to my children, even if they don't live with me."

"But ..."

"Okay," not wanting to sound a martyr because he didn't feel one. "Yes, I decided to stay because you decided to go away."

"Guilt feelings?"

"No, I don't think so," he said though he wouldn't swear to it; it was because reason demanded that Priti should have one of her parents nearby and reason also dictated that Veejala's needs deserved a higher priority than Len's; it was all as simple as that; and then, yes, he'd admit that hope had a part in the issue; he hoped that he might get to stay with his children, that Vithal might, just might become a little more responsible and ... he stopped ... it was better that they didn't get into that again.

Veejala knew what "that" meant. They'd had that argument countless times. Anant was too imbedded in his ideas about the indispensability and superiority of education ever to accept that a young man, especially his son, should be a dropout. His son — that's what rankled most, that a son of his should be so grossly insensitive to the values of education.

Anant always became irritated with Vithal, even with any reference to him. It was no use anyone talking of Vithal's strengths, his super-intelligence, his wide knowledge of music, of current events, of mechanical skills, his loyalty and affectionate nature. Everything, especially references to Vithal's talents, added to Anant's frustrations at the immense wastefulness. What good was anything if one failed to use it, and how could anyone use anything without the foundations of university education? If he were handicapped in some way, Anant would have no hesitation in accepting him for what he was. But the wastefulness, the utter wastefulness.

They had gone through this many times, and so Veejala let it run its course. Anant's hand was no longer on her knee.

Anant changed the subject. "Why did he want your car?" Veejala had taken a cab to meet them at the restaurant at lunch time because, she said, Vithal had asked her for the car that morning. She now replied that she wasn't sure, he had said something about pulling a trailer or something.

"A trailer? Is Donna moving again?" Anant liked Donna, for obvious reasons. She was conscientious about education. "She is too good for him," he said brusquely.

"No woman is too good for our son," she said lightly. But her mind was going over another line of thought that was as familiar and agonizing as their arguments over Vithal. If Vithal had moved away from home at the age of eighteen as so many youngsters did, would their life have been different?

Would it have been different for him, for them? At twenty-three, he was still living at home for practical purposes, probably living in two places without living in either. Maybe father and son would have been closer; maybe she and Anant would have been closer; the sound of the back door opening after they were in bed put him off lovemaking; more, even the subconscious waiting for the sound of the door to open bothered him; poor Anant, too indoctrinated to curfews and lights out and the *reveille* at Khadakvasla Military Academy, he couldn't function unless everything was in its place. On the other hand, maybe Vithal's waywardness had helped keep them together; maybe Anant's irritation with Vithal had taken the edge off his irritation with her at her way of life.

"Where do you want to go now?" he asked. "Home or office?" He slowed down, but the light was green at Grant so he went through the intersection.

"We could go home, if you are through with your work for today."

"It is past three; might as well call it a day. I think I'd enjoy a visit with Sharad this evening. I'm glad he's landed a deal; it could be rather depressing to go through a whole month without a sale."

"April is probably a lean month in the business. He's been doing well enough. How about if we go home, pick up Priti and go over to Savitri's for dinner?"

"I'll order pizzas to be delivered there at 5:30, how's that?"

"Good thinking, boss. That would leave us time for a nap or a shower together before Priti comes home."

"Let's make a bid for both. That reminds me, how about putting in a whirlpool? Richard was telling me ..." Anant turned on Corydon to backtrack to Grant.

"Ah, there he is," Donna said, as Jayant drove Veejala's car onto the driveway. Donna hastily put on her shoes and went out. "What a gorgeous tree, Jayant," she shouted with uncharacteristic enthusiasm. Jyoti joined them.

In a small U-Haul trailer behind the car was a six-foot Christmas tree, encased in burlap at the bottom, and filled with dirty brown gravel and snow.

"Quite a beaut, isn't it," Jayant shouted, "a perfect shape; your pal was nice to us, Donna, thanks for sending me to him." He was flushed with excitement and exertion. It had taken a lot longer than he'd budgeted for, and now they had to hurry.

Donna and he stood looking at the tree, and Jyoti felt a shaft of jealousy. She had to draw him away. "What's this for, Jai, a celebration, I hear?"

"Celebrating Shakespeare's birthday, let's say. Did you know his birthday is the same as his death day?"

Donna was looking up and down the lane, disappointment plain on her face. "Let's get this down, we have a way to go," she said, turning back to the work at hand.

Jayant cut the rope that held the tree in place. "Let me see, where shall we put it?"

Jyoti pointed to a corner of the backyard near the fence where the snow was still piled high. "There might provide some snow base, the ground is way too hard for digging."

"Nah, right in the middle of the yard would be a good place."

Donna got ready to pull at the tree.

"It weighs a ton. We wanted to do it in style, and so it's encased in solid ice. We'll just have to wait."

Just then, Sridhar's car nosed into sight, driven by Vithal. He jumped out and greeted the girls, both in the same way, as though he had seen Donna just that morning. Jyoti was looking out for something more effusive, more romantic. Vithal and Donna looked at each other, and suddenly Jyoti knew what was so familiar about them; it was the way her parents looked at each other, totally undemonstrative and yet deeply intimate.

"Pile out, you guys," Vithal hollered. "I'm sorry to say I could round up only these two morons."

Rajen and Sridhar rolled out of the car, pretending they had fallen asleep. "This is absolutely dimwitted, *yaar*," Rajen grumbled loudly. Sridhar escaped into clowning, slitting his throat with one hand and salaaming with the other.

“So where did you morons get the snow?” Rajen said, looking at the spade that Jayant had thrust into his hands.

“One can get anything under the sun and despite the sun if he goes about it the right way,” Jayant answered boastfully. They backed the U-Haul onto the grass — “Ruination, ruination,” Rajen said, “you are ruining the yard.” Heaved the tree to the ground, then positioned it. They couldn’t help it; it had to be in the middle of the yard, no point sticking it in a corner.

Jayant hacked away at the hard snow with demonic fury, Vithal with steady speed, and Donna hauled pails of water from the house to pack in the base.

Jayant looked at his watch. “Oh, jeesus! Jyo, do me a favour, drive to Mom’s school and hold her there till at least 4:20, then have her come in by the front door.”

Vithal said, “I wonder if it might work better if Donna were to go instead. Savitri would be less suspicious.” He looked at Donna. “Aunt S would be happy to see you,” and added, “So am I. Very.”

They continued to work, digging out snow to form a hole large enough for the bottom half of the ice base. They then shovelled back the gravelly snow around it, Jyoti packing it in, half fearing the water would only melt away the snow. Vithal parked the Lincoln Continental and U-Haul in the bay across the street, and Sridhar parked his car on the driveway so Sharad would have to drive around and come to the front.

At last it was ready. The tree stood gloriously in the yard, in full view from the kitchen window. They were sitting at the table drinking cola when Savitri came in with Donna. They quickly closed the curtain and waited for her. She was surprised but glad to see so many people around her kitchen table. “I called them for dinner, Mom. Hope that’s okay,” Jayant said, taking her books and coat from her and pushing her into a chair.

"Any time, *beta*, any time. Let me make you all some tea or something hot."

"Not today, Mom. You have to sit and watch us milling around."

"I do smell something very nice. Celebrating Mother's Day before you go?" Savitri was moved at the gesture, but felt a stab of pain that he would not be here for Mother's Day.

"Mother," Jayant spoke formally, "we are celebrating the cancellation of my departure for destinations unknown."

"But why, Jai?"

"I thought you'd be happy to hear I wasn't going."

"Oh, I would be, if it is for the right reason!"

Jayant spread his hands. "Well, Brendan wants to take his girlfriend along, and that has taken the wind out of my sails. I mean, who wants to be tagging a girl along? I mean, it wouldn't be the same, no offence to present company," he bowed to Donna. "Besides, there's enough work around here; they say there's going to be thousands of people coming into the city from the country, which means thousands of people will laver have to go home and rebuild; I'm sure they could do with some help. Jim definitely wants to postpone the trip because his cousin's family is in deep water."

"Haw haw haw," Rajen said, ridiculing his humour.

Krish came in by the back door with a big clatter. "Hey, what's this? Jay, how did you do it?" He was shrill with excitement. He stopped short at seeing so many people and greeted them before going on to shout, "Mom, did you see it?" He opened the curtain while Jayant put his hand to his head to show Krish what a bumblehead he was.

Savitri looked at the tree in astonishment. "It is lovely, Jai, how did you do it? I was wondering why you were guarding the curtain, Shri."

"Not just me, Mom. The native," he nodded at Donna, "told us where to get the tree, and the snow was Vithal's brainwave. The main idea, of course, came from the master mind." He bowed.

"Oh, you poor boys, you must be exhausted with all this hauling. Why aren't there any snacks on the table?"

Jayant pushed her back to her seat. "Just relax, Mom, we'll take care. Besides, the lady of the house shouldn't be working once her daughter-in-law comes home."

Savitri's heart leapt and sank at the same time. It wasn't Brendan after all but Jayant who had a girl. Why, he was hardly nineteen! Donna hit Jayant on the arm with a wooden spoon, and Savitri realized whom he meant. Vithal pretended not to have heard anything. Rajen slapped Vithal resoundingly on the back.

Krish wanted to know what was going on. "What was the tree doing in the yard so long after Christmas? How long could it stand there, anyway? Mom, could I wear just my windbreaker now on, I got toasted in my parka. Was anyone going to tell him anything?"

"It is an evergreen tree," Jayant said with a gentle clout on his brother's head, "and it will stand until the snow melts and then it will fall because it doesn't have roots."

Krish could see it was an evergreen, but why?

"Look at it, dumbbell, isn't it a beaut?"

"Sure is, but if it has no roots, that's a dumb thing to do. Why not get a little tree with roots from the woods at Birds' Hill or from Shelmerdine Nursery? It would be a real tree at least.

"This tree is real, kiddo, as real as any tree can be."

"But it doesn't have any roots! It's just one of those trees that they stick in the middle of boulevards at Christmas time."

"Exactly, exactly."

"Exactly. So what's the big deal?"

"Look, kiddo. Is it or is it not beautiful?"

"Yeah, kinda."

"Do you or do you not like it standing there?"

"Yeah, it's okay."

"That's all ye know on earth and all ye need to know. Now go do your homework."

"Not when everyone is having a jolly time here."

"Okay, stay. But keep your mouth shut and repeat after me, understand? An evergreen tree ..."

"An evergreen tree ..." he repeated.

"Is a thing of beauty ..."

"Yeah."

"And a thing of beauty is a joy forever. Say it."

"And a thing of beauty is a joy forever."

"Good."

"But rootless, I mean ... Jai, give me a break, what good is a tree without roots?"

Jyoti filled Krish's mug with chocolate milk and patted his head. "We will plant evergreens and oaks with roots, Krish. And grow mangoes on maples, and *jamuns* on birches, and *bilvas* on spruces. God willing, we shall." Krish and one of those little Indian girls born here, Romona's sister may be, Vithal and Donna, she and Pierre or ... whoever it was to be.

Jayant had his big hour later that evening. Sharad arrived a little later than usual; "Hey, Shri," he shouted as he came in, "your Cadillac has bit the dust, I see, blocking up the back lane."

With a lot of whispering and shushing reminiscent of make-believe Santas, Sharad was steered through his usual routine and brought to the table. Then Jayant pulled the curtain, unveiling the tree. Even though his speech was not rehearsed and he faltered occasionally, he spoke with passion: "That's us, Dad. Not just you and me with our memories of another land, another life, but all of us in this modern world in the year 1997, rootless but green for the length of our life, long or short; not a plantain tree that leaves a young one in its place, not an oak tree with its roots stretched a mile radius, this evergreen doesn't have one christly use, it isn't good even as firewood, but it is there, it is green, it is beautiful and therefore right."

Sharad was deeply touched. Jayant had brought home to him, he said, that trees could and would withstand even this eternally wintry Winnipeg, which was not god-forsaken after all, because no place graced by man can be god-forsaken.

"That's right, Dad," Jayant said. "Even in this eternal winter of a place one can ski cross-country in our fir and spruce woods even if dressed only in Stanfield briefs and Cougar boots that centrally heat one's soul."

"What does that mean," Krish said.

The doorbell rang. It was a pizza van. The delivery boy and Jayant sorted things, worked out the link between Moghe and Bhave on his order slip, and brought in pizzas. Veejala, Anant and Priti arrived just as the pizza van left.

"This is like Diwali," Anant said, pleased to see the whole family. "I can smell the pizza," Veejala said, "and a whole lot of other delicious smells as well, lasagna, mmm, it seems." She went to Vithal and gave him a bear hug. "Vithal, love, have you been working on a construction site? There's sawdust or something in your hair, and you've been perspiring." Anant was talking to Donna, his eyes full of affection for her. Veejala hugged her son again, this time for Anant, who would one day some day do it in person. "You absolutely stink, my love," she said.

"I know, ma," he said. "As soon as I tell you why, I'll join Rajen in line for a shower. Jayant, lord of the manor, has first dibs on the bathroom, and I am doing the proper host thing by letting the others ahead of me."

Jayant called them to the kitchen. Donna closed the curtain on that cue. Jayant unveiled the tree and went through his speech again. The light from the kitchen fell on the yard and lit up the tree.

“You missed the part about Stanfield briefs and Cougar boots,” Krish prompted.

“What does that mean?” Priti wanted to know.

“It means that as long as they are green and beautiful, that’s all you know on earth and all you need to know,” Krish said importantly.

“If your briefs are green! Oh, yuk,” Priti said.

A Selection of Our Titles

A Fredericton Alphabet (John Leroux) photos, architecture	1-896647-77-4	14.95
Avoidance Tactics (Sky Gilbert) drama	1-896647-50-2	15.88
Bathory (Moynan King) drama	1-896647-36-7	14.95
Break the Silence (Denise DeMoura) poetry	1-896647-87-1	13.95
Combustible Light (Matt Santateresa) poetry	0-921411-97-9	12.95
Crossroads Cant (Mary Elizabeth Grace, Mark Seabrook, Shafiq, Ann Shin. Joe Blades, editor) poetry	0-921411-48-0	13.95
Cuerpo amado/Beloved Body (Nela Rio; Hugh Hazelton, translator) poetry	1-896647-81-2	15.88
Dark Seasons (Georg Trakl; Robin Skelton, trans.) poetry	0-921411-22-7	10.95
Day of the Dog-tooth Violets (Christina Kilbourne) novel	1-896647-44-8	17.76
for a cappuccino on Bloor (kath macLean) poetry	0-921411-74-X	13.95
Great Lakes logia (Joe Blades, ed.) art & writing anthology	1-896647-70-7	16.82
Heaven of Small Moments (Allan Cooper) poetry	0-921411-79-0	12.95
Herbarium of Souls (Vladimir Tasic) short fiction	0-921411-72-3	14.95
I Hope It Don't Rain Tonight (Phillip Igloliorti) poetry	0-921411-57-X	11.95
Jive Talk: George Fetherling in Interviews and Documents (George Fetherling; editor Joe Blades)	1-896647-54-5	13.95
Mangoes on the Maple Tree (Uma Parameswaran) novel	1-896647-79-0	19.95
Manitoba highway map (rob mclennan) poetry	0-921411-89-8	13.95
Notes on drowning (rob mclennan) poetry	0-921411-75-8	13.95
Paper Hotel (rob mclennan) poetry	1-55391-004-4	17.95
Peppermint Night (Vanna Tessier) poetry	1-896647-83-9	13.95
Railway Station (karl wendt) poetry	0-921411-82-0	11.95
Reader Be Thou Also Ready (Robert James) novel	1-896647-26-X	18.69
resume drowning (Jon Paul Fiorentino) poetry	1-896647-94-4	15.95
Rum River (Raymond Fraser) fiction	0-921411-61-8	16.95
Shadowy Technicians: New Ottawa Poets (ed. rob mclennan) poetry	0-921411-71-5	16.95
Singapore (John Palmer) drama	1-896647-85-5	15.88
Song of the Vulgar Starling (Eric Miller) poetry	0-921411-93-6	14.95
Speaking Through Jagged Rock (Connie Fife) poetry	0-921411-99-5	12.95
Starting from Promise (Lorne Dufour) poetry	1-896647-52-9	13.95
Tales for an Urban Sky (Alice Major) poetry	1-896647-11-1	13.95
The Longest Winter (Julie Doiron, Ian Roy) photos, fiction	0-921411-95-2	18.69
These Are My Elders (Chad Norman; Heather Spears, ill.)	1-896647-74-X	13.95
The Sweet Smell of Mother's Milk-Wet Bodice (Uma Parameswaran) fiction	1-896647-72-3	13.95
This Day Full of Promise: Poems Selected and New (Michael Dennis, rob mclennan (editor) poetry	1-896647-48-0	15.88
Túnel de proa verde/Tunnel of the Green Prow (Nela Rio; Hugh Hazelton, translator) poetry	0-921411-80-4	13.95
What Was Always Hers (Uma Parameswaran) fiction	1-896647-12-X	17.95

www.brokenjaw.com hosts our current catalogue, submissions guidelines, manuscript award competitions, booktrade sales representation and fulfilment information. Directly from us, all individual orders must be prepaid. All Canadian orders must add 7% GST/HST (Canada Customs and Revenue Agency Number: 12489 7943 RT0001). Broken Jaw Press eBooks (in PDF format) of selected titles are available at http://www.PublishingOnline.com.

BROKEN JAW PRESS, Box 596 Stn A, Fredericton NB E3B 5A6, Canada